What's Worth Keeping

ALSO BY KAYA McLAREN

How I Came to Sparkle Again
The Firelight Girls
The Road to Enchantment

What's Worth Keeping

KAYA McLAREN

ST. MARTIN'S GRIFFIN
NEW YORK

First published in the United States by St. Martin's Griffin,
an imprint of St. Martin's Publishing Group

WHAT'S WORTH KEEPING. Copyright © 2021 by Kaya McLaren.
All rights reserved. Printed in the United States of America. For information,
address St. Martin's Publishing Group, 120 Broadway, New York, NY 10271.

www.stmartins.com

Library of Congress Cataloging-in-Publication data

Names: McLaren, Kaya, author.
Title: What's worth keeping / Kaya McLaren.
Other titles: What is worth keeping
Description: First Editon. | New York : St. Martin's Griffin, 2021.
Identifiers: LCCN 2020035339 | ISBN 9781250145093 (trade paperback) |
    ISBN 9781250145116 (ebook)
Classification: LCC PS3613.C57 W48 2021 | DDC 813/.6—dc23
LC record available at https://lccn.loc.gov/2020035339

Our books may be purchased in bulk for promotional, educational,
or business use. Please contact your local bookseller or the Macmillan Corporate
and Premium Sales Department at 1-800-221-7945, extension 5442,
or by email at MacmillanSpecialMarkets@macmillan.com.

First Edition: 2021

10 9 8 7 6 5 4 3 2 1

For my parents, Bob and Toni McLaren, for seeing me through the experience of breast cancer and doing everything in their power to make it as comfortable as it could be for me in all ways.

And for my whole team at Confluence Health in Wenatchee for playing a part in saving my life, but especially Dr. Julie Smith, Dr. Linda Strand, Nurse Ginny Heintz, Nurse Lori, Nurses Erica, Jen, and Rebecca in Infusion, Celeste the Breast Care Coordinator, Dr. Jesse Reignier, and Dr. Eric Leidke. Thank you for the compassion, the care, and the gift of more time you have given me.

What's Worth Keeping

Amy

It was as if an earthquake had hit, and now all of the contents of Amy Bergstrom's life had fallen out of her closets, cupboards, shelves, and drawers and onto the floor. Sometimes this was quite literal, like the pile of summer clothes that had lain folded and dormant in a storage bin in the back of her closet all winter but now sat next to her full-length mirror, where she courageously tried on every much-loved shirt and dress to see whether it would still fit her now. Her guesses about many pieces had been wrong, and relief filled her each time she discovered that she could still wear a piece that had been a favorite. Her long tan coat embroidered with flowers. Her maroon-and-black beaded cocktail dress. Three white summer shirts with eyelets and embroidery. Sporty knit sundresses with built-in padding where her breasts used to be. A long yellow halter maxi-dress that had made her feel a bit like a character in Greek mythology. Two peasant shirts. Of the things that were still worth keeping, she put a few in the large plastic tote she intended to take with her when she left and hung the rest in her closet, decoys to hide the true extent of her plan. The things that no longer fit would go in the large black plastic bag to take to a thrift store. Heartbroken, she held each piece in her hands, pausing to remember times she had worn it—a dinner out, a birthday party, a family vacation, a special day with her dad back when he could still remember who she was. Then she hugged each piece to her chest before saying good-bye and placing it lovingly in the bag. She had dreaded this task for months. Every part of it was difficult—letting go, even simply looking in the mirror. She missed her long hair as much as she missed her breasts.

Most of the things she needed to sift through, however, weren't nearly as tangible. Relationships. Work. Identity. Things even less tangible than that. Something along the lines of whether she had enough courage to live the rest of her life with the new set of fears she had, knowing how fragile and temporary life was.

Standing in the shower, she lifted her chin and stared at the ceiling in order to block her chest from her peripheral vision. It wasn't that she was in denial. It was simply that she couldn't handle it first thing in the morning. She ran her soapy hands over it, washing off the previous night's hot flash sweat. Her hands still remembered where they used to go, where the old contours were, what the weight of her breasts had been when she used to wash under them. Now, her hands felt like people trying to find their way home after their city had been bombed. Lost. Scared. Unable to imagine how anything would ever be all right again. Turning to rinse, she let the water strike her chest and paused to assess what she could feel and not feel. Nerves had been cut, leaving behind tingly sensations punctuated with occasional sharp phantom pain. Ten weeks. It had been only ten weeks.

A half inch of blond and white hair now covered her skull, muting the sensation of water hitting her scalp. She had hated everything about being bald except feeling so much more than she had ever felt before. Wind—even indoors when she was walking purposefully down the hall or an aisle at the supermarket. Cold rain. The bliss of a soft fleece hat. Warm water from the shower. She still used soap instead of shampoo most days, but on this morning, not knowing when her next shower would be, she indulged in the ritual she used to love, starting with pouring a tiny fraction of the shampoo she used to use into her palm, spreading it all over her head, and then lathering it all the way down to her scalp. Today, that was only a half inch. She massaged conditioner in next, then set about shaving her legs, the hair on which was significantly sparser and finer than it had been before chemo. After that, she turned off the water and began to dry her hair before she realized she had forgotten to rinse the conditioner; she marveled that a decades-old routine could have been broken in just a few months. With the water back on, she rinsed what remained of the conditioner and then, still looking at the ceiling, stepped out of the shower.

Paul had not said anything when she had covered the lower half of the bathroom mirror with wrapping paper and positive affirmations. She had banked on that. It had been a pretty safe guess. Twenty-six years ago, he might have. He probably would have. But people change. Things happen and people change. Now he didn't engage. And Amy knew there was something far more important he hadn't talked to her about.

Seven months ago, she had lain on the table in the clinic while a technician scanned her right breast with the ultrasound wand to assist Dr. Strauss, the radiologist, as she took needle biopsies of the tumor and a couple of lymph nodes. Amy asked Dr. Strauss the questions she'd formulated since reading her mammogram report online and then researching the meaning of new terms. "So, out of a hundred spiculated tumors you've seen, how many turned out to be benign?" she asked, truly expecting Dr. Strauss to say eight out of ten or even nine out of ten, leaving some possibility for hope.

"Not many, sister," Dr. Strauss replied frankly. "I will always be honest with you. I do not believe I am determining *if* it's cancer. I believe I'm determining what kind and what stage." When Amy started to cry, Dr. Strauss said, "You will get through this. I got through it. You will, too."

Amy wasn't so sure. Dr. Strauss seemed so much stronger than her.

When Dr. Strauss and the tech left, Amy dressed and found her sister, Alicia, in the waiting room. Alicia looked at Amy with deep concern as she approached, and Amy said, "This doesn't look good."

Alicia hugged her and then, stunned, they walked out to Alicia's car and drove to Amy's house. Once there, Amy didn't really want Alicia to stay. Alicia had a business to run—a natural foods store—and Amy didn't want her to lose any much-needed customers, but it occurred to her that this was a difficult day for her sister as well. After all, this very diagnosis was what had taken their mother. Alicia quite possibly needed to be with Amy right now, so Amy made her a cup of tea.

"I know someone whose sister cured herself naturally. You should watch *The Truth About Cancer*. There are all kinds of cures that Big Pharma doesn't want you to know about."

"Well, everyone I know who is still alive after cancer went through conventional treatment, so, if you love me, maybe don't steer me away from my best odds. This is not a time for experimentation. This is a time to save my life."

"Some people die of cancer treatment, not cancer. You remember what Mom went through. Just watch it—please. Perfect Health Supplements sent me to one of their seminars so I could learn about how their supplements have cured people."

"Right. That doesn't sound like science, Alicia. That sounds like a life-threatening pyramid scheme. Tell you what—when it's you with cancer, you can try those methods and risk your life. I want my treatment to be scientifically proven, not based on anecdotal evidence carefully selected to support the claims of snake-oil salesmen."

Alicia wasn't talking, but she wasn't budging either. She looked into Amy's eyes, imploring her to see the light as she saw it. Amy could see Alicia had the very best of intentions, but misinformed good intentions could kill her, and she was not remotely up for it. Doctors had a premed degree and medical school under their belts. They had seen a dozen patients a day for years. The vast majority of doctors could absolutely be trusted. How arrogant of a Perfect Health Supplements representative or a natural foods store owner like her sister to think they knew more. How dangerously arrogant.

"I need to be alone now. I really appreciate you going with me today and driving me home. Thank you for that. But I've got a lot of things to figure out and I don't need this."

"I am just trying to help. I'm just trying to help you. Why are you getting so mad at me for that?"

"Because your good intentions could kill me, Alicia. Good intentions are not the same thing as good decisions. Have you read the criticisms of *The Truth About Cancer*? A true expert would read the criticisms."

"Big Pharma gets researchers to write criticisms so they can keep making money. Do you know how much money Big Pharma makes on cancer patients?"

Amy took a big breath, having never been pushed so close to her limits. "Alicia, this is a moment that could forever ruin our good relationship. You need to go before that happens. I need all my energy to fight this and can't waste it fighting someone who is supposed to be on my side."

"I *am* on your side," Alicia said, following Amy to the door. "I love you, sis."

"I love you, too," Amy said, but she was too angry to hug her.

After Alicia left, Amy started worrying that the medical expenses would ruin them, that they would lose their house, and that after years of saving, they'd be unable to help their daughter, Carly, now in her senior year of high school, pay for college. Rifling through the drawer in the bottom of the desk, the one that held files, Amy searched for her insurance policy to see what exactly it covered. She found a file with homeowner's insurance and files with tax returns from the last seven years, and then she found a file containing do-it-yourself divorce papers and a list of all the assets she and Paul shared. Gasping, she looked closer, holding her stomach as if she had been kicked there. The pickup truck that Paul had bought only two months ago was listed. He had filled in the date June 10, 2012, the day after their daughter, Carly, would graduate from high school.

She was tempted to take the file and hide it or destroy it so that Paul would have to start the paperwork over, to buy herself more time, but it occurred to her that if he knew she knew, it might expedite the process. This was no time to make waves. She was going to need him in the months to come, and after years of cooking him dinner every night, doing his laundry, cleaning the house, raising their daughter, and loving him with an unwavering commitment, she felt he owed her that. He owed her more than that, really. She deserved a happy, lifelong marriage. She had earned that.

But then it occurred to her that "lifelong" might be before June 10. She didn't know and wondered whether Paul had a life insurance policy for her. Maybe he would lose his unwanted wife *and* hit the lotto. Wouldn't that be so great for him? She shook her head and fumed.

The moment felt like a gas leak in a house. So very dangerous. Such a high potential for an explosion.

So, she most likely had cancer. She had a well-intended but ignorant know-it-all sister whose help was going to come at the cost of listening to crap she didn't want to listen to and a husband who was waiting for their daughter to be out of the house so he could divorce her. There was only an extent to which she could count on him. Her father had Alzheimer's and had recently moved into a care facility for patients like him, and her mother had died when she was a teenager. She could absolutely count on Aunt Rae but knew her aunt couldn't leave her horses all alone on her little ranch in Chama, New Mexico, and if Amy went there, the medical care she would need would be hours away. Here in Oklahoma City, she had access to great care. It made sense to stay. She racked her brain, thinking of friends she could call on to help, but she felt so undeserving of all of them. Ever since her writing career had taken off, she had neglected her friendships. It seemed unfair to call on them now. Feeling so all alone, she pushed the file back into its place and shut the drawer. Paul would see her through this in all the practical ways. She was sure he would. He had a sense of duty. If it was strong enough to keep him married and in the house until their daughter was out of school, it was strong enough to keep him married and in the house while she had cancer. Duty wasn't the same as love, but if it was the best he could do, she would take it.

Now, it was June 10 and she was cancer-free. Paul had not abandoned her in her hour of need, and she appreciated that. She wondered whether he was still going to drop the bomb on her today but guessed that he would wait a little longer. He wouldn't want the world to think that he left his wife after twenty-six years because she no longer had breasts.

She, on the other hand, was not sure how much longer she could pretend that she had never seen the file, that something wasn't terribly wrong, or that she wanted to spend the rest of her life with a man who not only apparently did not love her anymore but these days often appeared to have no feelings at all.

She didn't trust herself at the moment. The combination of trauma and surgical menopause had left her feeling really unbalanced, to say the least. There was no doubt that it was a bad moment to make permanent decisions. She would have more time to sort it all out once she left. All she had to do was tell Paul about her trip without saying too much.

Picking through her toiletries, she collected a few minimal items to put in the tote as well. It was almost time. She would be free soon. Or freer, anyway.

Paul

Paul Bergstrom looked at the control panel on the treadmill as he ran, going over today's agenda in his mind and simultaneously counting down his last three-tenths of a mile. Pick up Carly. Take her to Rae's ranch in New Mexico. Ignore her fury. Check the Chama house he had once planned to retire in.

Just as he was finishing his last tenth of a mile, a woman just a little younger than him walked from the end of the Nautilus circuit to the treadmill that was right in front of him and progressed from a slow walk to a run. Although he tried not to stare as her buns jiggled with each step, for just a few seconds he couldn't help himself. He had cause to stare. First, since she appeared lean, he wasn't sure whether it was fat tissue or muscle or some combination that was jiggling and was intrigued by the mystery of that. And second, it had been almost eight months since he had had sex.

The night Amy had been officially diagnosed, he had held her. Something was different, though. She didn't melt into him the way she used to. She didn't look into his eyes for answers. She didn't look into his eyes at all.

When he had planned to leave her, he told himself she would

be better off without him . . . that after the initial shock and hurt, she would find greater happiness, someone who could love her more. His heart had been so heavy and numb since the day he had stood in the wreckage of the Alfred P. Murrah Federal Building, pulling toys from it. It changed him and everyone else who was there. Each day that had passed had left him either feeling as if he were letting Amy down for not being the man he was before or feeling like a liar in the brief moments he pretended he was. He had felt like human dead weight. But now that she had cancer, this idea that she'd be better off without him was no longer true. Quite the opposite. He would no longer make every day worse for her; he would be her hero. His heavy heart would not be a burden; it would be outweighed by his good deeds.

On that night, he supposed he was thinking that if he were her, he would want his breasts fondled and kissed at least one more time before anything happened to them and that he would want to feel pleasure while his body still felt healthy enough to feel pleasure. He supposed he was thinking that he had the power to make her feel better, to help her transcend the terror of this moment. And so he let his hands wander as she cried.

With an exasperated exhale, she said, "Paul, that hurts. My tumor hurts. It hurts even when you don't touch it. And Jesus, Paul, I may be dying. So, forgive me for not being in the mood. Tonight, it's not all about your dick." With that, she slipped out of his arms, locked herself in the bathroom, took a bath, and cried.

He just sat there on the end of the bed, so misunderstood, trying to untangle everything that was in just those few words. Dying. She might be dying. She probably wasn't. No one had said that, but still, he felt it was safe to believe she probably wasn't. But what if she was? What if he lost her? What if for the next several months she suffered and then just slipped away, leaving him to sleep alone, which yes, he thought he wanted but now couldn't imagine . . . leaving him to finish raising their girl and dealing with her grief all on his own.

Why couldn't it have been him? Her life, it seemed to him, would be a bigger loss. She had been happier than him on any given day, after all. She enjoyed life more. He would have taken this one for her. He may not have been good at loving her, but he did love her enough to take this from her.

Unfortunately, he couldn't.

And so, he sat next to the door to the master bath there in their bedroom and rested his cheek against it. It was the closest he could get to her right now. He just sat there, some of her words still stinging, the words about it being all about his dick. "Amy—," he began. "That wasn't what I meant. It wasn't about my dick. It was about making you feel good. About making you feel better. Because I don't know a lot of ways to do that. And I just wanted to be close to you."

From the bathroom came nothing but silence, and he knew she had already gone to the place where he could not reach her. It had already happened—he had already lost her. She was already gone. He knew it when he saw it because he remembered when he had been the one who had gone to the place where she could no longer reach him.

He looked across the room at their closet. Inside his side was a guitar he hadn't played in years, but there had been a time when he used to play for her every day when she painted or when she took a bath. For just a moment, he entertained the idea of getting his guitar out of its case and playing for her now. But she was silent. She didn't want connection. She wanted space. Slowly, he stood. He couldn't quite bring himself to go to the living room and watch TV. That seemed like too much space. Instead, he crawled into bed and turned out the light. He was there if she needed him or wanted him. Or they could both pretend he was asleep—whatever she wanted.

On the way home, he passed the Oklahoma City National Memorial and Museum. For many years, he would drive far out of his way to avoid it. Now, though it still seemed wrong for there to be an empty space where the federal building had stood, it wasn't as empty. The Field of Empty Chairs still evoked uneasiness in him, but at the same time he appreciated this memorial—particularly to those he knew and those he found. He liked the Reflecting Pool.

Something about this park mirrored what was inside him. At least he had thought that at the time. At first, it felt as if he had been blown open and destroyed just like that building. And then for a long time, he felt only rubble inside. He didn't know whether that had been demolished and removed in his heart—only that inside he felt as empty as that park. Not any emptier. In the way that the park had functional space, he had somehow figured out how to be functional as well. In the way that the park had soft grass and places for people to sit, he thought he was able to make people reasonably comfortable in his presence, even considering. But the memorial park would never be anything else. It was not a place for joy. It was not a place for fun. It wouldn't be a place where people wanted to have weddings. It wouldn't be a place for three-on-three basketball tournaments or music festivals. It was simply a big empty place to be solemn, a place to sit and think about how unfathomably horrible things can happen in an instant and how small and powerless we are, really, in the face of it all. Inside of himself, that was all he saw as well.

Turning on his signal, he waited at the light and then drove away from his reflection, drove on home to the woman he had planned to leave on this very day before he had come to his senses, the woman who had given him everything good about his life, the woman he had no idea how to reach right now. He had thought getting through cancer together would bring them closer, but he couldn't say it had. Still, it had counted. Surely it had counted.

He drove on home to shower and shave before picking up the daughter who was slipping away as well. Some things could not be fixed. Some things could only be made into something peaceful and still.

Carly

After a solid half-hour discussion of what their names would sound like combined, Kiara had gone off to "talk" with Kai, leaving Carly sitting on the edge of the pool alone, her feet in, watching member after member of the class of 2012 fly out of the long curvy tube feetfirst and, if they were smart, legs crossed. She pondered the irony of such a childish celebration following the ceremony that was supposed to make them all official adults. The hands on the clock had moved interminably slow all night. Six thirty felt like an accomplishment in endurance. Just two more hours. It was almost over. There was no denying that the other graduates were having a great time. Their hearts were all so much lighter than hers. They were like lightning bugs radiantly flying through the air, while she felt more like a spider, stuck in one place, waiting for something. If she was especially cross, as she was now, it might be fair to say waiting for her next victim, someone to take a tiny bit of her anger out on.

That turned out to be Billy O'Brien, Jr. This spring she had spent many class periods pondering what an unfortunate name that was the first time and trying to wrap her mind around why anyone would have thought it to be a name worth repeating.

Billy sat down next to her and smiled as he looked at her with his wolflike, silver eyes. "Carly! Aren't you having fun?"

She shrugged. "Sure," she said, because this was what people wanted to hear. As long as she said the words people wanted to hear, no one tried to fix her. God, she hated it when people tried to fix her. There were things that couldn't be fixed. She was one.

He either scratched his head or simply ran his fingers through his short, sandy hair, darker now that it was wet. She wasn't sure. "Carly, since it's graduation, I have a confession."

"Uh-oh," she replied with a smile, somewhat dreading the awkwardness that undoubtedly would follow.

"When we were in sixth grade, I had the biggest crush on you. I walked by your house every evening for a month just hoping to run into you so I could talk to you without all your friends or my friends watching."

"Only a month, huh? You call that persistence?" As she gave him a hard time, she noticed something change in his eyes, something that looked like excitement. This was the thing she had been surprised to learn this spring—the less she cared and the more she gave boys a hard time, the more they seemed to find her utterly irresistible. It wasn't anything she did with the intention of achieving that. She truly didn't care—not about anything—and it felt really good to be flippant with people who could take it and sometimes even with those who couldn't. It released small amounts of pressure before all of her stress caused her to blow up. Not blow up in a fit of rage—she meant physically blow up into a million little pieces, popped like a balloon that did not have the capacity to hold all of the air that it was expected to hold.

"You don't think a month is persistent?" He was incredulous.

She shrugged again. "All right, for a sixth-grade boy, a month is probably persistent. But why did you give up? Did you get distracted by another girl who grew bigger boobs?"

He looked up to the corner of the room wistfully. "Megan Frampton . . . but no, that wasn't why. I flunked a math test and when I looked across the aisle at your paper, I saw you had an A-plus and figured I wasn't smart enough for you."

She paused for a moment, trying to figure out how to unpack that sad story. "First, Megan? Really? Goody-goody, nicey-nice little Megan?"

"Yeah, she was stacked. She never paid any attention to any of us, but we all orbited around the gravitational pull of her. . . ." He directed his cupped hands toward his own chest rather than choose a distasteful word.

"Boobs," she said.

"Boobs," he repeated, now that he had permission to say that word.

"Issue number two: If you weren't smart enough to have a shot with me then, what changed? Did you get smarter?"

Smiling self-consciously, he said, "I don't think so. But a couple weeks ago, I saw that you flunked your math final and it gave me hope."

Burying her face in her hands, she laughed. Her life had come to this. And the worst part was that she actually preferred the attention of Billy O'Brien, Jr., to being holed up in her bedroom, stressed and alone, trying to be perfect and achieve everything.

She caught him glancing down at her boobs, but she didn't hold it against him. Her boobs looked undeniably great in her multicolor-striped bikini top. "Billy, I want to ask you something. If I had no boobs—I don't mean flat boobs, but no boobs at all—would you still be sitting here talking to me?"

He rubbed his jaw as he looked up at the ceiling and thought.

"Well, I suppose that would depend on how good you were at blow jobs," he finally said.

She rolled her lips into her mouth and bit them just enough not to swear up a tropical storm, then nodded, took a deep breath, and exhaled slowly. "Well, Billy, I do appreciate your honesty."

"I promise I'll always be honest."

Those words seemed to suggest that Billy was proposing a long-term relationship, which Carly found both strange and presumptuous.

Kiara and Kai came shooting out of the tube together just then, his arms around her belly, laughing as they flew through the air just before they plunged into the water.

"Go down the slide with me like that," said Billy.

Surfacing, Kiara and Kai smiled at one another and then swam to the side of the pool, where Kiara put her hands on his shoulders and kissed him quickly. Then she turned, grasped the rails, and climbed up the ladder out of the water, leaving Kai to study her behind, a look of pure bliss cemented on his face.

While Carly wasn't capable of feeling as happy as Kai looked, she supposed she could make Billy that happy. That was something. While she wouldn't have great memories of this night, he would at least have great memories of her. This was how she had revised the history of the end of her senior year as it was happening. It worked as long as she wrote in her journal as if she were someone else. Tonight's entry would be written from the perspective of Billy. One day she would by and large forget this night, God willing, but should she ever choose to go back and read an old journal, she would read the story of a boy whose dreams came true six years after he had dreamed them because in a moment when he felt he had nothing to lose, he had risked it all.

"Okay. But I'm not kissing you like that."

"Yeah . . . ," he said, unconvinced. "Maybe not the first or second time, but I suggest keeping an open mind." Then he shot her his best smile.

She laughed and walked toward the line at the bottom of the ladder.

As he walked beside her, he said, "Also, since I promised you honesty, I must admit that I have every intention of copping a little feel on the way down the slide but having the good manners to pretend it was an accident."

"So, like, a boob graze with your arm instead of your hand," she clarified.

"Well, if you're in front and my arms are around you, these things could happen."

"Eh, fair enough." While she had boobs, she might as well let Billy O'Brien enjoy them, and she might as well enjoy the attention she got from having them. There was a good chance that one day, that would all change.

Amy

As she toweled her hair dry, she studied herself in the top half of the bathroom mirror, the half not covered by wrapping paper. In it, she saw her short, masculine hairdo, somewhere between blond and white instead of the red it had been, and her green eyes that still reminded her of broken glass.

Any sense of control over her life that she had once had was long gone now. All the organic kale, beets, and blueberries she had eaten several times a week for most of her life, all the worthless natural deodorant and other natural products she had ever used, none of it had been enough to overcome her BRCA2 gene mutation and keep her cancer-free.

And all the good deeds, the acts of love, the effort and care, and the little family they had created together had not been enough to make Paul truly love her and want to stay. There was so much she had no control over, as it turned out. There was no rhyme or reason to this crapshoot called life.

She mused that no one had told her that even when breast cancer was technically over, it would leave her with unbearable intolerance for entire aspects of her life. It should have been listed in the side effects of her treatment plan.

She had expected to feel nothing but jubilant when treatment was over and the outcome was good. After all, so many people did not get such a good outcome. But often, it seemed that when her life was saved, it was also wrecked, and that made it hard to care about anything. She could not imagine any roads leading to happiness anymore, so there was nothing to lose. At least that was how she felt today. She didn't know whether she would feel that way in six months or in a year or in three years. She only knew that in this moment, she felt dangerously unattached to the few things that she hadn't already lost.

She watched as her face and scalp broke out in a menopausal sweat. Compared with the side effects of chemo, menopause was manageable, but it was one more thing that left her feeling irreversibly changed and so much older than she had been a year ago. What she missed most was sleeping well.

After opening the door to let the cold air into the steamy bathroom, she dressed and then began pacing the house, nervously, occasionally tossing another object into her tote—matches, a road atlas, a flashlight.

She paused in the doorway of Carly's room, a space Carly had just outgrown. The artifacts it held were reminiscent of the inbetween time when she wasn't a girl and wasn't a woman.

To say her cancer had been hard on her daughter and their relationship would have been an understatement. It had hit bottom nearly two months ago, in early April just before her second surgery, when Carly had asked, "If you had breast cancer, why are you getting all your other lady parts taken out?"

Amy had paused, still undecided about how to handle this. Out of time to make that decision now, she simply told the truth. "I have the BRCA 2 gene mutation. This means I had about a sixty to seventy percent chance of getting breast cancer in my lifetime, and it means I have a twenty percent chance of getting ovarian cancer, which is a really scary cancer. Often, by the time a woman knows there is a problem, it's too late. I want to live, so I'm getting rid of all my high-risk body parts."

"Is that the thing Angelina Jolie has that made her run out and get her boobs chopped off?"

Amy winced at Carly's word choice—*boobs chopped off*. As if it were done by a lumberjack with a big ax or maybe an ax murderer who hadn't finished the job. "She has the BRCA1 gene mutation. It's similar, but not exactly the same. I think she had an eighty percent chance of getting breast cancer."

Carly paused and then said, "You said gene. As in genetic."

"Yes. . . ." Amy watched Carly's face change as the implications hit her.

"Do I have it, too?" Carly had Paul's eyes, and Amy hoped like hell that Carly had inherited much more from Paul—namely, his ability to consistently repair both strands of his DNA instead of just one strand like her.

Immense dread filled Amy as she struggled to answer. "I don't know. There's a fifty-fifty chance. When you turn eighteen in August, you can have the test if you want."

Suddenly, Carly seemed angry. "Why would I want to know? So I can run out and get my boobs chopped off? Or just know that there's a gun pointed at my head? Why would I want to live like that?"

"You don't have to get the test now. But when you're twenty-five, you should find out so that if you have this gene mutation, you can get annual MRIs on your breasts. That way, if . . ." Amy couldn't even say it because it was too unthinkable. She choked up and then finished, "If you ever did get cancer, it would be caught . . . in time."

Carly froze in terror for a minute as she looked into her

mother's eyes and then said, "I am not going to be like you. I'm not anything like you. This is your problem—not mine."

Amy saw past the anger to the fear and wanted to reach out and hug Carly, but the wounds on her chest were still fresh and painful. If Carly resisted or fought . . . if she was anything but extremely gentle, she would hurt Amy. In that moment that Amy hesitated, Carly took off. With the exception of Carly's one-word answers, it was the last time they had talked. Carly had been avoiding her ever since, staying out too late or even spending the night at friends' houses without asking first, sometimes coming home drunk or smelling like marijuana, running wild and reckless as if she believed she was doomed so nothing mattered.

Even Paul, a police officer for twenty-five years now, could not rein her in, although in moments where Amy had been independent enough to be left alone, he had tried. The best he could come up with was a plan to ambush her after graduation and take her to Amy's aunt Rae in the mountains of northern New Mexico, where she would work in her aunt's outfitting business and hopefully straighten up before she self-destructed. When Amy and Paul had returned home from the ceremony last night, he had wordlessly packed a suitcase with things he thought Carly would need and put it in his trunk.

This morning, he had slipped out and gone to the gym before Amy was able to wake up enough to get the words out. Now the pressure of the words inside of her left her pacing around the house. She looked at family pictures on the wall. Disneyland. A trip to the Gulf Coast. Harvesting a small vegetable garden with Carly when she was just a little bitty thing. Birthdays, Christmases, and Halloweens. Togetherness. Traditions. Family. She was about to blow them all up.

With moments to spare, she walked out to drop bills into the mailbox, a detail she wanted to wrap up before she left. She waved to Jim, who was standing in his yard visiting with a neighbor who had just moved in on the other side of him, and he waved her over. The conversation started off normally enough. Jim put his arm around her and introduced her to Mark, the new neighbor. "Amy is a survivor," he said. That word made her bristle for so many reasons. In this particular case, her experience with cancer wasn't really what Amy would have chosen to lead with. Her struggle was personal, and this was a stranger. It was none of his business. The conversation got even weirder when Jim jokingly referred to her hysterectomy as being "field dressed." He didn't know her well enough to make a joke like that. And all of her suffering was no joke. She really had no sense of humor about it at all. Just when she didn't think it could get worse, he said, "When Helen first found out, she was thinking about shaving her head in solidarity with you, but I told her if she did . . . bye, bye!"

A lot of things went through Amy's head at once. First, that Helen had even considered it was touching. Second, that losing her own hair was so painful, she wouldn't wish it on anyone or gain any strength from having them suffer the same indignity. Looking at them would only mirror her own pain back to her. But then the third thought came, and it was less of a thought than a feeling of pure horror at what Jim had just said.

"Right," Amy said with a smile, "because a bald woman isn't worth keeping—even if you've been married to her for nearly fifty years and she's the mother of your children. I totally get it. Bald women are worthless and disgusting. Yeah, good call, Jim."

She held up her hand to stop him from saying one more dumb word, but he said, "I didn't mean that, Amy. I just meant—"

"I know you didn't mean to hurt me, Jim. It's okay. Nice to meet you, Mark. Welcome to the neighborhood. I gotta go." She turned around and walked back toward home as quickly as she could with her sore "field dressed" belly, quickly enough to escape before the angry tears came, letters still in hand.

"I really stuck my foot in it, didn't I," she could hear Jim say to his new neighbor, and then heard his uncomfortable laugh.

The thing was, she knew Jim had a kind heart and never meant to say anything so stupid. She did. Like him, many people made dumb attempts at humor when they were uncomfortable. It wasn't that she didn't understand; she just didn't want to be around them anymore.

Through the house, she heard the garage door hum as it raised, then Paul's car pull in and stop and his car door shut. She heard him open the laundry room door and close it behind him. Inhaling deeply, she bent her knees ever so slightly. Her heart raced, and then she broke out in another sweaty hot flash.

He walked in, expressionless as usual, glanced at her on his way to the kitchen, and stopped. She was as transparent as he was opaque. "What's going on?"

"I'm going to go away for a little while too," she said simply.

He waited for her to say more, which she usually did, but this time she feared she would say too much, so she remained silent.

"For how long?"

Even though she was clear about all of the reasons she was doing this, she felt a tugging at her heart. "A few weeks, maybe. A couple months. I'm not sure."

He studied her closely. "Are you coming back?"

"I don't know."

"I don't understand."

All the things she wanted to say were right there, but she couldn't figure out how to string them together in any way that made sense. *Because I found the file and I know how you really feel about me, and even though you feel obligated to stay now, I want more. You should have brought me a giant bouquet of flowers in the hospital after my surgeries, but especially after the first one. It would have made me feel like a woman when I just felt like a bald, sexless potato. You don't look at me the way you used to in the very beginning. You haven't for decades and I'm lonely. I'm so unspeakably lonely. There is always some emergency more important than me. I can't compete with humanity like that. There's not enough of you for all of us. And I know you know that. I intended to be your wellspring and your oasis forever, but then my well ran dry. And I can't imagine having sex ever again. I've tried and I just can't imagine it. Because even though I have no idea what another option would look like, I choose not to rebuild my isolated life. I am lonelier with you than I am alone.* All of those words were right there, and with every last ounce of her will, Amy successfully stopped them from tumbling out.

Taking a big breath, she decided to tell him only the parts that she knew for certain to be true and was willing to share. "I am going through something. And I have been through something. I don't even know how to wrap my mind around it. I look at my body in the mirror and I think, I have *been through* something, and I sob. And I know it's theoretically over now, but I'm completely overwhelmed by all the healing that still needs to be done. I can't figure out how I'm ever going to heal from all of this. But I know you can't help me. You've been here for me in very practical ways and I deeply appreciate it. I could not have gotten through this without you. You were absolutely my hero. I just know you can't help me with the emotional stuff."

His brow furrowed as he continued to stare at her, and she wondered how aware he was of his own limited capacity when it came to emotions.

"Where are you going?"

"Back to the forests where I spent my summers as a kid."

"Up in Washington State?"

She nodded. "I just want to be in the forest. I feel like nature is the only thing that might be able to heal me. For months, I kept thinking that if I could just be with the really big trees, I would be okay."

"You're leaving me for trees?"

"Yes."

"You could just come with us and spend time in the forest near Chama."

She shook her head. "It's not the same. I want to go home."

"I thought this was your home."

I found the papers! she wanted to say. *You intended to wreck this home on this very day! How can I pretend it's my home now?* But instead, she said, "I just want to be immersed in the gentlest, softest, kindest forest in the world. I want to visit my favorite tree."

"You have a favorite tree?"

She nodded.

"And then after that you'll probably come back?"

Amy nodded because it was easier—not because she really believed she would.

Paul

Paul vaguely remembered a time in college when he used to write song lyrics. Fragments of poetry would drift across his mind the way birds sometimes flew nearby. Life had changed all of that. The world, it seemed, was a chaotic and tragic place full of far too many problems to solve. Still, he tried to solve as many problems as he could each day, and that didn't leave room for poetry and songs. It demanded a person be as efficient as possible. No wasted time. No wasted words. Now he thought in lists.

When Carly disembarks, put her luggage in the back seat instead of the trunk, so she won't see the other bags I have packed for her.

Carry her bag for her so that she is less likely to see the small cooler containing sandwiches on the floor of the back seat.

Act normal.

Sitting in the front seat as he waited, he unfolded the map and reviewed the route he would drive. The bus pulled up eight minutes late. Graduates began to stream out of it while the driver pulled bags out from below.

Carly looked tired when she stepped off the bus. She was smiling with her mouth but not her eyes. Paul wished he could hug her and change it back. Even though this moment of graduation was all about letting go so his child could strike out into the world on her own, it felt wrong—not wrong because he was resisting it out of his own attachment, but wrong as if it were being done improperly. Her eyes had changed sometime last winter. He wanted his little girl back—the one with good judgment, the one with the best of intentions, the one with purity of heart and a mind full of idealism.

He stepped out of his car, casually strode over, and stood next to her as she said good-bye to her friends who walked by. She hardly acknowledged him at all. "Ready? Can I take your bag?" He put his arm around her for a sideways hug and gave her shoulder a little squeeze, looking at the boys in the crowd for one that looked guilty or scared when meeting his gaze. Carly had told him two years ago about how a group of boys in the cafeteria had joked that they were all scared of him and none of them would ever ask her on a date or to a dance. At the time, she had found it funny, but she had been his little girl still. "Did you have fun?"

Handing the handle of her duffel bag to him, she shrugged. "Yeah." It wasn't very convincing.

Not wanting to create any tension or resistance by asking her questions, he granted her silence as they walked to the car. She stepped into the front seat, and he put her duffel bag in the back seat, as planned. Then he got in and began to drive, waiting to see how far he could go before she would begin to ask questions.

To his surprise, she took off her coat, wadded it up and leaned it against the passenger window, rested her head on it, and closed her eyes, presumably to sleep but most likely to simply avoid conversation with him. He hoped she would fake it until she actually fell asleep.

As he drove, he glanced sideways at his little girl who was not so little anymore, looking for what had changed and what had stayed the same. Her nose and her lips looked the same to him as when she had been a sleeping baby, only bigger. Her face, though, was painted with makeup, showcasing her maturity and hiding her innocence. He wanted to see her innocence again. Maybe this summer he would. Her long blond hair had darkened over time. Suddenly it struck him as so odd that this young woman in the front seat had once fit in his two hands.

His mind drifted to Amy, wondering whether she had left yet, wondering how far she had driven if she had. He could check his Find My iPhone app if he really wanted to know, but it seemed out of line, a card he would hold until he had no other to play.

He remembered the night that he decided he would ask Amy for a divorce after Carly graduated. There was a block party. Around thirty neighbors gathered around tables full of food, their plates piled high, swapping compliments about so-and-so's chicken casserole and so-and-so's potato salad and so-and-so's biscuits. Below their feet, a few small children colored the street with sidewalk chalk, while the older ones shot baskets in the Jamesons' driveway. It was a Norman Rockwell painting, a picture of innocence, a moment reminiscent of another time, a time before meth, a time before human trafficking, a time when child porn was utterly unheard of.

"Hey! Paul!" his neighbor Jim shouted out as he made his way over to him. "Good to see you! How was your day?"

How was your day? It was a perfectly normal question. And yet when Paul thought about it, he did not come up with a perfectly normal answer. He had stopped a man that day—a man who appeared to be a pimp and had drawn a weapon on him. *Stopped.* That was the language they used when they had to shoot someone.

Stopped. And he had forgotten about it until Jim had asked about his day.

On Paul's third day on the job twenty-five years ago, he and his partner responded to a homicide call in an apartment. Brain tissue had dripped off the ceiling, lung tissue off the wall. A small group of first responders watched TV on the couch while they waited for the report to be finished and for someone from the coroner's office to come pick up the body. At the time, Paul hadn't been able to understand how these men could sit there and watch *Jeopardy!* as if this were nothing. For months, he would have nightmares about that ceiling and that wall.

And now, he could shoot a man and forget about it until someone asked him about his day. How remarkable, really, that someone could adapt to such horrors. The thing was, that to block out the ugliness, a person had to block out the good stuff too. It couldn't be selective. It was like watching TV and not being able to select the sounds he wanted to hear from the sounds he did not. There was just one volume button. And he had turned the volume on life way down, all the way down to where he rarely heard or felt anything.

There was even more to it, though, and that had something to do with the fact that he could not tell his neighbor about his day. He could not bring that ugliness into this pristine gathering. His neighbors would think he was a monster, killing people and then giving it no thought at all. That had to stay hidden. Washing over him was the sense that he did not belong there, that he was too impure to be there, and it was isolating.

"Pretty good," he answered, because that was true. He had stopped a man and still had a pretty good day. Until now. Until having it hit him again how different his daily reality was. How ugly it was.

Jim began to yammer on about nothing, while Paul shoveled pork and beans into his mouth and looked over at Amy farther down the street visiting with their elderly neighbor, Mrs. Farman. Amy was all smiles and sunshine. Nothing ugly ever stuck to her. She deserved so much more. It wasn't too late. She was still pretty. She could find someone new, someone who didn't shoot people and forget about it, someone who could love her the way she deserved to be loved, with the volume turned all the way up.

Since he didn't know what to wish for now, and since he had seldom seen the effects of wishing, he resolved to simply wait.

He made two left turns that were not part of the drive home, but Carly did not stir. It appeared she had indeed fallen asleep while faking it. For nearly two hours, he drove in peace.

The landscape around him took him back to when he drove this very route twenty-seven years ago, from Keyes back to Oklahoma City, after introducing Amy to his parents.

"So, how did you two meet?" asked Paul's mother, the first and only time he brought Amy home to meet his parents. "I mean, I know you met at school, but Paul didn't share the details."

Paul was the middle of three boys. John, the youngest, sat on the other side of him. Gary, the oldest, was grown and gone. His mother, it seemed to him, was excited to have another woman in the house to talk to.

Paul's dad had never been much of a source of conversation, all but ignoring Amy despite the fact that he was sitting directly across the table from her. Paul had wished his dad would try just this once to be nice. Instead, he served himself up a portion of mashed potatoes, giving it his full attention. On the wall behind him hung various honors from the time he had served in Vietnam, among them a Purple Heart.

Amy's hand trembled a bit as she served herself, revealing her nervousness. "Well," she began, "he used to play guitar outside of the art building, where I'd hear him while I was painting."

"Guitar," snorted his dad with some level of disgust. Turning to Paul, he said, "Just sitting on the grass playing guitar, huh? That sounds like something a hippie would do." He stared at Paul aggressively, but Paul didn't back down or fight, only met his gaze with a neutral expression. To his left, John hadn't looked up from his plate since he had sat down.

"Were you doing more than just sitting on the grass, son? Were you smoking it, too?"

"No, sir," Paul said, and although his expression was remarkably blank, inside he was feeling it all—anger, embarrassment, regret, sadness . . . and weighing the choice about whether to stay and endure his father or leave and hurt his mother.

"Here's an idea: Why don't you do something useful with your time, like work a little more."

"Yes, sir," Paul replied again, his obedience impeccable.

Paul looked over at his mother, again weighing his choice. She was staring at her plate as well. For the rest of the dinner, no one said a word and no one looked up. Paul didn't need to. Looking at his food, he could still see his family through Amy's eyes—his father's anger, his brother waiting for a safe moment to escape, his mother's noxious blend of terror and grief—grief for the family dinner experience she had thought she was going to have and had worked so hard for. With his peripheral vision, he thought he saw tears well up in her eyes from time to time. What a disaster. How he wished he had never brought Amy here.

Amy and Paul helped clear the plates when it was over, then thanked and complimented his mother in the kitchen. Paul made an excuse for them needing to get back and retrieved their coats from a bedroom, leaving Amy alone with his mother in the kitchen.

With coats in hand, he approached the kitchen but stopped when heard his mom whispering.

"I'm sorry. He really is a good man. He doesn't always act like it, but deep down he is. Please don't dismiss Paul because of this."

Horrified, Paul walked around the corner to stop any more damage from happening, but as he did, he heard Amy's reply.

"I love Paul." Paul's heart swelled. It was the first time he had heard her say so.

He took her hand, and together they walked into the family room, where his father rose to shake their hands.

"Thank you, sir," Paul said.

Amy was gracious enough to say, "It was a pleasure to meet you."

But his father grunted again and said, "I'll bet." Unbelievable.

Paul marveled at how he and his father could have such similar features—such a strong resemblance in the most basic ways—and yet be completely opposite in all the ways that mattered.

They shook John's hand too, and what Paul remembered seeing in his brother's eyes was a desperate imploring to take him with them. Paul wanted to, but he could not figure out how. There was no place for John in the tiny dorm room Paul shared with a roommate.

Once they were safely in Paul's car and on their way, Paul said, "I'm so sorry. I don't know why I thought that was a good idea. I guess I just had this fantasy that for one night of my whole life, my dad could be normal and I could bring my girl home like everyone else. I will never ask you to go there again."

"It's okay," Amy said, but he could see her relief.

Silence engulfed them for several miles, and then Paul said, "So, you love me, huh?"

He glanced at the road and back to Amy twice before she finally said, "Yeah, I love you."

"Even after all that," he said, marveling.

"Even after all that."

He pulled over to the shoulder of the road, leaned over, and kissed her long and tenderly. He ran his hand down the side of her face, gently brushing her hair, looked her deep in the eyes, and said, "I love you, too." Then, as he pulled the old car back onto the road and hit the gas, he added, "I'm going to marry you, Amy Jenkins."

"How do you know?" she sassed back to lighten the mood. "You haven't even asked me yet. You don't know what I'll say."

For a split second, he looked concerned before he glanced over and saw her smile. "I think I do know," he said, taking them down the road further and further from his roots and his fears and his inadequacies, taking them down the road toward the future they'd build together.

He was so glad that he hadn't known the future on that day. He would not have believed it, anyway. So sure had he been that he and Amy were for forever, he could not have fathomed it. He could not have fathomed the bombing of the federal building or the role he would play in its aftermath. He could not have fathomed how it would change him . . . how it would leave him feeling so isolated all the time. He could not have fathomed that cancer would happen to a person as good as Amy . . . could not have fathomed that he would come so close to losing her. And he certainly could not have fathomed that prior to the cancer he had actually filled out divorce papers. He thought of his twenty-one-year-old self, of how angry he was at his father, of how protective he felt of Amy, of how he was going to show his father that he was not just a man but a man of worth, a man worthy of Amy, and a man far more capable than his father had been of being a lifelong good husband. His twenty-one-year-old self would have kicked his forty-seven-year-old self's butt for not treating her right.

When Carly finally did wake, she looked with alarm at the wide-open spaces beneath a sky filled with cauliflower clouds rising and growing before their eyes. "Where are we?" she finally asked.

"I'm not sure," he replied because he thought it would be more fun to be coy.

"I don't understand."

"Yeah, it sucks not to understand, huh? Your mom and I haven't understood the choices you've been making for the last month and a half."

Seething, Carly looked at the dashboard and shook her head. "Where are we going?"

Paul paused before he told her, thinking that if she considered the possibility that he was taking her to rehab or a naughty kid wilderness camp, she might actually be happy when she learned that they were only going to Aunt Rae's.

Carly

It was unreal—her dad thinking he could just pick her up and take her to Great-Aunt Rae's like this, like he picked people up and took them to jail. So she had some beers, smoked a little pot, and spent a few nights at friends' houses without telling them—could her parents really blame her? After all, their home had become a sick ward of sadness. Everything was just cancer and sadness.

When her mom was going through chemo, Carly had been strong for her. Many nights, she alone had cared for her mom, a responsibility so great that she often felt she was buckling under its magnitude. She had cut up mangoes for her mom, opened cans of peaches, and kept her water glass full of lemon water. She had looked up recipes for new soups and then put them in the blender on days when her mom's mouth was too tender to chew. She had been the very best daughter she could be.

It had been day four of round one, the day they all learned that day four was the worst. It had caught them off guard. Her dad had stayed home on days one and two, the day her mom had the infusion and the day that followed, but her mom had felt much better than any of them had expected, and so, with a false sense of security, her dad had returned to work the graveyard shift. On every other day but day four, both before and after that round, Carly would wake to find her mom staring out the eastern window, waiting for the sun to rise, waiting alone for the long night to be over; but on day four, her mom stayed in bed and cried, unable to stop, unable to hide it. She just cried and cried into her pillow, her back turned to Carly.

Instinctively and tentatively, Carly sat next to her and rubbed her back gently through her pajamas, studying the rash on the back of her mom's neck and newly shaved head. "Can I make you a smoothie?" she asked.

Her mom shook her head. As Carly's hand reached her mom's shoulder, her mom's hand rose to meet it, patting the back of it, trying to comfort the daughter who was comforting her.

"Peaches?"

Her mom held still, thinking about it, and then nodded.

Carly practically ran to the kitchen to open a can, drain it, dump it in a bowl, grab a fork, and return. Her mom rolled over onto her other side and cried big teardrops into the bowl of peaches as she ate. It was the worst she had ever seen her mom. She wondered how much more her mom could take, whether she would make it through treatment, and she was scared. Her mom laid her head back down on the pillow next to the peaches, so Carly picked up the bowl before it spilled.

"How about I leave these right here so if you want more later, you have them?"

Eyes shut, blocking out the world, the light . . . everything she could block out, her mom nodded.

"I'm going to go get you some fresh water. I'll be right back."

She filled a glass with tap water, squeezed some lemon into it, and dropped in a reusable straw.

Her dad should have come home by now. That was the plan. He had arranged to work nights so that he could stay home with her during the day and Carly could stay with her at night. She wasn't sure when he would sleep. Maybe he would do what she did—sleep lightly and wake often, every two or three hours, to check on her during the first week after her mom's infusions. Night shift was hers and day shift was his, but this morning he was late. And it was day four, so she could not leave.

She walked around the bed and curled up behind her mom, resting her forehead on her mom's convulsing back, as if willing prayers to go directly from her mind right into her mom's body, wondering whether this was going to be the day they both broke.

Not too long after, her dad finally came home and took Carly's place on the bed so she could get ready for school. By the time she was done, both her parents were asleep and she didn't want to wake them—especially her mom—so she hopped on her bicycle and rode to school without a note excusing her tardiness.

On the way, she remembered that there was supposed to be a test in her precalculus class that morning, and she was missing it. She pedaled harder, arriving at school sweaty, then locking her bike and running directly to Mr. Long's class. She entered as quietly as she could so as not to disturb the others.

He looked up from his desk at her and held his hand out for the note from the office saying whether she was excused or unexcused. She approached and whispered, "Could we do this after the test? I've already missed so much of the time to take it."

He shook his head.

"Well, can I make it up later?" she asked, worried that this test could affect her grade and cause her to lose her chances at scholarships. Even with insurance, Carly expected the expense of cancer would wipe out the money her parents had saved for her college.

They would have to take out loans now, and she didn't want to burden them with any more debt than they surely would have by the time her mother's treatment was over.

"If you have a doctor's excuse. You know my policy. Sleeping in is not an excuse or a reason I should have to grade your test later."

Anger rose up within her. Anger and frustration. Couldn't anyone see that she was doing her best? "Sleeping in?" she said, tears brimming and then spilling over.

"Go to the office, Ms. Bergstrom. You know the rules. You have to check in whether you are excused or unexcused."

And there she was, standing in front of all of her classmates who were watching to see what would happen, crying in front of them because unlike most of them, she actually cared about the test, cared enough to pedal her heart out on her bike, and unlike all of them, she had been taking care of her mom, who had cancer.

"You know what, Mr. Long? You're a dick. You don't know anything about me." She slammed the door on the way out and instead of going to the office went to the girls' room, locked herself in a stall, and cried. No one understood. No one had any idea.

Between classes, students came and went. She silenced herself and listened to snippets of conversations, one of which was someone recounting how Carly had called Mr. Long a dick, while the listener expressed disbelief. She wasn't sure she recognized their voices and didn't really care.

Traffic subsided, much to her relief, and then she heard the unmistakable click-click-click of Ms. Hepworth's shoes. "Carly?" she called from the doorway, then entered.

Carly lifted her feet. She just wasn't up for this day getting even worse. The clicking slowed as Ms. Hepworth strolled by each of the six stalls, stopping in front of hers to peer through the crack. Busted. Carly didn't budge, though, curious about what would happen if she just didn't leave her sanctuary.

To her surprise, she watched Ms. Hepworth's shoes walk on to the end of the row, then turn and slide out as she sat down on the bathroom floor against the wall.

"Carly, I heard about what happened in Mr. Long's class. That doesn't sound like you. What's going on?"

What's going on? What's going on? Carly didn't even know where to start. She simply cried, reaching for toilet paper before her sniffles totally gave her away.

"Do we need to call your parents?"

"That would be unkind," Carly said quietly and deliberately.

"Oh? How come?"

Carly did not want Ms. Hepworth to call and wake them. "Because they're both finally asleep."

Ms. Hepworth was quiet for a moment, trying to make sense of that. "What's going on at home, Carly?"

Carly was cornered and she knew it. There was no way out. And so she said the words out loud that she did not want to say, the words that would make it even more real when shared, the words that opened the floodgates when she spoke them. "My mom has cancer." Sobbing, she opened the door and let herself be held by her principal, let herself cry, let her face be washed with a wet paper towel, let herself be led to Ms. Hepworth's office, where she was allowed to sit at a little desk in the corner, normally reserved for naughty kids but today reserved for one who just couldn't handle life, or pressure, or being seen by anyone.

Later, a precalculus test was delivered to her by the secretary and then classwork from other classes. Diligently, she worked her way through it, but when two o'clock rolled around, she made herself go to science class because she could not figure out how she would make up the lab if she missed it. Besides, Andrea was her lab partner, and she could count on her to carry her through it.

Feeling the stares as she walked through the hall and into her class, she looked down, trying to block out the world, the intrusion, the unbearable vulnerability, understanding something deeper about why her mom shut her eyes when she cried.

After that day, her dad took leave on day four, along with days three and five, and stayed home.

Yes, she had tried to be the very best daughter she could be, but each step led to another step and it seemed to be never ending. No matter how hard she tried, she never felt she was good enough. Not good enough in school, where she couldn't concentrate on much of what her teachers said. Not good enough at home, where she couldn't make her mother better.

Just when the chemo was all over, her mother had a double mastectomy. A couple of days after the surgery, lab results came back with great news. The cancer appeared to have been knocked completely out by the chemo. Her mother's lymph node had come back negative as well. For about three weeks, Carly had been happy. But still, it wasn't over. It was never over. Her mom had to have a second surgery—one to remove her uterus and ovaries.

It was Carly's senior year, the only senior year she'd ever have, and for the final two months of it, she just wanted to be a normal kid and go a little crazy. She just wanted to let go after holding on so tight. What was so wrong with that—especially when she might be the next one to have cancer?

Yeah, how about that memo? How about watching her mom suffer for months and then find out that that experience is genetic—

that she had better enjoy her boobs while she had them because one day they might need to be cut off? That very night, she had let Bryce Myers feel her up. There was no time to waste. Her chances of getting ovarian cancer were thirty times greater than for other women, and there were no mammograms for ovaries. In fact, doctors were now beginning to think that ovarian cancer started in the fallopian tubes, and those couldn't even be seen with ultrasound. So, she could live with a gun to her head until she had kids and then get her ovaries out, or she could do it sooner and adopt, or she could skip having kids because she was probably going to die early anyway. That was her takeaway. Because it wasn't just breast and ovarian cancer. She had gone online that night and learned a BRCA2 gene mutation gave her greater odds of other cancers too.

Suddenly, everything had seemed pointless. Good grades? Pointless. College? Pointless. All careful, healthy, or safe choices? Totally pointless. Her mom had made all the careful, healthy, and safe choices, and that had bought her a metric ton of jack squat. Yeah, when Carly looked at it, she realized that pretty much all of her goals had been long-term goals, and all of those were pointless when she might not be around long enough for the payoff. Delaying any kind of gratification seemed stupid.

As she sat in the passenger seat, scowling out the window at the flat, mostly barren landscape broken up only with the pumps from oil wells moving slowly up and down, she tried to formulate new goals for herself. Learn to ride a motorcycle. Get a fake ID so she could go to dance clubs. Maybe she would move to L.A. or New York City. After that, she wasn't sure what. She just felt so angry—so angry she didn't know what to do with it all. None of it was fair. Not one ounce of it.

As they approached a gas station, her dad asked, "Need to stop?"

"Yes," she answered. One-word answers—that's all he would be receiving from her in the foreseeable future. He could try to control everything else, but he couldn't control that.

She weighed her options. She could try to make a break for it at the gas station. Her dad would chase her. She could shout that he was not her dad and to help her. She could. It wasn't clear how that would work out, though. It would complicate things. So, she could do that . . . or she could work for Great-Aunt Rae, maybe earn a little money, and have that much more money in her pocket when she took off on her eighteenth birthday, when there would be not a damn thing anyone could do to stop her.

Carly began to pay attention later that afternoon when the plains turned into mountains, when the straight road began to wind and finally dropped down to Taos. She wanted to ask her dad to stop in the center of town or at least at the Pueblo so they could wander and explore, but that request would cause her to have to set aside her angst and her role as the victim and she wasn't remotely ready to do that. But she felt sad as they passed it and turned left onto another relatively flat road west, one momentarily interrupted by the colony of earthship houses, many more of which had sprung up since they had last driven through there. Eventually, they drove through another town—if it could be called that. It appeared to be little more than a restaurant and post office. And then they climbed over more mountains, dropping at last into an awesome, expansive view of a whole lot of not much.

Once in the valley, they drove through the tiny town of Tierra

Amarilla, past the houses of people who appeared to have enough and past the houses of people who it appeared did not. Then they turned right onto the highway that would lead them to Chama and drove north.

Although she had good memories of Chama, it now seemed entirely too small and too hopeless a place for her. A taco restaurant had taken over the large metal building that had been the feed shop. The Purina logo poked out from under the new sign. Farther up the road, a sign wishing Jesus a happy birthday sat on the roof of an abandoned building. There was a restaurant in an old, single-wide mobile home—not something she ever saw in Oklahoma City. Other things looked more normal to her—a small grocery store, two hotels, a Family Dollar store, and then a downtown so small that if she blinked, she'd miss it. Cute shops lined the west side of the street. The historic train was on the east. Her dad slowed after the restaurant they always ate at and before the bar they avoided, then turned up Third Street to the corner of Third and Pine, where he crept past the house on the northwest corner that her parents had bought years ago.

"You should fix that up," Carly said, breaking her rule about giving one-word answers only because she knew it would irritate him to have anyone, but especially her, tell him something he already knew about what he should do. *Let him see how it feels,* she thought.

He simply nodded.

Continuing north on Pine until the road ran out, they found Great-Aunt Rae's long gravel driveway and turned left onto it. Carly's stomach began to tie up in knots as the reality of all of this hit her. This was where she would be spending the summer against her will.

Great-Aunt Rae walked out of her barn and stood there

waiting in her overalls and T-shirt, a little smile on her face, her posture nonchalant. She looked like an old woman to Carly now . . . yet somehow still mighty. Carly sized her up as Great-Aunt Rae appeared to do the same. The look on Great-Aunt Rae's face seemed to say, *I could flip you like a cheese omelet, kid, but I'd rather have fun. What do you say?* Carly did not yet know her answer, but an early memory popped into her mind, a memory that should have been her first clue.

Carly had been tired. It wasn't easy being a toddler and out of her daily routine, and in new places on top of that, new places that smelled all wrong—nothing like home.

Her road-weary parents each thought the other was looking after her, her dad as he strolled the horse trail on the property line and her mom as she visited with her aunt. And so it was that she had no obstacles when she saw and smelled the perfect place to sleep and the perfect napping companion all rolled into one.

It was big and round, covered with fur, and on the ground, like her giant teddy bear at home but better because it was warm, and it moved ever so slightly up and down like her mom or dad when she fell asleep on one of them. This one was already asleep, just like she wanted to be, and so she crawled right on top of it, worked her fingers deep down into its fur, laid her head down, and fell fast asleep.

She did not hear the whispers of Great-Aunt Rae when she walked around the corner with Carly's mom and, much to her horror, saw Carly's napping place, the horse wide-awake now, not moving but looking at this tiny creature on its side with a wild and confused eye, then looking at Rae, imploring her to do something. She did not see her mother freeze on Rae's command, terrified tears running down her face as helplessness overwhelmed her. She did not hear Rae swear under her breath and say, "Of all of the horses, she had to pick T. Rex," and then swear some more. She only remembered being lifted swiftly off the soft warmth and opening her eyes to see a sky full of hooves as the giant horse rolled once, twice, and then got its feet under it and stood, taller than her very tall great-aunt.

Carly looked at that broad back, broad enough to go back to sleep on, and she reached out for the horse.

"I know. I know, little one. I know," was all Great-Aunt Rae said.

The horse turned to sniff her, blowing hot air on Carly's bare arms and face. She remembered that—all that hot wind. Then the horse turned and pranced away.

When Carly stepped out of the car, the smells on the wind confused and disarmed her momentarily. Pine. Hay. Horse manure. Horses. And then as she and her dad were circled once, then twice, by Violet the Australian shepherd, there was the smell of dog too. She wanted to squat down and get her fingers in all that fur, but she didn't want to give her dad the satisfaction of seeing her happy. If he was going to treat her like a prisoner instead of a daughter, she was going to act like a prisoner instead of a daughter. *You reap what you sow, Dad,* she thought.

But turning over her shoulder and looking in the field beyond the barn, she scanned until she saw T. Rex, her favorite, and since no one could see her face, she smiled in spite of herself.

Amy

Back when Amy was receiving chemo infusions, she had leafed through an old issue of *National Geographic*—the one with the feature article about national parks. On the cover was a picture of Great Smoky Mountains National Park, and she recalled her dad telling her about how in early June, people came from all over to watch the lightning bugs put on their light show. Somehow all this time had passed and she had never made time to see that. Not that or much else. Her eyes had welled up with grateful tears because there was still time to change that. The chemo she was receiving was going to save her. Not everyone in the infusion room had such a good prognosis. Not everyone still had time to see the lightning bugs in Great Smoky Mountains National Park.

In 1986, the year the little books were first published, her dad had given Alicia and Amy both a copy of *Passport to Your National Parks* for Christmas. It was only their second Christmas without their mom, and the grief was still so acute, but just opening the tiny book and seeing pictures of Mt. Rainier had evoked happy memories of a time when they were all together. Amy, Alicia, and their dad swapped memories, and then her dad said he hoped that his girls would always share his love for the national parks and enjoy documenting their adventures at every new place. Flipping through the little book some more, she dreamed of visiting every magical park and monument listed.

As the years passed, though, something always took priority, it seemed—finishing college, getting married, starting their careers. Before Carly was born, Amy had taught a weekly painting class in two different senior living communities and at a YMCA after-school program. When she wasn't doing that, she was painting or peddling her paintings to furniture and home decor stores and sometimes at the farmers market. Then she rushed home in time to make dinner for Paul—not because he expected it necessarily but because she loved showing him love in this way. They bought a house they could barely afford in preparation for a family they hoped to have. After that, there was no money for traveling. It seemed they never had both freedom and money at the same time. After Carly was born, Amy remembered the dream, hoping to share her dad's love of the national parks with her daughter; but then the bombing happened, and Paul changed, leaving her just wanting to give him whatever he needed to be happy. The beach seemed to make him happy.

One spring break back when Carly was seven, they did take her to Carlsbad Caverns, though, and it was far more magical than Amy had dared to dream it would be. Instead of taking the elevator, they had walked in, climbing farther and farther down until they were in a completely foreign world, one covered in jewels. The cave was unimaginably large, with an opaque turquoise pond in the middle, and she had stared in wonder at it all, trying to absorb every little detail as she walked behind her husband, who held their little girl's hand. That night, from the campground, they had watched as millions of bats flew out of the cave to hunt for mosquitoes. Amy had felt like a girl again, immersed in the joy of discovery. Although Paul had seemed to enjoy himself, she'd noticed how tired he was. He'd yawned while driving and while wandering through the visitor center, and it had hit her that while she craved stimulation on vacation, Paul needed relaxation. He was so deep-down weary. He needed time away from humanity. So after that, they went back to the beach or occasionally visited Aunt Rae.

But now Amy didn't need to take anyone else into consideration. Mt. Rainier National Park was her goal, but there were opportunities to check parks off her list between there and Oklahoma. Tonight, it was Great Sand Dunes National Park in Colorado.

She pulled in just as the sun was illuminating the sand, casting an orange glow on the western-facing sides, enhancing the forms with highlights and shadows. After finding a camping spot, she went for a short walk on a nature trail and marveled that here in the middle of the country so close to mammoth peaks, there would be giant sand dunes of all things. In the waning light, some visitors still surfed down the dunes on boards cut and shaped for that purpose, while those who were done for the day walked together through a wide but shallow river and back up the hill toward her, smiles on their faces. For a moment, she forgot about her painful year and simply felt the joy of discovery, but then as she saw the difference in how people looked at her now, she became acutely aware of how she appeared in the eyes of the visitors who passed her, and it was painful. She missed her hair. She missed being beautiful. Her mood darkened, and she kicked herself for thinking she could run away from any of this when it was so obvious that the vessel for the emotional distress wasn't her house but her very own body and mind. Breathing deeply, she told herself she would feel better after some sleep.

After visiting the restroom, she made her bed in the back of her Honda CR-V station wagon with the same small pad and sleeping bag she had used on camping trips as a teenager. Before crawling in, she dug through the tote that sat on the passenger seat to find the flashlight she had packed, and then, ready for sleep, she dove in. Her bed was hard, so much harder than she had imagined it would be. Hard and hot. As soon as she zipped her sleeping bag, she had a hot flash and abruptly unzipped it, turned on her flashlight, and awkwardly reached over the seat to dig for a hand towel in the tote to blot off her excess sweat before it soaked into her sleeping bag. A lot of things were better in a person's imagination, she mused as she lay back down. She had no idea how she was actually going to sleep on such a hard surface, and as she tried, her whole trip felt like a big mistake.

She had been so certain that it would feel so good to put miles between her and the pressures at home—the pressure to be who she was, to feel normal and act normal, to be a good wife when she knew she surely repulsed her husband, and to be a good mother when her daughter clearly wanted nothing to do with her. Yes, she thought she would feel better, but now that she was away, she felt very little relief at all. She still felt weary and irreparably broken.

After she watched the first stars emerge from twilight, she closed her eyes to sleep but just sweated instead. Her own home at least offered the comfort of familiarity, after all. Familiarity and a little fan on her bedside table just for moments like these. She could have stayed and had the house all to herself while Paul and Carly were gone. But what would she have done with the house all to herself? Cry some more?

She rested her hands on her chest, on top of her T-shirt, felt the uneven ridges and bumps where her breasts used to be, the asymmetry, the giant dimple on the stump of her left breast that reminded her of a manatee's mouth, and she moved her hands in small circles to help her nerves recalibrate. The tingly, electric sensations spread, and she followed the sensations up her chest and into her armpits. They weren't the good kind of tingly sensations she used to get in the early days of her relationship with Paul when he touched her there. They were the high-voltage kind that followed nerve damage. "Heal, heal, heal," she whispered to her body as she touched it, both an order and a desperate prayer.

It was all in the region of her heart, in the part of her body where she used to hold and feed her child, in this place that touched the heart of another when she hugged them. All this numbness. All this loss. All this emptiness. It was all right there where she used to feel so much.

Carly

Carly couldn't untangle all the things she felt so anxious about. Sleeping in a new place. Being seen as a failure now. Failing tomorrow. Disappointing Great-Aunt Rae. Difficult decisions about her future that she would need to make starting in about a month and a half. The likelihood that she would go through what her mom went through. Control. Having no control now. Having little control later. Then having no control again at the end of her surely too-short life. Being unlovable. And undesirable. Being lonely. That last thought was what actually hit her hardest.

On the bedside table, Great-Aunt Rae had left a small stack of books for Carly, and since she was unable to sleep, she picked up each one and examined it: field guides for birds and flowers; *The Milagro Beanfield War*, which was set in northern New Mexico; a novel called *The Death of Bernadette Lefthand*, set on the Jicarilla Apache Reservation nearby; plus *The Bean Trees, Cowboys Are My Weakness*, and *How I Came West, and Why I Stayed*. And even though she and Great-Aunt Rae were leaving on a pack trip the next day, Great-Aunt Rae had put a few wild roses in a jar there too. They smelled like cotton candy. Great-Aunt Rae was trying. Carly remembered what it felt like to try.

Great-Aunt Rae had explained when showing Carly to this

room that next to her bed were a pair of old riding boots that she had bought on sale and found to be uncomfortably just a little too small and that she hoped they would fit Carly. And in the closet, she had put a few cowgirl shirts she had outgrown, uncertain whether Carly would like them or wear them. Guests liked it when the guides dressed the part though, so she always made an effort and hoped Carly would as well.

Over the doorway hung an angel that someone had hand carved from wood. It looked down over Carly as if keeping watch. If it was meant to comfort her, it didn't. It only left her wondering why. Why her mom. And probably one day why her.

She slipped out of bed and tried on one of the cowgirl shirts—red with white trim on the yokes and pockets. It was a little big, but fine. Then she pulled her curtain open enough to peek out. Under the nearly full moon, she could see the shapes of the gentle giants in the large paddock. Feeling the pull, she slipped on jeans and socks and carried her shoes as she crept down the little hall to the stairs. Boards squeaked like tattletales, but neither her dad nor Great-Aunt Rae opened their doors to check on her. That was a surprise. Usually her dad was more vigilant than that, and a light sleeper too. Surely a part of him had to be anticipating that she might run away. Maybe he was giving up on her. She was surprised to feel that possibility turn her stomach like bad fish.

Violet barked once and then recognized her enough to suspend judgment. Maybe the shirt and boots still smelled enough like Great-Aunt Rae to convince the dog that Carly was okay. As she sat on the porch steps and put on her shoes, Violet wriggled up next to her, shaking her back end, happy to have company. Carly put an arm around the furry dog, surprised to find a feeling of comfort wash over her. It was similar to when she drank water after not realizing she had been so thirsty. Memories of all the moments she had needed a hug in the last several months bubbled right up to the surface. Worried someone would catch her before she made it all the way to T. Rex, she patted Violet's shoulder and walked out to her destination. Unable to tell whether the horses were sleeping, she leaned on the rails of the fence and quietly talked to them. She certainly did not want to get stepped on by startled Clydesdales when she approached them.

Violet ran back toward the house, and for a minute, Carly considered hiding, but she wasn't doing anything wrong, really. She figured that if it was her dad, Violet would have barked, so it was probably Great-Aunt Rae. It seemed best to just stay put.

Soon she heard footsteps, and then Great-Aunt Rae stood next to her and leaned on the same rail. At first, she didn't say anything, and then she asked, "Do you remember your first ride?"

Carly thought and then answered, "I don't know. A lot of memories blend together."

"It's one of my very favorite memories. I remember sitting on Tea for Two, yes, a dumb name for a good horse, but on this occasion, rather appropriate. Your dad climbed the tractor tires I used as a mounting block with you in tow. You were only four years old. I will never forget the look on your face—the perfectly appropriate mix of terror and euphoria as your dad lifted you up and out to sit bareback right in front of me. I said, 'Hold on to the mane there, cowgirl! We're going on an adventure!'" Smiling, Great-Aunt Rae paused for a long moment before she continued.

"I remember the feeling of your little ribs against my own as you nearly hyperventilated with excitement, your little body so rigid. . . . I knew you were apt to slide right off if you didn't learn to sink in. I said, 'Here's what you need to know, cowgirl. Relax your low back so that your tushie moves with the horse and the rest of you floats along above it. Breathe in one, two, three, breathe out one, two, three. . . .' And what I remember most was feeling the moment you synchronized with that horse, and I knew that you were hooked. I remember thinking that you were one of my tribe now—the tribe of horse-crazy girls and girl-crazy horses, my spirit tribe."

Again, Great-Aunt Rae paused. It gave Carly a moment to consider whether she was going to allow the belonging that was being offered to sink into her heart or whether she was going to resolve to be impermeable and let the belonging that was being offered slide off. Before she made up her mind, Great-Aunt Rae began to speak again.

"It was something, you know. This little child sitting in front of me, her dreams coming true right that very instant . . . such a bitty thing in the space between my arms. For just an instant, I had a taste of what my life might have been like if there had not been a war going on during the one time in my life when I had really been in love. I wasn't sure whether to feel sad at what life hadn't given me or grateful for the little taste of pure sweetness that it was offering me in that very moment. Tea for Two walked through the long loop with us on his back and your dad following on foot and taking pictures until your mom reached out and touched his arm. She knew. She remembered. There were moments too sacred for pictures, too sacred for the distraction of having them taken. There were moments that should be allowed to be the pure magic they were.

"We wandered away on our own, our noses full of the scent of horse and wild roses, your little hands full of fur and mane . . . soft, well-oiled leather reins and a little girl in mine. I had wanted that ride to last forever, but when you began to head bob just a little, I broke the sacred silence and asked you all of the questions I saved just for the rare moments that I met a four-year-old, questions about how you thought it all worked. The big questions like where horses came from and where wildflowers came from and why you thought you were born a girl and not a horse. This woke you up, and you rattled off ideas in fragments that sometimes made sense all strung together and sometimes did not, but you stayed awake until we were safely back at the barn." Great-Aunt Rae took a long breath. "Not a lot of things in my life softened me. But that moment was one thing that did. Softened me all the way to the very center of my beat-up heart."

Great-Aunt Rae kept her eyes on the horses even when Carly turned to look at her with a small smile. A smile like a peace offering. She had never considered that Great-Aunt Rae had ever been in love, or that she might have wanted anything out of life other than what she had gotten, or that her heart might have felt beat-up.

"Well, kiddo, child of my tribe, don't stay out too long. Tomorrow is a big day. Life is more fun when you've had enough sleep. It's safer, too." Great-Aunt Rae gave Carly a pat on the back and a little smile before leaving her to remember something about who she was in the presence of girl-crazy horses.

T. Rex turned to face her. Moonlight shone on his back, illuminating his outline like a halo. And even though she had hated having her dad's will imposed upon her, she couldn't help it. She was glad she was here.

Paul

Paul came down the stairs with his things and found Rae sitting at the kitchen table. "Good morning, Rae. I woke up early and got to thinking that if I left before Carly woke, you two might get off to a better start."

Rae nodded in agreement. "Leave her a note, though." She poured him a cup of coffee and set granola and milk on the table along with two bowls and two spoons. "Did you stop by your house?"

"Drove by. That's all."

"You going to?"

He nodded. "It's high time I assess the situation." He dreaded it—dreaded seeing his dream ruined, possibly beyond repair.

"You know, if you wanted to stay, Carly and I won't be back here for a week. Key to the garage is right there. I've got plenty of tools. And you can use my truck if you need to buy anything that won't fit in your car."

Paul chewed and thought about it. "After Amy's . . . you know, winter, I used up a lot of my leave. I need to let it build back up. Plus, it's such a big job. I wonder how much difference a week of just me working on it could make, you know? But do you keep a key to your house hidden in case I get there and change my mind?" He was confident he wouldn't, but it never hurt to have alternative plans.

Rae gestured for him to follow her and led him outside to show him the nail under the eve where it hung.

"Thanks, Rae," he said. "Hey, if this doesn't work out for any reason, call me and I'll come back out as fast as I can. Amy has taken off, so call my cell phone."

"What do you mean Amy has taken off?"

"Uh, she's gone on a trip back to Washington State to visit trees."

"I have trees here," said Rae.

"I mentioned that to her, but she wanted to visit those trees."

Rae's eyes narrowed with concern. "Is she slipping away?"

"I don't know," he answered.

Rae paused and then asked, "Is she slipping over the edge?"

A few weeks after the bombing, she had asked him the same question about himself. Amy had driven him out here to visit, knowing getting out of the city would help. Paul had given Rae the same answer then. "Maybe."

"After the bombing, you did a lot of walking by yourself out here. Sounds like she's doing the same thing. Did it help you?"

There were too many thoughts in Paul's mind for him to process all at once. He hadn't considered the ways in which his experience and hers might be similar. Once Amy was cancer-free and the surgeries were over, he had expected all would be well—joyous, even. Why wouldn't someone be happy about a second lease on life? But before he could finish that train of thought, it was interrupted by her last question, *Did it help you?* He didn't know. On the one hand, maybe. It surely hadn't hurt. It probably allowed his nervous system to calm down and his lungs to clean themselves out. But on the other hand, nothing had really helped. Not even time. He could only shrug his answer.

"Well, maybe it will help her," Rae said, and led the way back into the house, where Paul rinsed his coffee cup, gave her a little good-bye hug, thanked her again, and then carried his bag to his car. Rae stood on her little porch, waving, as he drove away.

He found it hard to drive away from his still-sleeping daughter. Life was short—too short not to make good memories with the ones he loved the most. He saw it all the time. Every day. People's lives cut unexpectedly shorter. He hoped Carly knew how much he loved her just in case it was his life that would be cut short next. It was his preference to leave things in better order than this.

As he drove down the road and into town, the old narrow-gauge train whistled like a ghost and then whistled again, this time even more emphatic, before beginning its journey into the Rocky Mountains along the Continental Divide. And maybe because he wasn't used to hearing it and hadn't learned to tune it out as he had all the other noises in his life, it struck him as such a haunting, lonely sound. It was the sound of a loved one leaving, growing farther and farther away until they could no longer be seen or heard. For a moment, he envisioned himself on the platform, looking at one train taking his wife away in one direction and another train taking his daughter away in the opposite. It still felt to him as if they were growing farther and farther away with each passing moment until one day, he'd be unable to see them or hear them at all. They were leaving him. He could feel it, and there was really nothing he could do about it. And perhaps there was nothing he *should* do about it, because it was the natural course of things. Nonetheless, he pulled out his phone and texted Amy, *Thinking about you,* because he really didn't know what to say.

The distance between Aunt Rae's ranch and his house was not more than a mile. He passed the Laundromat, both the Catholic and Episcopal churches, then the elementary school, and one more block. There, he parked and just sat in his car for a moment. This had been his dream, this dilapidated old Dutch Colonial house that he had bought two years ago, thinking he would fix it up so he and Amy could move there when he retired. It was far from the urban troubles and chaos and the heat of Oklahoma City, and close to Amy's aunt, whom Amy wanted to be near as she grew older. He had been more excited than he had been in years when they bought it, because it made retirement seem so close and so real. His escape route was in his sights. He supposed it still was. In a few months he would turn forty-eight, and then it would just be three more years. But it was different somehow when he had this place to go to the day after he retired.

He had taken three trips out here and made a little progress on some basic upgrades, but then last October, not even a week before Amy knew something was wrong, whatever progress had been made was erased when the upstairs bathroom had a water leak that showered the house until a neighbor noticed water running out from under the door and called city hall. He'd come out for a few days and gutted all of the saturated drywall and floorboards before they molded.

And then he got the call from Alicia, Amy's sister, who knew Amy wouldn't tell him what was going on—that she wouldn't want to cause him worry if it turned out to be nothing. Amy had found a lump and gone to the doctor. The doctor was concerned enough that he got radiology to get her in for a mammogram that day. And after the radiologist looked at the images, she was concerned enough to slip her into someone else's canceled appointment for a needle biopsy the very next day. Alicia was going to take her. But it was all happening so fast, Alicia said. Nothing ever happened that fast. It had to be serious.

It was as if the house had been an omen of what was about to happen. To her. To him. To them. Cancer, as silent as water rotting the inside while everything on the outside looked normal. Destroyed. Then gutted.

As Paul pulled up to the house now, what he noticed was the darkness on the other side of the windows where there should have been light. The windows were just like Amy's sad eyes.

But while the changes Amy had been through showed on the outside of her, the outside of this house still looked as it always had—rather charming. The covered porch was supported by scalloped posts and embellished with gingerbread. While it did need a new coat of paint, the old paint didn't look all that shabby. Squares of leaded stained glass framed the front windows. The old front door was welcoming, with a doorknob embossed with intricate flowers and, below it, an equally elegant plate with two holes for skeleton keys. This had always been Paul's favorite part of the whole house, this doorknob like a person in their Sunday best shaking his hand for just a moment before he came in. There was something very polite and formal about it. But now that he had started to entertain the notion of this house as a reflection of his wife, he thought about Amy's delicate, feminine hand in his as he touched the doorknob. All the times he had held her hand . . . in the beginning, during the vows, while she gave birth to Carly, when she was so sick and he lay on his side facing her. Her eyes looked so scared, so weary . . . he held her hands and hoped she felt all of his love flow from him into her through this place where their bodies met. He had hoped she would absorb his strength. His resolve. Because he could feel her surrender and it scared him.

He held her hands as if he were holding her here to earth when she had ambivalent hours.

For a long moment, he simply stood there, holding the floral doorknob, as it occurred to him that he might never hold Amy's hand again. He probably would, he told himself. Probably. But it wasn't certain.

In the middle of the door was the doorbell, like a bicycle bell on the inside but with a knob on the outside. He turned it to wind it up and then released it so that the striker repeatedly hit the bell, as if he could call out to Amy in this way. As if he could say he was so sorry for the neglect prior to the big disaster, so sorry. But he was here now. And he wanted to fix things. Fix them and then maintain them better.

Paul unlocked the door and opened it. Inside, the complete wreckage overwhelmed him on a new level now that the metaphor was taking root. Paul shook his head in disbelief. What a nightmare. "Fix" was the wrong word for what had to be done. There was not enough left to fix. "Rebuild" was more accurate. Starting anew in an old structure was so much harder than just building an entirely new house. It was so tempting to just bulldoze the whole thing and start over, but then he thought of all the details he could never re-create in a new structure, the touches that had charmed him in the first place.

As Paul set down the skeleton key on a nearby windowsill, he marveled again how no one locked their doors here in Chama. For a cop like him, this was unimaginable. This house in this community seemed like a portal to another time, a simpler, more honest time.

He walked into the house on the exposed floor joists and examined the giant tree root that had grown under the structure. Someone had cut it long ago. He looked out the window in the direction from which the root had come. A large elm tree seemed to be just fine despite the injury.

An elegant old light fixture was mounted to the ceiling by an intricately embossed plate. If he still wrote songs, he would have been inspired by that, by how people used to make practical things beautiful instead of cluttering their lives to make up for functional things that were not beautiful. But he hadn't written songs in nearly two decades, and so he turned his mind back to creating a list of everything that needed to be done and all the tools and materials that would be needed for each job.

This was his chance to start all over, to redo the ancient knob-and-tube electrical wiring, greatly reducing the chance that the house would burn down on its own, to examine the plumbing and see whether more disasters could be averted by changing out parts, to put in a really good floor, one tight enough to keep mice and drafts out, and to install good insulation. He could do all that or he could cut his losses, get rid of it, maybe find something else. Making all the repairs seemed like it would either take him a lifetime to do himself or cost him a fortune to contract someone else.

Hopping from floor joist to floor joist, he realized that he wouldn't be able to use a single power tool to do the work until he put in a new circuit breaker box. That would be step one. The old electricity had been run through the attic and under the house, not so much through the walls, so the studs didn't have holes for wires to run through. He would need to drill holes through all of them. That would be step two, and that alone could take weeks. Looking at the cluster of exposed asbestos fabric–covered wires connected to the old fuse box, he marveled that the house hadn't gone up in flames a long time ago.

He walked back out the door to the porch and sat down. Although he would have liked to stay a week, make some progress, and be here in case things didn't work out between Carly and Rae, there really was no decision to make. He simply didn't have sick leave to waste.

Music interrupted his thinking. At first it seemed as if one of the neighbors were listening to a Spanish guitar recording, but at some point he realized, no, someone was actually playing it. He followed the sound to the backyard, but the neighbor's border collie barked at him through the back fence and the music stopped. A moment later, after he retreated back to the front porch, the music continued.

The first time Paul had seen Amy, he was playing his guitar outside the art building at the University of Oklahoma early one September evening, shortly after fall quarter had begun. He thought he was alone out there, but the window to the room where she was working on a painting was open.

She applauded for him when he finished each song, finally standing and peeking out the window when the music stopped. He was bent over, snapping the final clasp on his guitar case. "Hey, thanks for the concert," she called out the window, her smile competing with the sun. "Your music inspired great things."

Well, he had to see that. "Yeah? Can I see?" he asked.

"Um, okay. Sure," she answered, her demeanor changing to shy and self-conscious. "Room 105."

Paul entered with a smile and admired the landscape painting. There were trees that served as a windbreak on someone's farm, rippling wheat, and sky. "It reminds me of the national grasslands near where I grew up," he said. "Have you ever stood in the middle of wheat or tall grass when it's rippling like that?"

Amy shook her head.

He smiled, remembering the experience, looking for words. "Hard to describe," he finally said.

He was aware of her proximity as they stood near the painting, of the electric current passing back and forth between them each time they looked at each other and even when they didn't. He knew even then that something significant was happening, but he played it cool, giving her painting a nod, and said, "I like it. Thanks for letting me see it." With that, he gave her a little wave and left, stepping into the hall to catch his breath before he passed out. She had that effect on him from that very first moment—she took his breath away.

Years later, while they were lying in bed in each other's arms, trying to figure out on what day they had first met and recounting the story, she told him she had wondered whether she had somehow blown it, whether she should have proposed getting some coffee or something, wondered what she might have said or done differently so that her visit with him might have lasted longer. She said she kicked herself all night and all the next day, until he showed up again the next night and serenaded her again and every night after that, until it finally got so chilly that he would come directly inside room 105 and play for her there. Something about that confession—vulnerability, he supposed—had made Paul love her even more, which he hadn't thought possible.

From the step where he sat on the front porch, he dared to dream of life after retirement, of staying there in Chama, of fixing up this house that had once been his dream, of taking guitar lessons from the man with the border collie, of going for runs out the dirt road past Rae's house, out into the seemingly infinite Edward Sargent Wildlife Area without locking his door behind him. He imagined each room in its perfected state, the remodeled bathroom with a floor tiled in white and black octagons and the stately claw-foot bathtub put back where it belonged, hardwood floors in the main room, a copper backsplash in the kitchen.

But then he remembered his caseload at work. As reality hit him, his shoulders sagged. He had to go back. The other officers on the force had covered for him enough throughout Amy's battle with cancer. It was time for him to come through for them, to take extra shifts so that they could take vacations with their families. Yes, that was the responsible thing to do. Of course, he thought, it would be better for the structure of the house if he put a floor in to keep the moisture out next winter. . . . He would have to consider either doing that this summer or hiring a carpenter to.

Reluctantly, he locked up the house, walked to his car, and began the ten-hour drive home. After all, he had a shift tomorrow. Criminals weren't going to stop committing crimes just because he had a daughter that was somewhere between at-risk and off the rails and an old house to fix up.

Carly

Watching carefully, Carly tried imitating Great-Aunt Rae's circular movement with the curry brush, firmly enough to remove dirt clods from Mister T's fur but slight enough not to scratch his skin. Then she picked up the stiff bristle brush to brush over where she had just curried and a softer brush with longer bristles for the horse's face and legs. Finally, she combed out his mane and tail. He was a massive black Clydesdale with a white blaze down his face and white "feathers," the long, fluffy fur, on the lower part of his legs.

Great-Aunt Rae picked through the grooming box until she found a hoof pick. Then she bent over, tapped his ankle, and said in her best Mr. T voice, "I pity the fool who doesn't pick up his foot!" Mr. T the horse picked up his foot and she picked the mud and rocks out of the massive cavity between his shoes. "See that?" she asked, pointing to a V-shaped structure on the bottom of the horse's hoof. "That's the frog. Don't try to pick that out."

Carly wasn't sure what she had expected. More warmth? Great-Aunt Rae had been warm. Carly knew that her great-aunt was glad she was here. Pity. Carly supposed she had expected pity. And maybe the allowance to slack that went with it. That was clearly not happening.

She groomed two more horses, and in the same time, Great-Aunt Rae groomed four. As Carly glanced over at Great-Aunt Rae's progress, she said, "Don't worry. You'll get faster," as if it were pure encouragement, as if she weren't clearly telling Carly that in the future, she expected her to work faster.

Carly's dad was gone—left before she even woke, left without a good-bye. Although a part of her was glad to have the freedom of his absence, another part felt offended and abandoned—just a problem to be cast off onto someone else, no longer the little girl that he loved. She knew that was likely baloney, but still, those feelings echoed around inside of her as she worked.

In light of his absence, there was no real point in putting on a show of rebelliousness. The truth was that while Chama was otherwise lame and she already missed her friends, she was pretty excited to ride these giant horses every day. She kept her excitement hidden, though, just in case she needed to play martyr at some point in the future.

She followed Great-Aunt Rae into the tack room, where she picked up the saddle, pad, and blankets on the rack labeled "Mr. T" and the bridle on the hook next to it. Her arms full, she returned to the horse and began saddling him. Great-Aunt Rae came over and moved the blanket and pad forward a little bit before Carly attempted to lift the heavy western saddle high up onto the horse's back. She wasn't quite able to make it.

"Swing it like this," said Great-Aunt Rae, lifting the saddle as she twisted a quarter of a turn. "Or use that ladder. I think it's safer to stay off ladders whenever possible." Once the saddle was on, she reached under the horse to grab the girth and cinch it up. "Some people tie a knot. I use the buckle so it lies flatter. Just be sure to sort of back it up once it's buckled so there's tension on it." Sticking two fingers under the girth, she said, "About this tight. Two fingers."

Back in the tack room, Carly picked up the next saddle and tried to do better as she saddled T. Rex, her favorite. Great-Aunt Rae saddled three horses in the time it took her to saddle one.

Just then the guests arrived, spilling out of a rental car, big smiles on their excited faces. Carly watched as Great-Aunt Rae shook their hands and welcomed them, then pointed them to the pile of saddlebags and gave them some time to transfer their belongings. The guests' excitement was contagious, and Carly smiled in spite of herself. She was going to get paid to do something other people paid a lot of money to do. Quickly, though, she dialed that smile all the way down to obligatory politeness so she wouldn't show Great-Aunt Rae too much enthusiasm. After all, she still wasn't completely sure how this was going to go.

"Okay, kiddo, time for a quick driving lesson," said Great-Aunt Rae.

"I already know how to drive," said Carly. "I've had my license for almost two years now."

Great-Aunt Rae laughed. "I'm glad to hear that," she said as she walked into the barn and placed her hand on the chuck wagon. "This handles a little differently than your parents' car, so I suggest you take me up on my offer to teach you how to drive it."

Unable to stifle a chuckle, Carly smiled and said, "Yes, ma'am."

In a nearby stall stood two black Clydesdales Carly hadn't seen before. Rae clipped ropes to the bottom of one's halter and led him out. The other tried to follow, but she said, "Not yet, Drake." She handed the rope to Carly and said, "I just got these two last year since Mr. T is getting old and I didn't want him to have to work this hard. Their official names are Frankenstein and Dracula. Ugh. I wish everyone would just name their horses 'Buddy' and call it good. I would have completely changed their names if they weren't already nine, but since it's a little late in the game for that, I call them Frank and Drake because animals perform better without negative names." Great-Aunt Rae began to put all kinds of straps all over him, and though Carly tried to make some kind of sense of the order of things, she could not. As if reading her mind, Great-Aunt Rae said, "Don't worry about learning how to harness them. I'll do it for now. It's a fine art."

When the harnessing was done, Great-Aunt Rae stepped up onto the bench in the front of the wagon and motioned for Carly to sit next to her. Then she gave the reins a little flick and called, "Ha!" It seemed like with a command like that, the horses should have shot out of the barn like bullets, but instead they simply plodded forward with no drama.

Once out of the barn, she pulled back on one set of reins and turned them to the left and then to the right. "Not so complicated, right? Not a steering wheel, but not so different from riding. To stop, pull back like this. Ho!" Handing the reins to Carly, she said, "Now, you try."

It took Carly a few tries to flick the reins in such a way that Frank and Drake responded. When they walked forward calmly, she felt victorious. She turned them to the left, then turned them to the right, and then stopped them just like Great-Aunt Rae.

"Well done, Carly. Now, that all seems pretty easy, and it is. But horses are horses, so freak things can happen. Say they smell a cougar or a bear and decide to run. You can pull back, but since they're each about fifteen times larger than you, you're probably not going to outmuscle them on a good day and especially not in a panic. Nonetheless, pump the brakes like this because that's your best chance. You can also try it one hand at a time so they think about turning this way and then, oh, no, now you're asking them to turn that way, and then this way and that way, back and forth until they're so confused, they stop. Worth a shot. If this happens on a straight road with no large areas to turn them, try to just hang on and keep them on the road. Eventually, they'll get tired. If you run them up to a fence or something in hopes of stopping them, they may stop suddenly, sending you flying, and you may land where they can trample you. If you turn them too sharply, the wagon may roll. That would be bad for everyone involved. You want to be able to turn them into a wide circle until they calm down, but that's rarely possible when you need it most. Out here, you are going to have a hard time sticking to the bench, should you decide to leave the road at high speeds. The really good news is that I've only had this happen twice in my lifetime, so the odds of it happening to you in the next two months are slim. When we go out, you'll be driving behind the riders, so I expect there will be no problem. Should something like this happen, other riders will bring their horses under control pretty quickly and Frank and Drake will want to stay with them instead of strike out on their own. But again, this is all very unlikely."

Unlikely. A lot of things were unlikely. A mom with breast cancer. A gene mutation. The Oklahoma City bombing. They were all unlikely, and they all happened. Pump the brakes, hang on, and try to stay on the road. Carly wasn't sure there was any value in this advice because what she knew to be true was that it didn't actually matter what anyone did. Life was more or less a crapshoot. It could deliver all kinds of unlikely things. And when they happened, some would live and many would not. At the end of the day, that's the way it was. It reminded her of a video game where she tried to stay alive, the one where she'd made it to the eighth level only once. She would try to stay alive, and she might make it to her eighties if she was really lucky. But at some point, the game ended. It just did. There was no "unlikely" to that. It was certain.

She flicked the reins again and drove the horses down to the road and then back, because even though disaster was inevitable, as it turned out, there was no choice but to move forward. It was what people did.

Amy

The next morning, Amy poured lukewarm water from her thermos into a bowl of instant oatmeal and into a mug of herb tea. She had gotten hot water from a gas station the night before while fueling up. It had seemed like a good idea, but as she choked down her oatmeal and water, it became clear she was going to need a camp stove. A camp stove, a pan, and a fat foam pad for the back of her car. Her back, hips, and shoulders all hurt from her eight-hour attempt at sleeping. The bright side was that it distracted her somewhat from the pain in her abdomen.

She walked down a trail to the river, then crossed it. Walking uphill toward the dunes caused pain deep in her vagina and below the incision near her left hip where the camera had been inserted. Still, she pressed on until she found a spot on the east slope of a dune, where, bundled in a coat and hat, she lay back in the early morning sun, closed her eyes, and tried resting. After some sweating, followed by the removal of her hat, she fell into a light sleep, enough to recharge her for the day ahead.

By the time she woke, the visitor center had opened, so she stopped in to buy four postcards and stamp her little book. As she pressed the gold ink onto a select spot in her copy of *Passport to Your National Parks,* she smiled. If her dad were here and still himself, this would make him so happy. Maybe it still would when she returned and showed him.

On one postcard, she wrote, "Dear Dad, I just stamped my passport book here at Great Sand Dunes. You probably don't remember giving it to me. That's okay. I just wanted to thank you for it and for teaching me to love the national parks and for being my dad. You were a wonderful dad. Do you remember being a park ranger? You were really great at it. I love you always. Your Younger Daughter, Amy."

To Aunt Rae, she simply wrote, "Thank you for taking my girl under your wing and helping her heal. I sure do love you. Amy."

Carly was harder to write to. There was so much she wanted to say, but every single word seemed risky, as if it could push her away forever. "I wish I knew how to help you through this difficult time. I love you and I miss you. Wishing you great adventures. Mom."

And then, there was Paul. She had no clue what to write to him. "Wish you were here"? No. That was a lie. She didn't wish he was there, and she had no idea how to write something normal to him when nothing was normal. In fact, just writing to him felt like a lie in itself because she didn't want to. She was tired of pretending that everything was okay, and now that her survival didn't depend on it, she didn't have to. No, she didn't have to even pretend long enough to send a postcard. She tucked it into her purse, then addressed and stamped the others and dropped them into a receptacle before she got back in her car and headed toward the Black Canyon of the Gunnison.

After nearly five hours, Amy turned off the highway and drove up the road to the visitor center for the Black Canyon of the

Gunnison National Park. Along the canyon rim was a sparse forest of mostly ancient junipers, twisted and gnarled like the hands
of old women reaching toward the heavens. It felt good to Amy
to be among them, but it was nothing like being dwarfed by the
ancient trees closer to the coast.

The Black Canyon itself was every bit as twisted and gnarled
as the junipers, strata in the canyon walls as random as abstract
modern art. She had read that this gneiss and schist was some of
the oldest rock on earth. The very rock she was looking at used to
be almost a mile underground. How remarkable that something
she saw as so static, as stable as the earth itself, could move so
much. She thought it was something she could count on, but she
should have known better. After all, she had seen the aftermath of
Mount St. Helens just a month following its eruption back in 1980
when they had returned to Washington after her freshman year
of high school. Still, this notion that she was floating on pieces of
the earth's crust as it slowly shifted always astounded her. Stripes
in the canyon walls contained newer basalt, from where magma
had crept into the cracks of the ancient gneiss when it had been far
below millions of years ago.

She walked along the rim for a little bit, pondering how little
it mattered that shifts happened so slowly that they were imper-
ceptible. In the end, the ground under her feet shifted, whether
it was the earth or the foundation of her marriage or her very
life. Everything in nature changed, both things that were alive
and things that were not. How foolish she had been to ever think
things could have stayed remotely the same or even on the same
trajectory.

She found a place to perch where she looked down on the
slightly iridescent blue of the black wings of white-throated swifts,
which flew acrobatically below her. While she knew birds didn't

have human emotions, she wondered whether they did experience some kind of happiness, because they appeared happy. If they experienced, say, the stress of avoiding predators and the stress of enduring cold weather, wouldn't they enjoy the times when living was easier? Sometimes two individuals flew together, flirting, perhaps, before parting ways, watching from afar, and singing. Then, as if on cue, they would do it all over again, coming together and drifting apart. Maybe that was part of nature too. It was possible that if she waited long enough, she and Paul would come together again. Yes, it was possible, she knew, but she sure couldn't imagine it.

Back at the visitor center, she stamped her passport book and wished she could share this moment with her dad. Perhaps she should have taken all the risks that would have come with taking him out of the care facility and bringing him along. Surely the part of him that had awareness would have enjoyed these places. But then she remembered how scared he was of her the last time she visited, how unkind that visit had been for both of them. The reality was that taking him on this trip would not have followed the script she had in her mind; it would have been even more unkind than the visit.

"Hi, Dad," she had said with a polite knock before walking into his room.

Startled by her bald head, he shrieked. Then he barked, "Who are you?" accusingly.

It was the first time she had visited him after losing her hair, and she marveled that she had made it this far, really—that she had gotten out of bed, showered, dressed, walked out the door, and driven. Each step had been a huge accomplishment. Physically, she did not feel great, but emotionally, she felt even worse. It was real now. Being bald made the cancer so real. She could no longer have moments where she pretended it was all just a bad dream. The whole world could see what she was going through. It was her new identity. The days when people looked at her and saw a beautiful woman were over. Now, they looked at her and saw a cancer patient, a reminder of how tough and scary life could get. And she hated that—hated reminding people of their own mortality or of the loss of someone they had loved. It felt like being a dark rain cloud that ruined everyone's day.

But this moment was far worse. Until now, her dad had always recognized her after a few minutes or, on a bad day, after a little while. Now, he couldn't.

"Dad," she said firmly, "look at my eyes. It's still me. I have cancer. My hair fell out because I have cancer. It's still me. Your daughter. It's still me." But there was no recognition. Tears welled up in her eyes and spilled over. "Please, Dad. Please don't abandon me right now. I need you. Please recognize me. I'm sick and I need my daddy. It's me. Amy. Your daughter."

The combination of her baldness and her crying agitated him. "I don't know who you are, but you have the wrong person. I'm not your dad. I don't know who you are. You should go. You should go find your dad. I'm not him."

She paused for a moment and covered her mouth, still hoping that he would see her underneath all of her baldness, see her and recognize her, still hoping he would recognize her voice, maybe. "I am Catherine's daughter. You used to be married to her. I am Alicia's sister. I am your daughter." She knew better. On every other day that he hadn't recognized her instantly, she had simply sat quietly next to him and played backgammon. Eventually, something sparked a memory within him, one from long ago.

Today, she had been too desperate for that, and now she was going to pay the price.

"I know who you are . . . ," he said, and for an instant she dared to hope he did, despite the darkness in the tone of his voice, because she just wanted him to hug her so badly. She just wanted to crawl right up in the arms of her daddy. But then he said the worst thing. "You're an alien, aren't you? I've seen you on TV. Well, you're not going to kill me!" With that, he hopped out of bed and threw a cup of water on her. "Somebody! There's an alien in here trying to kill me!"

Sobbing, she turned and walked out his door. The young nurse rushed in to calm her dad while the grandmotherly one embraced Amy and said, "Alzheimer's is the cruelest disease. It really is. His brain is all haywire, but his spirit still loves you. I promise, it does."

Unfortunately, there was not one single ounce of big girl left inside of her. She had used it all up being brave on so many recent occasions—every diagnostic appointment, her first chemo, the day her hair fell out. "I want my daddy," she cried, sobbing onto the nurse's shoulder.

And the nurse just cooed, "Oh, sweet girl. Oh, sweet girl," because sometimes there were just no words. No words at all that could fix anything.

She knew she couldn't go back—not for a long time, if ever. If he was still alive after her hair grew back, maybe she would try again, but until then, she couldn't see how it was kind to either one of them to do that again.

Even though she couldn't imagine writing to Paul, she bought four postcards anyway.

"Dear Dad," she wrote on one of the postcards. "You would love the white-throated swifts here that fly in the canyon below. I'm on an adventure back to Mt. Rainier to come home to the places we loved. On the way, I'm visiting other parks and monuments. I wish you were with me. You would love this. I love you. Love, Amy."

"I hope your reunion with T. Rex was wonderful," she wrote to Carly, "and I hope you're having fun. Love, Mom."

To Aunt Rae, she wrote another thank-you. After she addressed, stamped, and dropped them in the receptacle, she inquired about available campsites in the park and learned there were none. The ranger asked questions about her plans and then enthusiastically encouraged her to consider Colorado National Monument, just a little farther to the north. "National monuments are some of the best-kept secrets," she said. "It's beautiful there. I promise you won't be disappointed."

Nearby, in Montrose, she stopped at Walmart and picked up the camp stove, pan, and thick foam pad she had wished for the night before, along with more food and a box knife to cut the foam down to size.

A bakery caught her eye before she left town, so she pulled over abruptly and ordered a sandwich. It was too late for lunch and too early for dinner, but that didn't matter because there was no one else's needs to consider. All that mattered was that she was hungry now.

With time to kill, she checked her phone more out of habit than a true desire to hear from anyone. Paul had sent a text: *Thinking of you.* Amy bristled as she read it because it was bullshit disguised as sentiment and she knew it. *Thinking of you, too,* she considered writing back, because she was. She would just leave out one key word—leaving. *Thinking of leaving you, too.* Annoyed, she put away her phone, deciding against any action that might lead to dialogue that resulted in permanent decisions when she might be temporarily not quite balanced enough to make decisions she wouldn't regret.

Across the room sat two women and a man who all appeared to be in their eighties, and Amy found herself trying not to stare at one of the women in particular. In the old woman's eyes, Amy saw peace and happiness, and she wondered how . . . how that was possible . . . what that woman's secret was. Amy's fear of dying was so acute, a dragon she slayed several times a day but one that just kept coming back to life. It startled her to think it was entirely possible for cancer to resurface somewhere in her body and that her life could not only be cut short but involve unthinkable suffering before it was. The three old people laughed now— despite the fact that they probably didn't have another decade or even another five years . . . despite the fact that so few people got a quick death anymore and unthinkable suffering likely lay before them. For now, they were happy. They had figured out a way to simply eat their sandwiches together and not think obsessively about death. Was this what happened when people had the luxury of a slow boil instead of being microwaved into this reality as she had? She desperately wanted to ask them how . . . how to simply live . . . how to cope with this fear.

The young woman at the counter called her name, jolting Amy out of her spiral downward into unhealthy thoughts. She rose, thanked the woman, took her bag, and pressed on.

In just over an hour, she was beyond Grand Junction and a little west, entering Colorado National Monument. Driving up the narrow mesa on the windy road, she found herself suddenly a world away from the civilization on the valley bottom. Her eyes widened and her heart fluttered with excitement as each bend in the road offered her new and better views of enormous red rock cliffs below. Something about that red rock struck her as wildly exotic. More and more effort was required to stay on the narrow road as views became more expansive.

When she stepped out of her car at the visitor center, she was aware of a dull ache where her most recent surgery had been, undoubtedly irritated from the core muscles she had used driving such a windy road. Still, it was worth it. The beauty in every direction filled her and inspired her.

As she walked through the visitor center, she stamped her little book and bought more postcards, then walked on out to the back deck, where a ranger was telling a little girl about the leading causes of death in bighorn sheep—slipping, dental problems, and being killed by a cougar. Across a fork of the narrow canyon in front of her, she saw three bighorn sheep perched precariously on a cliff. They did not appear to be thinking of these three possibilities, although they might have been. Instead, they appeared to simply be finding the next place to take a step, and then the next, as they walked forward.

And later, when she crawled into her new, improved bed, she knew she hadn't made a mistake at all. If beauty itself couldn't heal her faster than she would have healed, it surely would distract her while she healed at her own otherwise intolerably slow pace.

Carly

Four hours hadn't seemed like very long to drive the chuck wagon, but every single second of it had been like being in a centrifuge, where all of the molecules in her body were separated according to atomic weight. The ride jostled and shook her that much. Ahead of her, the six women from Florida who were their guests for the week chatted merrily with each other and with Great-Aunt Rae, who rode in the front. They were all having a great time.

It wasn't a completely hopeless situation. Great-Aunt Rae had tied T. Rex to the back of the wagon to follow along so that when time allowed, Carly would have a horse to ride. Frank and Drake hadn't been trained under saddle. Just knowing T. Rex was there with her made Carly a little happier—even if she never had time to ride.

After they arrived at the spot where Great-Aunt Rae always camped with her groups, Carly helped unhitch Frank and Drake and lead them and T. Rex to the stream to drink, while the guests dismounted, stretched, and led their own horses there. Great-Aunt Rae showed Carly how to set up a canvas wall tent after they tied the horses, then left her to set up the three other tents and put two cots inside each one. As Great-Aunt Rae set off on horseback with the six women and Violet the dog, Carly was envious. Images of Cinderella came to mind. Had she really been so bad that she deserved this? She didn't think so. Rolling out the canvas of the next tent, she remembered that Cinderella had not been paid, and Carly would be—even if it was only two hundred dollars a week. She struggled with posts, the ropes, and the stakes but eventually erected tent number two. Unlike the crisp, tight tent Great-Aunt Rae had set up, Carly's tent sagged. Trying to pull this rope tighter and then that one, she saw some improvement, but still, a line of wrinkles cut through the middle of the roof. Surely Great-Aunt Rae could tweak it when she returned. Repeating the process again, she set up the third tent and then the fourth, but just as she was carrying a cot from the chuck wagon to the tent, a stiff breeze blew and the third tent collapsed. Any sense of satisfaction she'd had with her progress fell along with it, leaving her feeling once again like she couldn't do anything right. The guests would come back, see their tents on the ground, and know that Carly's secondhand cowgirl clothes were nothing but a make-believe costume, nothing more than Cinderella's ball gown. She imagined how stupid she was going to feel.

For a moment, she turned her back to it and took some deep breaths, undecided about whether she was collecting herself or preparing to leave. That was the upside to failure. If she failed, she might be allowed to return home to Oklahoma City.

But as soon as she thought it, the feeling of failure hit her in the belly. This failure would be different from ones at school, because she could leave behind school and everyone in it. It would be different from her perceived failure at home too. After all, at some point she would either redeem herself with her parents or not, but regardless, she was going to have to leave them behind too. That was nature. That was expected. But with Great-Aunt Rae and the horses, it was different. There was nothing kicking her out of here. There was no expectation of high levels of academic achievement, expectations that if met would lead to even higher expectations. No, there was just wind and a few trees, and horses. And if today was any indication, there wasn't going to be anyone standing over her judging her all day long—no teachers, no parents, not even friends. The truth was that she did not want to return home, where each night she had to figure out where she could sleep if she wanted to avoid her own bed in a house that held all the joy of a mausoleum. Sleeping at friends' houses came with the pressure to bring the party, or at least act normal or fine, which she wasn't. She was actually freer here. She knew where she was going to sleep even if it was a cot in a tent, and she didn't have to work to stay socially relevant. Here, she had the freedom to simply be neutral. With her next breath, she breathed in all the wide-open spaces around her. She walked over to T. Rex, touched her nose to his, and reached up and petted his enormous, sweet face. Yes, she definitely preferred him to human friends. Stepping forward, she wrapped her arms around his big neck and shoulders, and he rested his head on her back. It had been so long since she had been hugged like that—slow and indefinite, quiet and still. It was such a relief—just such a relief to be hugged, that a couple of tears slipped out of her eyes and down her face. Begrudgingly, she admitted to herself that she very much wanted to stay.

Resolved, she erected the third tent again, lugged two cots over to each one, and set them up. Then, back at the chuck wagon, she looked at the list Great-Aunt Rae had left for her and began accomplishing those tasks. She set up a long folding table, put a red-checked tablecloth on it, secured it with clips, put two decks of cards on the table in case guests wanted to play while they waited for dinner, and unfolded eight camp chairs. After that, she filled two five-gallon buckets with water from the stream and carried them to the firepit, then began some of the prep cooking until everyone returned.

Great-Aunt Rae took over then, and Carly simply followed her lead, and though she didn't say so, Carly appreciated that Great-Aunt Rae was happy—not happy the way Carly's friends were happy when some boy or another liked them, not temporary like that, but solidly happy . . . not superficially happy, but deep-down happy. It wasn't dramatic. It wasn't euphoria happy. It was contentment happy. Carly made no effort to join her in happiness, but she observed it and appreciated it nonetheless, even if she didn't laugh or smile the way Great-Aunt Rae did.

And later, after a dinner of steak and potatoes with a side of peas and carrots, Carly watched Great-Aunt Rae and the guests as she washed all the dishes. She listened to them tell funny stories, watching their eyes smile even in the rare moments their mouths didn't. They felt light—light in a way Carly hadn't felt in months, if ever . . . light in the way a person could feel only when she didn't fear that she wasn't good enough and destined to die early.

Before bed, as Carly brushed her teeth and spit toothpaste into some bushes, Great-Aunt Rae handed her a small package of earplugs. "Sorry," she said, "I snore." As Great-Aunt Rae brushed her teeth next to Carly, Carly wondered whether this summer might be punishment after all.

After the centrifugal experience of the wagon, it seemed funny to Carly that crawling into a sleeping bag on a cot would be the most uncomfortable part of her day, but it was. It was here that she was most in unfamiliar territory . . . most vulnerable, perhaps.

She remembered T. Rex's fur under her hands as she took long, deep breaths and began to relax. Just as she was on the brink of sleep, Great-Aunt Rae's snoring began. Carly squeezed the foam earplugs and put them in her ears, but finding both the pressure of them in her ear canal and the sound of white noise unpleasant, she took them out.

In the distance to the west, a coyote howled. It was the first one she had ever heard that wasn't on the TV or in a movie. She rolled over to look down and see what Violet's reaction was. The dog had taken note of it but wasn't alarmed, so Carly figured everything must be okay. Just then a group of coyotes answered from the east. Shortly after that, another song came from the west, but this time there was more than one voice. For the next hour, at least, the two groups of coyotes called and answered each other, moving closer and closer to the middle ground, which Carly suspected more and more was in fact her tent.

"Great-Aunt Rae," she whispered. "Great-Aunt Rae." Great-Aunt Rae did not even stir. If it was possible for a dog to have an expression, Violet's would have been that any attempt to wake the old woman was pointless. Instead, Carly patted the sliver of space next to her, inviting the dog up, and to her surprise, Violet accepted.

When the two groups of coyotes converged, the middle ground was not exactly her tent but a site not too far away. Calls became happy yips.

Her thoughts turned back to an unsupervised night at Kaylee's house when, after drinking some vodka they'd found in a cabinet, it seemed like a good idea for Kaylee to drive her parents' remaining car while Carly held a waterski rope that was attached to the rear bumper and skateboard behind it through the neighborhood. She'd felt wild then.

But here in this tent, where there really was no escaping her fear and discomfort, she suddenly knew the difference between being wild and being reckless. One took courage. One took vodka. Being wild wasn't the complete absence of self-control. It was actually quite the opposite. It had something to do with acute awareness, knowing the best way to respond and having the self-control to respond in no other way than that. Being reckless was easier. And more fun. For just a second, she fantasized about jumping on T. Rex's back and galloping all the way back to Great-Aunt Rae's house.

When the twilight before sunrise finally came, birds began singing loudly. Had there not been guests, Carly would have yelled at them to go back to sleep until the sun was up. Instead, she put on her clothes, emerged from the tent, and found Great-Aunt Rae in a camp chair facing the east, drinking coffee and waiting for the sun to crest the mountains. Violet sat next to her, nudging Great-Aunt Rae's free hand with her nose, wanting to be petted.

Carly wandered off to answer nature's call, returned and brushed her teeth, and sat with Great-Aunt Rae for a moment of stillness before work.

"How did you sleep?" Great-Aunt Rae asked her.

Carly hesitated for a moment the way someone did when they didn't sleep well but didn't want to say so. "Fine, thank you." Then she added, "Did you hear the coyotes?"

"Eh, I sleep through them now."

"There was a group that came from over there," she said, pointing, "and a group from over there. They seemed to come together over there."

Great-Aunt Rae nodded. "That happens sometimes." Then she added, "Were you scared?"

Carly didn't know why it was such an uncomfortable thing to admit. She considered a few answers and then simply said, "No."

Great-Aunt Rae could see she was lying. "If you're not a goat or a sheep . . . or a dog," she said, opening her hand to pet Violet's head, "or a cat, or some kind of rodent, you don't have to worry about them. There's been no documented cases of coyotes attacking people."

"Maybe the coyotes ate the evidence," Carly said with a laugh.

Great-Aunt Rae smiled as her expression said, *Hey, that could be*. Then she changed the subject. "Well, eggs this morning. Let's get cracking! Pun intended!"

Carly winced at her bad humor, then smiled despite herself.

"If we can get all the guests fed and the dishes done quickly, you can join us on our ride this morning. Some days, we'll be riding too many hours and will need to leave you behind, but I like to start the guests off gradually, so today will be shorter than the others. Let's see whether we can make that happen for you."

With a little smile, Carly said, "Thanks," and in that moment saw a look of confidence wash over her great-aunt's face—confidence in her, as if she had a feeling that whatever tailspin Carly had been in, she could still pull herself out of it.

Paul

Now that Amy was well, there was no reason to continue to work night shifts, but Paul had to wait a few more months for another day shift to open up. Another officer would be retiring soon, and then Paul could return to his old schedule. This morning, Paul was initially grateful to have a little more time to rest from the long drive the day before. Later, not long after his shift started, though, he missed the slightly quieter day shift. Evenings, it seemed, were when a lot of unfortunate things happened.

After word from dispatch, Paul and his partner, Mark, sped to the house that neighbors had reported for a possible active domestic abuse situation, arriving before the other team of officers. They paused for just a moment to listen to the sound of a woman shrieking, "I'm sorry! I'm sorry!" followed by a heavy thud before knocking on the door of the otherwise rather ordinary house. Silence followed and then a child crying.

Paul knocked again, shouting, "Police!" and hoping that the residents would make this easier by opening the door before he and Mark had to force their way in.

The knob turned and a man cracked the door just enough to reveal himself. He said nothing, as if he had been read his *Miranda* rights before.

"Open the door wider," said Mark.

The suspect opened the door all the way. A woman sat on the couch, blood dripping from her nose. "I fell," the woman said. Beside her sat a child, not quite two, Paul guessed. She bore a striking resemblance to his own daughter at that age. Sensing the tension in the room, she buried her face behind her mother's bruised arm.

"Put your hands behind your head," said Paul to the suspect. The suspect complied, and Paul cuffed him while reciting his rights, starting with, "You have the right to remain silent," which the suspect chose.

Mark stepped in to get the woman's statement for the report, but she stood and walked toward the doorway to watch her husband or boyfriend be taken away. "He didn't do anything. I fell," she said simply. With the threat now gone, the crying child ran to her and she picked up the little girl.

Just as Paul and the suspect reached the car, the suspect turned forcefully, spit in Paul's face, and then headbutted him hard enough that Paul saw stars, but not so hard that it knocked him out. Disoriented and unsure about whether he was going to remain conscious, he feared what would happen to him and everyone else if he didn't get the suspect secured into the back of the patrol car. Because of this, he forced the suspect into the car quickly and without the usual care. In the process, the suspect's head hit the roof of the car hard as he went in and he shouted the f-word. Paul shut the door and put a hand on his own head where he had been struck, and with the other hand, he reached in his pocket for a handkerchief to wipe the spit off his face.

Just then, backup arrived, and Paul let them assist Mark and interview any neighbors for statements.

Since he knew he had taken a good hit to the head, Paul asked Mark to drive back to the station and book the suspect.

Paul was finishing his report on the computer and icing his head in the cubicle reserved for this purpose when Captain Lopez walked in. "Mrs. Miller, the woman from the domestic abuse call you just responded to, is saying that you said, 'Take that!' as you slammed her husband's head into the doorjamb of the car."

"You know me better than that," said Paul.

"Yeah," Captain Lopez said, nodding. "I do. Any witnesses? Mark was inside. Juan and Vince hadn't arrived yet. Mr. Miller isn't cooperating. Did you happen to notice any neighbors watching?"

Paul shook his head. "I was seeing stars."

"I have to put you on administrative leave while we do an investigation. The team will call you in—maybe more than once— and when they do, you need to show up in a timely manner, so stick around. I'm sorry, Paul."

Paul nodded, then stood to leave, unsure of whether he really should drive himself home. *No good deed goes unpunished,* said his father's bitter voice in his head. He was annoyed but not terribly concerned. The truth usually had a way of coming to light. So, he would have about a week of mostly paid vacation, and then he'd be found to have done nothing wrong and return to work. It might not be such a terrible thing.

Amy

There were so many choices. Too many choices. Amy looked west over the red rock rim of the butte near where she had camped. She was only a couple of hours at the most from Arches National Park, which she very much wanted to explore. She did. But mostly she just wanted to go home. Not the home in Oklahoma City where she had lived for most of her life. No, the home where her soul dwelled—the kindest forest. Her endurance was low and she knew it. She knew it was likely going to take all of her energy just to get to Mt. Rainier by way of Yellowstone. There was a spot there in Yellowstone that had been magic for her during the one summer they spent there. By the time she came back through this region of the Southwest, she would feel stronger and her abdomen wouldn't hurt so much. There would be time to come back. That was the thing. There was time now. She didn't know exactly how much. People's cancer came back sometimes. And sometimes people got an entirely new cancer. That could happen. That and a thousand other possibilities could happen. But they probably wouldn't, she told herself. It was just that "probably" had lost its meaning after being the exception to all the probable outcomes during each step in her diagnosis. A person's concept of probable was what kept their somewhat irrational fears in check. Without it, all she could do was resolve to act like a sane person even if she didn't feel like one. With that, she walked a short nature trail near the visitor center before getting back in the car and heading north.

Just two hours later, she neared her first stop. Dinosaur National Monument was on the way to Yellowstone. She passed by the visitor center in the Colorado portion of the park and continued driving to Utah, since that's where the quarry was. On the road, she'd noticed a strange mountain, twisted and swirled, the strata that should have been horizontal lifting straight up to the sky. Sure enough, the road ended there.

At that visitor center, she went through her routine, buying postcards and stamping her passport book, before catching the shuttle bus to the quarry. She imagined her dad sitting next to her—not the dad who didn't recognize her, but her old dad, the dad with unconditional love and plenty of questions about the natural world. She imagined what she would say—*Hey, Dad, look at that! How do you suppose that formed?* And she imagined just looking into his eyes, seeing him cognizant and happy, and feeling connected with him.

After a short drive, all the passengers disembarked and walked into the quarry building, where an entire excavated hillside was both exposed and protected in the structure. Large bones poked out of the sediment everywhere. Strolling along, she read interpretive signs, still imagining her dad was next to her enjoying the experience as well.

When a young mother looked at her, ruled her out, and then asked someone else to take a picture of her family, the spell was broken. A year ago, that woman would have asked her. Now, she scared people, it seemed.

It would have been nice to have Paul there right then to put everyone at ease. She became keenly aware of her aloneness. It felt exposed. But that wasn't a good enough reason to be with Paul.

She walked out of the building and onto the next shuttle bus, hoping the woman who hadn't chosen her wouldn't be on the bus. Although she knew there was no hour or minute of her life to waste hiding, she couldn't help it. She wanted to hide until her hair grew and she felt better. Instead, back at the car, she did the next best thing. She pulled out the wig that she'd had made out of her own hair before it had fallen out. It wasn't comfortable even now that her scalp was no longer unspeakably tender from chemo rash. Although it was her hair, it didn't look like her hair the way it came out of her scalp naturally. She put a hat on over it to hide that and just enjoyed seeing it frame her view of the ground below her as she walked a short nature trail. It reminded her of digging out her blankie after a bad day in second grade . . . knowing she was too old to need this thing but finding so much comfort in it that she didn't care. Inside, she scolded herself for this moment of weakness. There was no shame in surviving. None. The fact she had just survived cancer and cancer treatment was nothing that she should have felt any need to hide. She supposed she was simply tired of being so exposed all the time. Her history, her struggles, they were nobody's business—and yet there they were, written on her body out there for the whole world to see. What a cruel joke—to be so sick, so close to dying, and then, following being bald, have ugly hairstyles for the next two years.

A breeze picked up some strands of her hair from her wig. No, she shouldn't need this disguise to hide behind, but sometimes it was just such a relief to see the world the way it used to look— framed by strands of red hair blowing in the wind.

For the last four and a half hours, Amy had driven on roads where she rarely saw another person. The visitor center at Fossil Butte

National Monument in Wyoming was open for only ten more minutes, so she stamped her book and looked around at the many fossil displays before it closed. She had planned to camp here for the night but was surprised to find that in order to prevent fossil theft, no camping was allowed.

One of the two rangers in the visitor center warned her that there was a moose nearby that had charged her just the day before. Fortunately, she had been near one of the only trees in the area and had been able to take cover behind it until the coast was clear. All signs were pointing to moving on, which was fine. There was national forest land between there and Grand Teton National Park where she could find a campground that still had available spaces.

Before she left, she walked around the porch of the visitor center where the rail had been turned into a time line of life on earth. She walked past all the labeled points, past ferns and but-terflies, past fir trees and dogs, all the way up to humans. Resting her finger on the rail, she felt that it all came down to this spot. Whether her life was long or not so long, it was just part of this, part of this tiny dot on the time line of earth, fairly inconsequen-tial, she supposed, in the grand scheme of things. It didn't bother her and it didn't comfort her.

Instead, she redirected her attention to listening to the song of an unfamiliar bird. She was here now. Here with this bird. Here discovering something new—a new birdsong. That was all. And it was enough.

Carly

Carly's sore muscles woke her again, but this time a faint light illuminated the eastern sky and the birds were singing. Great-Aunt Rae was still in her cot, her fingers in her ears. The birdsongs were loud, but lovely. Carly rolled onto her side to study Great-Aunt Rae more closely, to try to determine whether she had actually fallen back asleep plugging her ears or whether she was just resting like that.

Sensing something was staring at her, Great-Aunt Rae opened one eye and smiled as she lowered her hands.

"Birdsongs?" Carly asked quietly so as not to wake the guests.

"Yep."

"It's not like they're crows squawking or anything. They're pretty songs."

"Too pretty. They break my heart." Great-Aunt Rae shut her eyes tightly and shook her head. Opening her eyes again, she said, "American robins. Most mornings I can handle it, but this morning is the anniversary of the day I met my one and only true love. The birdsongs take me back to that summer. You'd think they'd have lost their power by now, but all these decades later, they still haunt me."

"Oh. I'm sorry."

"Yeah, I was your age. Sometimes it's strange to watch you do some of the things I did that summer. That takes me back, too. But boy, things were different for me. I didn't have all the choices you have. After high school, the plan my parents had formulated for me involved going to secretarial school, which was one of the three options available to women at the time, nursing and teaching being the other two."

"That's it? Three choices?"

"Yes, ma'am. However, I wanted adventure and so I spent the little bit of money I had received as graduation gifts not on books for secretarial school, but on an Amtrak ticket to Whitefish, Montana."

"Your parents must have flipped."

"That is an understatement, but to their credit, they did not drive up there and get me. They let me figure it out for myself. For the first month, I waitressed in a café, and that was where I met Cal, my future boss, who liked my service, and offered me a different job—one with housing." She laughed. "And by housing, he did mean a tent—cooking on horse-packing trips. Well, that sounded just fine to me! Far more adventurous than working in a café."

"I didn't know that."

"Yes, pretty daring for a woman in my day."

"Pretty daring even now."

Great-Aunt Rae smiled. "Smartest decision I ever made. Sometimes I rode with the tourists, followed by a pack string that carried all the things we needed for meals. Oh, that was great, riding for miles and then cooking in Dutch ovens and frying pans over the campfire. That was relatively easy because I was riding with the group, you know? But other times, I hitched the chuck wagon to a team of Clydesdales and drove up a dirt road to meet the tourists—usually hunters—at a designated spot, and that was far more involved than I had initially imagined. I had to learn to do all that by myself.

"Sam—he was the boss's son—showed me how to catch, brush, pick their feet, on this very day back in 1968. . . . I was so scared of those giant horses."

Carly imagined what it would be like to stand next to a Clydesdale for the first time if she'd never been around them before. It would be intimidating, to say the least.

"And then, there was the seemingly impossible task of making sense of all of the straps involved in their harnesses so that I could put them on right."

Carly nodded emphatically. "Yeah, I have no idea how anyone does that."

Great-Aunt Rae laughed. "And when that was done, I had to hook the horses to the wagon. All of that was in addition to packing the wagon, checking four times to make sure I hadn't forgotten anything. Sam was patient and encouraging with me as I gained confidence in handling the horses. But just when I thought I had a handle on it all, it was time to head up the road with a topographic map and try to identify the meeting spot. Well, I'd had no experience with topographic maps and could not figure out the scale. The first three times, Sam rode with me, his saddle horse tied to the back of the wagon, coaching me on how to drive and making sure I found the correct place, and marking little landmarks on the map to help me when I would have to do it alone. I tell you, I was straining to concentrate on what he was trying to teach me because I was so distracted by his smell. Is that too much information?"

Carly laughed and shook her head. "Some guys smell really good."

"Mm!" Great-Aunt Rae smiled and shook her head. "We talked about the different places we were from, you know, comparing and contrasting the culture and geography of Oklahoma and Montana, telling stories about family, school . . . embarrassing moments, and stuff like that. God, I loved his smell. He'd had a very distinctive smell, an earthy smell like dirt and musk but sweeter. Whenever I was around him, I found myself breathing in his scent with long, deep breaths, trying to name it, getting drunker and drunker on his intoxicating scent."

Carly laughed. It was so hard for her to imagine her great-aunt under the spell of some boy's smell, and it was amusing to see a different side of her.

"He was not particularly handsome, nor was he particularly homely," Great-Aunt Rae continued, and this frank statement made Carly laugh. "He wore these thick glasses with black frames that made his eyes appear larger . . . kind of slightly bulged at times. They seemed to domesticate him in an otherwise wild setting. His skin was not his best feature either. If a woman stopped looking right there, she would have missed the magic. He was strong and well built, and utterly magnetic. Yeah, that was the start of something wonderful. You know, there are moments in life that are golden, and if you're smart, you know when you're in one of those times and just drink it all up like you might never drink again."

Carly didn't know what to say. Great-Aunt Rae shut her eyes and a few moments later rolled over with her back to Carly, an invitation to go back to sleep for the remaining hour.

It was strange to imagine that Great-Aunt Rae had ever been in love. Carly could only picture her alone. She had once overheard her mom and Aunt Alicia arguing over what they thought Great-Aunt Rae's gender preference was, and even then, Carly thought it was irrelevant because Great-Aunt Rae was simply alone.

The next thing Carly knew, it was morning again, but this time brighter and without the loud songs of American robins.

The previous morning, Carly had been amused at the guests from Florida when they hobbled out of their tents, sore from being on horses for the first time in a long time. Today, however, it was Carly who could hardly move.

Great-Aunt Rae was sitting in a camp chair outside, drinking coffee and laughing at her when Carly hobbled by on her way to the outhouse. "You're staying in camp today!"

"Twist my arm!" Carly replied without turning around. It was true: there were muscles a person used only when she rode horses.

Amy

Amy had been too excited about returning to a place that held family memories to stop for more than a bathroom break in Grand Teton National Park. It was beautiful, for sure, but her heart ached for something else.

After she crossed into Yellowstone, she did stop to watch Old Faithful blow, amazed at how reliable it had been over her entire lifetime and probably many others. She stamped her passport book at the visitor center there before driving on a bit further to look at the Grand Prismatic Hot Spring, a pool of water that was nearly all the colors of the rainbow, with red tendrils of water radiating from the outside of the circle. One day, this very spot was rumored to be the center of a massive volcanic explosion that would wipe the western half of North America off the map and cover the sun with ash for years. No one knew when. It was like cancer recurrence, but on a much grander scale, a grave, hidden danger that lurked deep within. Despite that, hundreds of visitors a day still came to stand at the very edge of it and appreciate its beauty. And in the same way, she supposed, there were many, many people every day who stood on the edge of their lives, or who stood right on ground zero in some way, and instead of thinking about the end of their life chose simply to admire the beauty of it. She wished she could be like them. Maybe one day she would be.

After driving a little farther north, she wandered through the Morrison Formation on boardwalks, looking at strangely colored hot springs and the bursts of steam rising from fumaroles. One misstep, one slip or trip, could leave a person dying in boiling mud, yet the boardwalk was filled with people, people who brought their children out here in this dangerous place, and they all seemed to explore joyfully and unscathed. She supposed it was ignorance, really, that allowed everyone to live so happily—ignorance and denial. She wanted hers back desperately. Of all the things she had been robbed of, this perhaps was the very worst of all.

Then she moved on to Mammoth Hot Springs, taking a detour past the employee housing where she had lived with her family for one summer. She paused for a moment, waiting, she supposed, to see whether her mother would open the door and call her in for dinner. Then she looked around to see whether her dad might be walking home from work. Neither of those things happened, so she drove on.

She had only the vaguest recollection of the place she was looking for and little hope she would find it. It had been thirty-five years since she had been there. As she drove the road leading toward the magical place, her mind traveled back in time.

At the end of the summer before, on their way back to Oklahoma from Mt. Rainier, her parents had driven a little out of their way to stop here in Yellowstone so her dad could say hi to a ranger who had worked at Mt. Rainier with him the year before. After exploring Mammoth Hot Springs and the Albright Visitor Center, where her dad saw his old friend, they piled back into the car and drove east—how far, she could not say. She remembered only that it was a while, whatever that meant. There was a place on a curve where her dad pulled off the road, and then the three of them walked down a little hill into an aspen grove. There, nestled in the trees, were the remains of wickiups left behind by the Sheep-eaters, a subgroup of the Shoshone tribe, long ago. The poles were similar to tipi poles, set in a circle, but instead of being covered by hides, they had been covered in reed mats, bark, or brush. The poles, although they were rotting into the ground, still stood nearly ten feet high.

In the middle of the wickiup remains, her family sat together, eating sandwiches and thinking about those who had made the structure and had lived there. Had the trees been all around it then? Her dad thought the trees were too young. They speculated about the foods the Sheepeaters might have eaten in addition to the bighorn sheep they had been named after. The wickiup seemed almost like a portal to another time to Amy, like the books she had read a few years before where the kids entered an enchanted land through a magical closet. Sitting in the wickiup made anything seem possible like that.

When they were done eating, they lay back and gazed at the early evening summer sky through the leaves. That was when the aspen grove looked like a kaleidoscope, partitioned off into sections by the radial lines of the poles above. What she remembered was peace. Peace and a sense of possibility.

More than anything, that was what she needed now.

As the day began to reach its end, she knew she needed to find a place to camp that night. All campsites inside the park had surely been booked for months, so she would have to drive west, possibly quite a long way. But first, she turned right instead of left, in hopes of finding the wickiups where perhaps peace awaited her.

Truthfully, she had no idea whether the wickiups were even

still there. It seemed likely that sometime in the last thirty-five years, they might have finally buckled and fallen to the earth and become part of it.

When a curve in the road seemed to feel familiar, she pulled over and stopped. It was getting late in the day, so she needed to be extra careful not to get lost. Stepping out of her car, she thought about the megafauna—the bison, the cougar, the grizzlies—and something about taking the risk of walking alone among them felt like a relief to her. Maybe it was because it offered her the opportunity to die in another way, a way that was somehow more natural. A way that was certainly faster. But she didn't think that was it. She thought it had something to do with being freed from the percentages that haunted her. No one would tell her what her chances were of surviving her trip to Yellowstone the way her doctor told her what her chances were of still being cancer-free and alive in five years. She was allowed to visit Yellowstone in ignorant bliss, and it felt like truly living.

On the downhill side, she wandered across the side of a hill into an aspen grove. There, she looked for a bench level enough on which to construct shelters but found none. Instead, she stopped where she was and lay down on the hill. After all, there was something sacred and cathedral-like about any aspen grove. Through the leaves that had fallen the year before, she dug her fingers all the way down to the earth and into it, as if she were clinging to it. As if she were holding on for her dear life.

As she had suspected, there was no camping to be found anywhere near Yellowstone and no vacancy in any hotels either. She had been willing to spring for a room. Exhausted, she drove on to Craters of the Moon National Monument, where she felt bad for driving through the campground so late and with her headlights on. Not even bothering to brush her teeth, she just crawled into the back of her car and fell fast asleep.

The next day, sunlight and the sound of the other campers woke her from a deep sleep. She rose and surveyed her otherworldly surroundings. Although it was black instead of white, the landscape did indeed look like the surface of the moon. While eating a granola bar and drinking her cup of herb tea, she walked an interpretive trail through pahoehoe lava fields, reading educational signs about the volcanoes that had once erupted there.

It happened, and then it was over, and then it was safe for her to be here. She had to learn to believe that about her health . . . about cancer. It happened, and it was over, and she was safe.

By tonight, she would be in the big trees. Excitement filled her. She stopped by the visitor center on her way out to stamp her book and learned there was a cave to explore, but eager to finally reach Mt. Rainier, she decided to skip it and press on.

A little bit before Boise, she stopped at Hagerman Fossil Beds National Monument and learned that there had been a horse ancestor right there on that land. Some of those horse ancestors had crossed over the Bering Land Bridge and become today's modern horse in Asia, while others had migrated down into South America and become today's llamas and alpacas. That very spot of earth had been closer to the equator long ago. Time had moved it that far. That struck Amy as hopeful. In time, she would surely shift and come a long way too.

The next time she was ready for a stop, she was near Baker City, Oregon, home of the Oregon Trail Interpretive Center, which was also part of the National Park System. Perched on a hill, Amy surveyed the beautiful valley below and the Wallowa Mountains rising straight up beyond. Ruts from wagon wheels still scarred the land after all this time. Time and revegetation had faded them, but still they traversed the expanse before her, telling a story. She didn't see these scars on the land as beautiful or ugly and hoped that in time she'd see her own scars in the same way.

Inside, she stamped her book, examined bonnets in the gift shop, and then wandered through all the dioramas that walked her through the journey of coming west. In the past, the westward movement had always seemed like a difficult but grand adventure, but now she knew something about trauma and saw it everywhere. She imagined being a woman leaving her parents behind, highly unlikely ever to see them again . . . the grief people must have felt. She imagined losing a family member along the way . . . burying a child, perhaps, or finding herself a widow in a strange place on a horrible journey, grief-stricken and terrified. She imagined the moments the travelers regretted their decision but were in far too deep to go back, and she imagined finding herself in a new and unfamiliar land at the end of it all, figuring out how to survive.

No one survived breast cancer then.

Wandering back outside to the wagon display, she let that sink in. How strange it seemed to her sometimes to still be alive. It seemed obvious, but it wasn't—maybe because she didn't feel alive; she felt beat-up. She wondered how it all worked in the grand scheme . . . what the implications to still being alive were after a person was destined to die. Is that why she felt so disoriented . . . because she'd missed her flight home to heaven? Could medical intervention also be part of a person's destiny?

Regardless, here she was—alive. Alive, here near Baker City, with a car instead of a wagon. With every comfort and convenience. With every advantage. With an oncologist who would check on her every few months. She was alive. Her daughter was alive. Her husband was alive. And because of that, there was still the opportunity for change.

Paul

If only he could have used this week to work on the house in Chama, Paul had thought with each passing day. Such wasted time. He had cleaned and reorganized the garage during the first two mornings while it was still cool out, but on the third morning, he was called in to speak in front of an independent investigative panel in the conference room at the station. Lamar Green, the union rep, met him just outside and walked in with him, notepad and pen in hand. At this point, he was just a witness to the process.

Even though Paul hadn't done anything wrong, he felt embarrassed. It seemed to him that his colleague, Rich, had been particularly smug as Paul had passed him on the way to the conference room, perhaps knowing that when it came time for one of them to get promoted, this stain on Paul's record could cost him and give Rich the edge he needed to outcompete Paul. That was tough to think about—how this lie could cost Paul actual money in that way, and in the five years before his retirement, the most important five years in determining pension payments for the rest of his life. But he did his best to have faith in the system.

The panel reviewed his report and Mrs. Miller's statement. All Paul could do was deny her account. These people didn't know him, didn't know his character, and suddenly he began to feel scared at being at the mercy of this process.

"After he spit in your face, were you mad?" asked one member of the panel.

"I didn't really have much time to think about it. It surprised me, I suppose, and then he immediately headbutted me." Paul pointed to the large goose egg on his forehead.

"And did that make you mad?" the panel member asked, staying on that tangent.

"I was scared, actually. I thought I might go down, and I wanted to make sure he was in the car before I did if I did. He was clearly violent, and not safe to be left unattended even if he was cuffed. So, I was rushing, and I was seeing stars. With my vision temporarily impaired, I didn't have my normal coordination."

"Did you use the standard technique for putting someone in a car?"

"I'm guessing I did not because of the result, but again, I was seeing stars and disoriented, so I don't really know what I did."

"If you don't really know what you did, is it possible that you said, 'Take that!'?"

"No," Paul said, "because I didn't even think that. I was only thinking about whether I was going to lose consciousness."

"Mrs. Miller is the only witness."

"Mrs. Miller also said she fell when Mr. Miller had clearly been assaulting her, so I would argue she's not known for her truth telling," said Paul.

The five members of the panel looked neither convinced nor unconvinced. They only looked concerned.

"Lieutenant Bergstrom," another member of the panel began, "do you use any drugs or alcohol?"

"Sometimes on a day off, I have a beer with a buddy or two," he answered.

"Just one beer?"

"Just one."

"You never have more than one."

"I never have more than one."

"Is that because you've had a problem with alcohol in the past?"

"No." He could tell they wanted to know more about that, but he didn't think they needed to know that his dad was an alcoholic so he did not offer a reason.

"Do any other members of the panel have further questions for Lieutenant Bergstrom?"

After a pause, Paul was dismissed. He thanked the union rep and walked stone-faced through the maze of cubicles back to the door. He told himself he didn't need to be worried because the truth was on his side, but still, as he left the building, he was.

A year after the bombing, ninety of them had received a Medal of Valor at a banquet at the National Cowboy Hall of Fame and Western Heritage Center. Just that morning he had been at the funeral for Sergeant Terrance Yeakey, only thirty years old, who had chosen to end his life three days before. On the day of the blast, he had worked beside Paul. None of the ninety officers knew how to begin to deal with the trauma of every single minute of those days and nights. Some had just been willing and able to wait a little longer to see whether the intensity would die down to something more manageable. Yeakey hadn't been able to, possibly because in addition to this experience, he had served in Iraq, where one of his duties had been the mass burial of civilians. Once, he shared with

Paul that he was haunted by images of dead children and afraid to sleep because his nightmares were so horrific. Paul understood. Every single one of them receiving the medal understood.

As they sat in their chairs and listened to a letter from President Clinton be read, all of them simply wondered how to go on, how to live with all of these images etched in their minds forever, how to live with the possibility that if they had only done something differently, stepped there instead of there, gone to that spot sooner, if lightning hadn't stopped work with the large cranes on that fourth day after the blast, maybe they could have saved one more person or a few more people. President Clinton said they "set the standard for perseverance," but they knew they were not that special. Any other officers would have done the same thing. They weren't doing their job; they were simply being human. They did what humans do for one another. That was all. And now, because they were human, they were not okay. The chaplain of the Oklahoma City Fire Department had eighty suicide interventions for first responders of the blast under his belt. Eighty. And there were ninety of them receiving the medal.

Eager for the obligatory ceremony to be over, Paul, along with the others, watched a video from Reba McEntire, Vince Gill, Jay Leno, and Chuck Norris congratulating the department—*congratulating* them . . . as if they had *won,* as if they hadn't in fact *lost*—lost everything by being unlucky enough to have been part of this horror . . . lost their innocence, sanity, their ability to sleep or to ever feel normal again, lost their ability to connect with other people, with their spouses and children, with everybody, lost their capacity for happiness and joy, and, for many, lost their very will to live.

Everyone called them heroes, but those who did hadn't heard all the muffled moans that grew silent under their feet as they tried their best. Sure, they were heroes to those they pulled out and to their families, but their successes seemed dwarfed by their failures. They were so aware of all the people they hadn't been able to save, so aware of the devastation of so many families.

Yeakey had saved four people, and Paul knew that just like him, he never returned phone calls from any of them. And like Paul, he never wore his gold memorial pin either. People wanted to believe they were special, that they were superheroes, but Paul, Terrance Yeakey, and others wanted people to see that they were just humans. Humans that break. Because humans can't cope with that level and scale of tragedy. Listening to Chuck Norris, Paul thought about that—about how Yeakey was just a human, one who felt that if he had been the superhero everyone thought he was and wanted him to be, he would not have fallen two floors and injured his back, halting his ability to keep saving lives. If only. If only he had been a superhero. He would have saved so many more lives. They all would have loved to be the superhero that everyone thought they were and wanted them to be. They would have flown around in their capes and hovered over the wreckage, searching out still-living people with their X-ray vision instead of walking on the rubble that covered those buried below. . . . They would have vaporized the bricks with laser beams that shot out of their fingertips instead of digging blindly brick by brick, hoping, just hoping, for one more miracle.

Paul sat there in his formal uniform, willing himself to be still, willing himself to just stay there in his seat and wait until it was over, willing himself to act like the hero for the people to whom he was a hero, willing himself to act normal. Somewhere in the audience was his wife and two-year-old daughter. He had to keep it together. Affixed to the podium was the Oklahoma City seal, and in the center of that was a cross. He stared at the place where the two lines intersected. If all the other parts of the seal were taken away, this part would look like the crosshairs of a gun.

Apparently, his Medal of Valor wasn't going to buy him any credibility from this independent panel. The very service that President Clinton and others praised was now a liability. The statistics were in, giving basis for some to suggest with their questions that he might be unfit for duty.

Several of them had gone off the rails. He couldn't deny that. It would be easy to think he was just one more, he supposed. Except that he wasn't. He had worked so hard not to go off the rails.

In the weeks that followed the search-and-rescue effort, he and the others had attended mandatory small-group sessions. Maybe they helped. Maybe they didn't. Paul didn't know for sure. But he had kept an open mind and he had tried. Sometimes it had been helpful to remember that he wasn't in it alone. But he also knew talking wasn't enough. He didn't know what else there was, but he knew it wasn't enough.

More help was offered, a term he found ambiguous and likely based more on intent than on effect. He was desperate enough to accept any help offered, but some of the officers who had asked for this "more help" felt stigmatized by their supervisors and found their fitness for duty questioned. It may have been appropriate, because it was possible that none of them were fit for duty after that—that they were all too traumatized. But that job was their livelihood, their security, and the central part of their identity, so very few of them were ready to give it up. As a result, most of them had done their best to slip under the radar, and most of them, fit or unfit, had functioned. They had. He had. And for that, he would have liked a little more respect.

Back at home, he felt both tired and restless at the same time. He went back to bed, hoping to calm himself enough to nap so that he could have the sense of restarting the day when he woke, but lying there with his eyes shut, he realized he wasn't tired—he was weary, and they were two different things.

So, he got up and deadheaded all the flowering shrubs that Amy had always taken care of up until this year—the lilacs, hydrangeas, camellias, and roses. One after another, he removed what had run its course, what had blossomed and then died. When he got to the roses, he felt far more comfortable because he had complete confidence in their resilience. The more a person let go of what was done blooming, the more he was rewarded with new blooms. He hoped Amy was like the roses . . . that letting go of her now would lead to a rebirth of their love before summer was over.

Amy

Sometimes things seem so much larger to a child than an adult, and as Amy drove away from the U.S. Forest Service campground where she had pulled over the night before, she wondered whether that would be true of Mt. Rainier. However, as she drove over the summit of Chinook Pass and under the log arbor welcoming her to Mt. Rainier National Park, the giant dormant volcano consumed the southwestern sky over Tipsoo Lake. It was every bit as enormous as she had remembered. Patches of snow several feet deep still clung to the north sides of the hills and mountains and blanketed the basin in which the lake sat, giving Amy the strong suspicion that Sunrise wouldn't even be open yet. Snow. How long had it been since she had seen deep snow like this? Decades. Her younger self would have jumped right out of the car and made a snow angel. Her older self would have cared what people thought. Pulling over, she tried to figure out what her postcancer self wanted, and didn't know. She stepped out of the car and took a picture with her phone. Up and down the road, other tourists had pulled over and now took the same photo. Studying them for a moment, she determined that she did not care one tiny bit what any of them thought. With that, she lay down on the snow with the intention of making a snow angel, but once she was there, she didn't feel like moving her arms and legs. She just didn't have the heart. Instead, she wondered what life would be like if a person could just lie on ice and freeze moments of life like meat in the freezer, freeze them before they spoiled, freeze themselves before their own bodies turned on them. She found herself wanting to be very still like that, wanting to pause without the world still turning all around her. And then she had this little thought—that she could. She could find a quieter place to lie down in the snow and just go to sleep and not wake up. Instantly, her eyes bulged with horror at her own thought and she sat up. No. No permanent decisions until she was sane. That was the rule. And if she was even thinking these things, she was not completely sane.

Just stick to the plan, she told herself. *Just stick to the plan and you'll pull out of this.*

Knowing she needed help, Amy had tried going to a support group for cancer survivors less than two weeks after her last surgery. Most of the women were a generation older than her, and as they went around the circle, each of the dozen or so shared her cancer story and the challenges she was facing now. One woman had been cancer-free for eighteen years, but she needed a knee replacement and her husband had just been diagnosed with Alzheimer's, so he could no longer drive. The woman next to her had survived pancreatic cancer, and then breast cancer, and then a weeklong coma after surgery for that because of the tamoxifen, and now she had just been diagnosed with Parkinson's. She was mad and trying to make spiritual sense of her misfortune. The woman next to her spoke about choosing to be a victor instead of a victim, which seemed to Amy perhaps not so much an ignorant scolding of the woman who had just spoken as simply what the woman told herself to stay sane. Someone else had had nine rounds of chemo. Amy could not imagine. Another woman said she was a five-time member of the cancer club. Most recently, she had had a lung removed. The final woman who spoke, Mary, seemed to try to give the group some tough love about how whining and crying would not lead to happiness. She showed off the Christmas present her husband had given her—a T-shirt that said, "This girl doesn't retreat—she reloads."

Mary's tough love hurt Amy because she had cried when it had been her turn to speak. It seemed unreal to say these things about herself, to say that she had had stage two, type three, invasive-ductal breast cancer, four rounds of chemo, a double mastectomy ten weeks ago, and a radical hysterectomy less than two weeks ago. She had been through *all that*. All of it. And it was a lot. And it was still so fresh. She still could not believe that all of that had happened or that it had happened to her. It was horrifying to say it and horrifying to hear herself say it. Now, on top of it all, it felt as if she were being shamed and scolded for it, even though it was clearly with the very best of intentions.

She thought about a time a few years ago when Carly was upset about how one of her friends had turned into a mean girl and had begun to exclude her. Amy had sat next to Carly on her bed, where she sat crying. "Well, forget her!" Amy had said. "Just forget her! You deserve better friends than that, and now there's room in your life for those better friends! Good riddance, I say!" She had wanted Carly to rise up and fight—not physically fight her old friend but fight the thoughts that were going through her own head about her worth. Instead, Carly had just cried harder. She hadn't had any fight inside her at the moment. Carly had still been in the stage where she couldn't believe this loss was happening to her. Now, Amy understood perfectly.

And she understood Mary's good intentions too. But tough love wasn't what was needed. What Amy had been looking for were examples of happy women leading full lives, women who had it on good authority that, like them, she would be okay. Women who could honestly tell her that her mastectomy wouldn't make any difference in whether she was loved by her husband or anyone else.

The leader of the group said final words about how it was okay to whine and cry when it was new, as it was for Amy—that they all had been there. However, the second the meeting was over, Amy got out of there as fast as she could. The leader of the group asked with a friendly smile, "Well, did we scare you off?"

And with a friendly smile, Amy said, "I don't know. . . ." But she did know. She would not be going within a three-block radius of this support group. She told the leader it was nice to meet her, which it had been, and slipped out.

As she drove home, she thought about all of the tragedy, all of the suffering, in the stories she had heard, and she thought that if that was all she had to look forward to, then saving her life had been a waste of time, effort, and money. And then for just a split second, for just the tiniest of moments, she had this other thought: that she had enough Percocet, oxycodone, and sleeping pills at home to end it now. Immediately, she recoiled in horror at this thought and the fact she'd had it. It made no sense. She had fought so hard for her life in the last six months, so why would she give up now? How did that make any sense at all? How had she sunk to these depths?

Surgical menopause had to be playing a role in it. Rationally, she knew her body was surely in shock from all it had been through. It made sense that she would be wildly out of balance. It made sense that this imbalance would be reflected in her brain. Pain used up a person's serotonin, she knew, and she certainly had coped with her share of that in the last six months. Certainly, there was a part of her depression that was biological, and maybe it was a big part.

But it was also true she was overwhelmed by the changes she'd had to adapt to. And the grief she had for how her life and body had been was real.

As fragments of the support group fiasco replayed in her mind, she began to ask deeper questions still. What purpose did the support group serve? Was retelling one's cancer story each month actually helpful? Maybe it was. Maybe it helped a person come to believe it had happened. Or maybe it picked an emotional scab. People seemed to think talking about things was the answer, and maybe it was. But maybe it wasn't. Maybe her tears had come in part because a shift was happening that had to do with cancer becoming part of her identity. Certainly, that was reasonable. After all, the world had been able to see her struggle and treated her differently—not badly, but differently—when chemo had made her bald. Even now, with such short hair and the tiniest remnants of her breasts, she could not deny that her outward identity had changed. But she'd never wanted this experience and she never wanted it to be part of her identity.

A couple of weeks before her last surgery, when she had been at her presurgical appointment, her surgeon had come in and said, "Well, let me tell you what I know about you, and you tell me if I left anything out." She'd launched into Amy's diagnosis, treatment, and mastectomy, and Amy, listening to it all, had started sobbing. Yes, she had gone through all of that. But the other piece was her doctor's word choice: Let me tell you what I know about *you*. Not, Let me tell you what I know about your medical history—let me tell you what I know about *you*. Amy had wanted to stop her right away and say, *Wait, that's not me. Let me tell you about me. I love nature. Growing up, I spent my summers in two national parks and even now dream of visiting them all. I have a daughter who is a senior in high school this year. I'm terrified to let her go—terrified. I grow a beautiful garden. Tomatoes, irises, and geraniums are my favorites. I'm lonely in my marriage. My husband used to serenade me when we were young. I loved that. I miss it. Now I just write books about it, about all my romantic wishes, because even though they don't come true for me anymore, I want other people to imagine them coming true for them. I used to love to paint when I was in college, but I haven't done it in years. I want to get back into it. I am kind. I am giving. I am creative. And six months ago, I would have told you I was health conscious and healthy.*

But she hadn't said any of that. She had just listened and cried.

Maybe the support group would have served a better purpose if it had been structured differently. What would it have sounded like if each woman had said, *Hi, I'm _____. I'm _____, _____, and _____. I also survived cancer. This month, this is what gave my life meaning and purpose, and made me so glad I was able to stick around: _____. This is still a challenge to me: _____. When I get discouraged or down, here is how I find my way back to happiness: _____. I am here. You are here. We are all still here. There is still joy within us and ahead of us.*

What would it have been like if there had been little or no talking about cancer at all, but just an activity they could do together? Just an unspoken understanding while forging on with life together?

She was a woman who had survived cancer. She could not deny that. It was part of her experience and part of her story and part of the fears she still carried with her now. But while it would always be a part of her, she didn't want it to be a *big* part of her. She didn't want it to be her identity or be her new hobby.

When she returned home from the support group, she packed up all of her old prescriptions and returned them to the pharmacy, even though she really believed she would never actually act on that impulse she'd had. It just felt safer to have them out of the house, because she didn't know whether she had bottomed out yet.

As she drove home from the pharmacy, she realized she wanted to have Paul's guns out of the house too, but they were locked up in a safe, and she could put the spare key in the glove compartment of his car so that both keys would always be with him. Yes, she would do that. It was probably unnecessary, just like taking the pills back to the pharmacy, but taking these measures felt like a loving thing to do for herself. These were things she would do for Carly if Carly was going through a time of extreme imbalance like this. This imbalance was temporary, she reminded herself.

That moment she decided to save her own life was the same moment she decided to take the trip. It was when she knew with absolute certainty that she needed to go back to the places that would hopefully remind her of who she had been before all of this and who she still was deep down. The birdsongs and the beauty would hold her safely on the shore of the present moment so she wouldn't drift back out into the stormy sea of the recent past.

She checked the map before starting the car again. The park had four main entrances: Paradise on the southwestern side, where most people went and most climbers began their ascent; Carbon River on the northwest side, where fewer people went; Sunrise high up on the northeast side, which had expansive views and was one of the two places her dad had worked; and Ohanapecosh on the southeast side, a lower-elevation site that used to be a hot spring resort tucked into a temperate rain forest. That had been her primary childhood summer home. That was where Amy most wanted to be.

Not even a half hour later, she was there. She was finally there! Stepping out of her car, she first noticed the sound of the rushing river, a sound like a mother gently shushing a crying child. Closing her eyes, she could hear her own mother's voice woven into it. She took a big breath and let it out, softening into the comfort and assurance of the sound of her mother and of Mother Earth herself.

Next, she noticed the smell, earthy and sweet like Douglas fir needles, the western red cedarwood, and service berries. Rich and heavy and moist. Wafts of the scents of campers' breakfasts traveled through the air as well, mingling.

Everything was covered in moss here in the gentlest forest. It was as if the spirit of the forest herself liked to knit and made pajamas for the trees and blankets for the large boulders. Everything seemed lovingly cloaked in softness and tucked in for a peaceful sleep.

All around her she noticed plants that she hadn't seen in decades and had mostly forgotten about. They seemed like familiar old friends—lady ferns and oak ferns, salal and kinnikinnick, trillium, vanilla leaf, bunchberry dogwood, glacial lilies, and bear grass.

She made her way from the parking lot to the visitor center, inhaling deeply, breathing this place that she loved right into the very center of her body. According to the ranger, there was one campsite left for that night. The next night was Friday, though, and the campground was booked. All the weekend nights for the rest of the summer were, in fact. Amy made reservations for all of the weeknights for the next three weeks, not terribly inconvenienced that she would need to change campsites every night or two. She was going to sleep in her station wagon, after all, so it wasn't as if she would have to take down a tent and put it back up each time, moving all its contents as well. Sleeping in her car was easier than that and safer too. It had been one thing to sleep on the lawn outside of employee housing or in the clearing with the fire ring when she had been a kid, but it was quite another to sleep in a tent in a crowded campground full of people, many of whom knew nothing about keeping a clean camp. Ohanapecosh had plenty of bears. And even though she was clear that they wanted ice chests and not her, she had a hard enough time sleeping these days without the added element of listening for bears walking outside of her tent.

It was fine that the campground was completely reserved on the weekends all summer long because by then she would be badly in need of a shower. Maybe she would stay in a hotel at Crystal Mountain Resort or go on down to Enumclaw or Yakima and re-stock her food supplies. She would figure it out.

After she parked at her campsite and put her food in the large bear-proof box provided there, she set off first to the employee housing. At the far end of the campground, a trail led up the hill to the two two-story apartment buildings that housed the seasonal rangers and maintenance workers. Each year, they had stayed in the downstairs apartment on the far end of the complex farthest from the maintenance garage. Now, there were Tibetan prayer flags hanging outside of it and a bicycle parked near the door. In that moment when she could not go in, could not walk through the door and see her mom making pot roast and potatoes or something equally hearty, she realized that home wasn't just a place but a time too. There was only a limited extent to which she was going to be able to come back home. She hoped it would be enough.

Around back was the big rock, the one where she and Alicia used to meet the other kids.

She patted it like a faithful old dog. Denny had given her her first kiss on top of that rock—a harmless peck, the summer they turned nine. If she could have gone back and done it differently, she would have married Denny Swensen. He had been as absolutely sweet as they came.

Walking on to the large stone campfire ring in a clearing just across the road, she found the trail to the Grotto after two attempts. The Grotto had been their name for a swimming hole at the bottom of a steep hill. Stepping on or over small fallen branches, she made her way to the part of the trail that involved hanging on to a rope while descending a series of rocks for about ten or fifteen feet. She had done it before. But she paused, unsure of whether her weak body would make it down safely and make it back up later on when it was time to return. If she fell, who knew how long it would take for someone to find her. The sound of the river would drown out her calls. Feeling too vulnerable to try, she sat on the edge among the sword ferns and lady ferns and looked down at the bright, aqua-colored water far below. She listened to the long, high, lyrical songs of the wrens that flitted about in the trees closest to her, their bodies small and brown, with a little white spot behind their eye. Sometimes, she thought she heard a hermit thrush in the distance, with a similar song that also had rapid highs and lows. Although she saw no flashes of yellow, from time to time she could hear a western tanager singing alto to the sopranos of the other birds.

It was then that she began to feel the weight of her body settle deeper into the earth, began to feel herself slow her rhythm, her breath, and her heart. When she walked, her footsteps slowed too. If she stayed on that trajectory of slowing down, she thought, she would eventually be in sync with the natural world around her. Slow enough to listen. Slow enough to smell. Slow enough to be back in the rhythm of peace.

Carly

As the days ticked on, Carly began to fall into a rhythm. Parts of the routine were still clumsy. There was definitely room for refinement. For starters, she would bring one or more of the books Great-Aunt Rae had left in her room to help pass the long days when there wasn't enough time to join the guests but too much time to sit and think. All in all, she was pleased with how time had passed. There had been moments that had moved painfully slowly, like the moments she had lain awake at night listening to Great-Aunt Rae snore despite the earplugs. There had also been moments that passed too quickly, like when she had been trying to complete all her prep cooking before Great-Aunt Rae returned with the guests. And then there had been times that had moved at just the right speed, like when she brought up the rear on a trail ride on T. Rex, the gentle rocking of his walk soothing her like a baby in a cradle.

After she prepared what could be done in advance for tonight's dinner, she crawled on T. Rex bareback while he was tied up in the shade of a tree, leaned forward, and just lay on him like that, like a baby monkey would cling to its mother. When she opened her eyes, she saw a coyote in a break in the trees quite a ways off, its eyes fixed on her. It was large and silvery, its winter coat not completely lost yet. Had she felt no fear, she would have found it quite beautiful.

Unsure of what to do, she slid off T. Rex, stood near the horses, and stared back, breaking only for moments to scan her surroundings, assessing whether there were others. If there were, she never saw them. The coyote sat down, but Carly did not. She held its gaze until at last it stood, turned, and walked back into the woods. She didn't know whether it was gone for good or just gone for a while.

That night, after she had served the guests, she sat down at the dinner table to join them. One of the women stood, her glass raised. "I'd like to propose a toast—to Kathy, who has been cancer-free for five years now."

The other women raised their glasses and cheered, "To Kathy!" but Carly froze. Just hearing that word, here where she thought she was safe from it, caught her off guard and threw her.

Great-Aunt Rae, astute enough to suspect it would, turned in time to catch a look of devastation on her face and said quietly, "Quick, go get that thing in the kitchen."

"What thing?" Carly asked quietly, looking at her, unable to interpret the look on her great-aunt's face.

Great-Aunt Rae whispered her response: "It doesn't matter."

Carly understood. This was a happy occasion for the guests. If she was going to have a moment, Great-Aunt Rae wanted her to have it privately for the sake of everyone involved.

She stepped inside the chuck wagon, held her head in her hands, and took some deep breaths. When she thought she was ready, she rifled through a drawer for a large serving spoon, which she carried with her as she walked back to the table. She put it in the cubed potatoes next to the other spoon, as if there were supposed to be two. No one seemed to question it.

But later that night, after Kathy's friends were immersed in a game of cards and Great-Aunt Rae was taking horses to the stream for one more drink for the night, Kathy approached Carly while she finished up the night's dishes.

"Rae said you've had a hard year." Her hazel eyes were deeply compassionate.

Carly waited to see how specific her great-aunt had been with the guests.

"Six years ago, my daughter had a hard year, too."

Oh no, Carly thought because she could feel it coming and she knew it was important to be happy around the guests. *Oh, no.* But it was too late. Kathy could see it.

"Come here, sugar," she said, opening her arms. "Come here."

Carly walked into Kathy's embrace, laid her head on her shoulder, and cried.

"There, there, sugar. It's all right. It's all right," Kathy murmured. "It's all right now. Your mama's all right."

"It's not that easy," Carly whispered.

"I know, sugar. Believe me, I know."

Later that night, after all the guests had gone to bed, Carly and Great-Aunt Rae sat next to the campfire in their camp chairs.

"I should go to bed," said Great-Aunt Rae, "but that would mean getting up, and right now I'm too tired to get up."

Carly laughed. She understood. Not that her day had been exhausting in the same way Great-Aunt Rae's had, but crying made her sleepy. It had been a long day, one mostly too slow. "I had a stare-down with a coyote today," she said.

"Yeah? They're curious animals. So are cougar. Sometimes they just like to watch people."

"I would poop my pants if I saw a cougar watching me. I don't even know what I'd do."

"Sometimes when I go for a hike out and back on some dirt road, I see their tracks in mine and know they've been following me, but so far, that's all they've ever done. I don't know whether that comforts you."

"No. Not at all. I hadn't even thought about cougar until a couple minutes ago."

"My mistake. I'm just saying that I've pretty much lived with the cougars for decades and none have eaten me yet. Haven't eaten any of my dogs yet either," she said, leaning forward and knocking on a piece of firewood.

They were quiet for a bit, and then Great-Aunt Rae smiled and said, "Sam and I used to sit by the fire like this. Sometimes when I'm alone, I look up and still see him. And in my mind's eye, I'm still eighteen."

"Hm," Carly said with all the understanding she was capable of at this point in her life. She wondered whether life would be kinder to her or whether, like Great-Aunt Rae, she would just get a taste of the good stuff and then have it taken away . . . or whether someone else would be remembering her the way Great-Aunt Rae was remembering Sam, whether she would die and leave a hole in someone else's life. She assumed that's what happened to Sam.

"Pretty risky, flirting with the boss's son," Carly said.

"Sure seemed like it at the time," Great-Aunt Rae agreed. "But when it's the real thing, you can't stop it any more than you could stop a freight train coming straight at you. When it happens to you, you'll see it in his eyes. For a long time, all Sam and I did was catch each other looking at one another across camp.

I'd be preparing food while Sam and the other guide helped set up tents and entertained the guests. Eventually, everyone seemed to gather at the fire. Sometimes Sam would help cook—flipping steaks or stirring stew while I tended to something else. After the guests ate, I ate, and then washed all of the dishes. Usually Sam would help me, because you know, up there in grizzly country, it was in everyone's interest to get the food cleaned up quickly." Great-Aunt Rae laughed and then continued, "Oh boy, when he rinsed dishes next to me, he sometimes stood very close—close enough to feel the heat radiate off his arm. We'd chitchat about nothing—the dinner, the weather, the rate at which summer was passing—nothing that would be embarrassing or inappropriate if overheard, you know, but really all I could think about was his arm heat." She laughed at herself.

"Yeah, I had no clue arm heat was a thing."

"Oh Carly, when you fall in love, you will enjoy yourself some arm heat."

Carly laughed.

"One night, when there were a lot of dishes and the group of visitors was very tired, Sam and I had been the last two remaining up after everyone else had gone to bed. When the last dish was put away, Sam asked—with a sweet smile I could not resist— whether I might sit by the fire with him for just a few moments before turning in. I was so in love with him that I could not have denied any request he made, so I sat down on a log and to my surprise, he sat right next to me. When he asked whether I was cold, I told him just my back half because my front was warmed by the fire, so he put his arm around me. I never would have guessed that something as simple as an arm on my back would be as thrilling as it was. Electrical thrilling. Driving-too-fast thrilling. Diving-into-an-icy-mountain-lake-with-abandon-despite-knowing-the-end-result thrilling. Oh, Carly, that is the good stuff." Great-Aunt Rae smiled as she inhaled. "Mm, I breathed in his sexy scent, felt the warmth of the fire on my face, and leaned into him, resting my head on his shoulder. I could hear the uneven way he breathed, almost as if his breath was stuttering, and I knew he was feeling it too— the thrill. It was only mid-July. I knew I was in trouble . . . that the only thing I could do was try to make sure things didn't move too fast, so I said, 'I hate for this moment to end, but I should go to sleep,' all casually, as if my heart wasn't racing a hundred miles an hour, as if I had a chance of sleeping at all. He held my hand as he walked me to my tent. Hand heat. Oh, Carly. Hand heat with the right person is intoxicating too. Usually I was a bit scared going to my tent at night because it was on the other side of the chuck wagon and in the shadow of the fire, always seemed so dark. Generally, I tried to make sure I was in my tent before it was dark, with my cowbell nearby in case I needed to alert the guides that a bear was nosing around the kitchen. So, anyway, I appreciated him walking me to my tent. And then he asked if he could kiss me."

"Ooo!"

Great-Aunt Rae smiled broadly. "It was quite a kiss." She paused and then said, "So I asked for another. And before he kissed me again, he whispered, 'Girl, you are playing with fire.'" Great-Aunt Rae exhaled. "Wasn't that the truth! To his credit, he said, 'Good night, beautiful Rae,' and as he turned to walk away, he held my hand until the last possible moment, and then let it slip from his. I remember crawling into my tent out of breath and with my heart beating out of my chest and thinking the odds of me being unmarried and pregnant by the end of summer seemed very good, and man, I did not want that."

How many times, how many thousands of times, had Great-Aunt Rae replayed that night over in her head? Carly wondered. It seemed to her that to recall that level of detail all these decades later, a person would have to retell herself that story at least a couple of times a week.

Great-Aunt Rae shook her head. "Within a month, he was sneaking into my tent, and we'd kiss all night. Sometimes he'd whisper, 'I'm going to marry you, Rae Zakow,' but I knew the difference between those words and, 'Will you marry me?' One set of words was meant to begin a life together. The other set of words was meant to simply coax the next piece of clothing off a girl. Remember that. I'd wake up in the night so peaceful in Sam's embrace, but when the American robins started singing, he'd untangle himself from me and sneak out. I hated those birds.

"Before I got up and made breakfast, I'd lay there for a few more minutes, wondering how this all was going to end, or whether in fact it never would. I'm not sure everybody gets to experience that kind of love."

"Do you think I will?"

"I think it's inevitable. I think it will happen later for you, though. Right now, no one could get through."

Unsure of what Great-Aunt Rae meant, Carly looked at her, puzzled.

"You've got a lot of armor on. It's invisible, but still very real. You'll need to take that off before you can experience the really good stuff in life. The land of the good stuff is a risky place. And sometimes it leaves you utterly devastated . . . completely destroyed. But you can't have it both ways. You can't get into the land of the good stuff with armor on, and I suppose that's why I've never been back. You've just got to jump in with your heart wide open. I don't know that I have it in me to go to the land of the good stuff again, but Carly, I am so glad I went there once. Don't miss out." With that, Great-Aunt Rae stood. "I've imparted enough wisdom tonight. I'm going to bed. Don't stay up too long." She walked off to the outhouse, leaving Carly to wonder how a person takes off invisible armor when it's welded on.

Amy

That morning, Amy had woken early, maybe too early, cold and sweaty from hot flashing all night, wondering how sustainable camping was going to be. Campgrounds were much noisier than she remembered. She'd had to wait until quite late before enough people nearby had fallen asleep that she could sleep too. As she had lain awake waiting for sleep to find her, she had savored the sounds of the forest.

The morning was chilly, so she put on a warm hat and set off to the restroom, but later, when she walked out of the stall and to the sink to wash her hands, she saw her reflection in the mirror and panicked. With a hat on, she looked the way she had when she was going through chemo, and for a split second, she forgot that it was today and not a day six months ago. Her heart raced, and she felt as if she were going to cry. Quickly, she whipped off her hat. *It's over now. It's over. It's okay, it's okay, it's okay,* she told herself, but her body didn't quite believe it yet.

Walking outside, she found the cold air on her head as disturbing as the sight of herself in the hat, so she put the hat back on. She loved that hat—she did. Her sister had brought it back from Trinidad, Colorado, where she had gone one weekend to buy Amy some marijuana edibles to help with nausea. The hat was off-white cable knit on the outside so it had matched anything she wore, which she appreciated. Just because she'd had cancer didn't mean she wanted to look like she was going to make a snowman. But best of all, it had a layer of very soft fleece inside, like short fur but even softer. The first time she had put it on her bald, tender head, she had closed her eyes in a state of pure euphoria. Hats had been such a challenge. Almost all of them had been somewhere between painful and uncomfortable. What had felt soft enough to ordinary people had felt unbearably scratchy to her. They had to be loose enough not to hurt but tight enough not to fall in her eyes. If they were too thick, she would get too hot indoors and the prickling rash on her head would worsen. She remembered one in particular, one she had wanted to wear in front of the woman who had knit it for her to show her appreciation, but she had felt every yarn in every knit cable pressing against her head and it had hurt. And then there had been the ones that were supposed to be funny, and maybe had been funny to other people going through the same thing, but those had hurt Amy—not on her scalp but in her heart, because she was unable to comprehend how her cancer could be funny to anyone, how what she was going through and would go through in the weeks to come could be a big joke to anyone who cared about her. There was nothing funny about going bald. There was nothing funny about being so close to death.

Feeling a hot flash coming on, she took the hat off again. How long would it be before the hot flashes were over and her hair had grown back enough that she wouldn't need a hat any longer? How long before she really felt and looked like herself again? Would she ever?

Then she looked up at the branches of the trees above her and breathed in the scent of Ohanapecosh deeply. She listened to the river shushing her busy mind and felt the earth give just a little under her boots. It calmed her as she continued to walk down the little path, veering up to the hot springs.

Long ago there had been a bathhouse nearby, but now the springs had been restored to their natural state. One pool near the trail was large enough and cool enough to put her feet in, so she took off her boots, rolled up her pants, and did just that. When she had been going through chemo, the bottoms of her feet had burned, but in recent months they had felt all right, and for that she was grateful. Many people had permanent nerve damage in their feet after chemo. She gripped the sediment on the bottom of the little pool with her toes the way a tree sends down roots, and she simply noticed details in her surroundings. Elk tracks, some large and some very small. The songs of black-capped chickadees waking up. Hot water gently babbling down the hill and into her pool. The smell of sulfur and earth. Tiny rocks under her hands. She noticed her feet again, immersed in this warm water, and stretched them, noticing her right foot was tighter from stepping on the gas and brake pedals so much in the last week. What a discovery it felt like to notice a body part other than her chest and abdomen. What a relief, really. This awareness of all the parts of her body that had not changed this year struck her as revolutionary.

It seemed the whole world slowed down to a speed that was merciful, slow enough that her own life would feel as if it were lasting forever no matter how much or how little time she actually had left. In this state of awareness, she felt like she was living. For the first time in months, she actually felt as if she were truly living . . . here in this system of living organisms, all of them living together.

Packwood, Washington, was a town that just wanted to be left alone. On the outside it had changed a little bit since her teen years, the peak of the spotted owl controversy, when signs could be seen in the front yards of loggers and others who depended on the logging industry—signs that read, "Save a tree. Wipe your ass with a spotted owl," and, "PNW loggers: an endangered species." Families who had logged for four or even five generations just wanted to peacefully cut trees in the rain five days a week and hunt and fish on the other two. Despite the welcome signs outside motels, Amy could feel it, this internal war Packwood had been having with the outside world since the eighties. She could feel the energy of prickly annoyance and residual anger.

It was not the kind of community where an average woman went out and got a pixie cut. For starters, they weren't practical. They didn't offer enough warmth in the cold rain. Pixies were more of an urban phenomenon. They weren't considered feminine here. She knew Packwood well enough to know this. Some locals felt kicked around by liberal environmentalists and were looking for an opportunity to kick a liberal back.

So, when she was filling up at the gas station and a large pickup with two men in front and two motorcycles in the back pulled up, followed by another pickup truck with one younger man and one motorcycle, Amy felt nervous. She looked at herself, in jeans, running shoes, and a green fleece shirt. Since she was hiking and camping, she wasn't wearing makeup or earrings. In her mind, she ran through how she would protect herself if it came to it, since she was still recovering from surgery and too weak to actually fight. She decided she would lift up her shirt and yell, I'm recovering from breast cancer, you stupid a-holes!

It wasn't a completely unwarranted thought. Her college friend Viviane, who had been through breast cancer a year before Amy went through it, had contacted her after Amy had first been diagnosed. She gave her all kinds of reassurance, practical advice, and information about what she might expect, with the disclaimer that every woman's experience was unique to her. When the topic of hair came up, she said, "Yesterday I went to the gym for the second time since all of this happened, and afterward I stopped by the grocery store. When I was in the produce section, I noticed this little old lady giving me the stink eye, but I couldn't figure out why. Eventually, she came up to me, wagged her finger in my face, and said, 'I don't approve of your lifestyle!' Now I realize that, yeah, I was wearing my gym clothes and my hair is just beginning to come back. . . . I was so proud of it, you know? Just to have hair again. . . ."

"That's horrible!" Amy said. "What did you do?"

"I was so stunned, I couldn't do anything. I couldn't speak. She stormed away, and some other shoppers said supportive things to me, but I just had to go. I left my cart there, went to my car, and cried."

Since hearing that story, Amy had played it out a hundred times in her head with all of the things she would have liked to say in order to make that mean old lady feel as small and stupid as possible. So, she supposed she had been expecting to have her moment of being on the receiving end of bigotry.

But the rednecks fueled up without paying her much attention at all. She didn't know whether they thought she was a man or a woman. She didn't know whether any of them had had a mother, a sister, a wife, or a friend who had been through the very same thing she had and perhaps recognized what they were seeing. And in that moment when she no longer felt threatened, she realized it was she who had been judgmental. She wondered how many times she had misjudged someone—assumed someone in the very same shoes she was in now was gay (even if she didn't have a negative judgment of that), assumed someone who was skinny was anorexic instead of recovering from an illness, assumed someone had a boob job instead of reconstruction, assumed to know anything about anyone, really.

It was easy to forgive herself for the kind of judgment that stemmed from survival or safety concerns, but harder to forgive herself for the other misjudgments she had surely made. Well, now, she knew. From now on, she would do better.

She wished it were as easy to let go of the vulnerability she still felt in the world, but it wasn't. She still felt so weary and so vulnerable.

Since it was Friday night and Ohanapecosh was full, Amy returned to the forest service campground where she had stayed two nights ago and pulled into the same slot. Familiarity was what she needed tonight. As she unpacked her stove and box of chicken-rice soup, she noticed an older couple sitting in lawn chairs outside their RV, their little dog at their feet.

Later, when she took her trash to the bear-proof dumpster, she crossed paths with the couple as they walked their dog.

"Cute dog," Amy said.

The woman who held the leash had neat, short white hair and soulful brown eyes, and her expression reminded Amy that she did not look the way she normally did.

Her husband was tall and bald, with blue eyes that sparkled. "We found this dog on the streets, starving, and we saved her. But then a couple years later, I got cancer, and I felt like she saved us. She was just such a comfort, you know?"

Amy felt she could use a little comfort, so she asked, "Can I pet her?" And with permission, she bent down and let her fingers travel through the dog's soft gray curls. The dog looked into her eyes, and Amy knew it was ridiculous to project this much onto a dog, but it seemed to her that the dog understood something she couldn't quite name—something other humans couldn't understand. When she stood, there were tears in her eyes.

"Are you okay, honey?" asked the woman.

"I survived it this year," she replied.

"It shakes you up, doesn't it," the man said.

Amy nodded and then said softly, "I didn't know I was going to feel this way after it was all over."

"Yep. It shakes you up." And then, before she could ask him how to handle it, he patted her on the shoulder and said, "We've got today," and then, looking at his wife, he said, "And today is pretty good, isn't it?"

"It sure is," his wife agreed.

The next day, Amy drove to Crystal Mountain Resort. Needing a shower and a place to call Aunt Rae, she decided to splurge on a hotel room there.

"Could I check in early?" she asked, thinking that since it was off-season and there was plenty of vacancy, the clerk might say yes.

"Sure," replied the clerk. "ID and credit card, please."

Amy fished both out of her wallet and laid them on the counter. The clerk picked up her driver's license and took longer than normal to look at it.

"I went through chemo last winter," she explained. "That's why I don't look like my picture. I was bald two months ago."

Even though the clerk was young, she had the sense to look Amy in the eye and ask, "Are you all good now?"

"Yes."

"I'm glad."

"Me, too."

These moments were so many things. A reminder of a time she wanted to forget. An invasion of her privacy, because her medical history was not a clerk's business. But they were also moments to be human with a stranger—just be human and accept the good wishes of someone that didn't have to care about her and yet still did.

After dropping her things next to the door as it shut behind her, Amy stood in the doorway of the bathroom. It had such a large mirror. And no wrapping paper on the bottom of it.

There had been a counselor who came around to check in on people during their first chemo infusion and ask them whether they wanted to talk. He was a resident, which mattered only because he was young enough that Amy made assumptions about the life experience he had not had, which may not have been fair or accurate. Or it may have. She didn't know. It surprised her to have him say something that was helpful then—something about the parts of who she was that would stay the same even though she was having a transformative experience.

Almost three weeks after her mastectomy, she had simply wanted to know when most women felt better. She figured he could likely tell her that. He didn't immediately answer her question, though. First, he looked through her answers on the questionnaire that was on her intake form, then said, "It looks like you're having a hard time."

"Some days I can handle it. And some days I just . . . I just look at the ceiling from the moment I take off my shirt to the moment I get out of the shower. I just don't want to see what has happened to me. I just don't want to see what I've been through."

"I find that people who have this avoidance behavior take longer to come to acceptance," he said.

Amy wondered what was the chicken and what was the egg. Maybe he had it backward. Maybe people who took longer to come to acceptance needed to adopt avoidance behavior.

And she wondered where a young man got off telling a middle-aged woman about how she should handle the trauma of cancer diagnosis, chemo, and losing her breasts. What did he know about any of it?

"I had a massage two days ago," she told him. "It was so wonderful to feel all the parts of me that had not changed . . . it was such a blessed relief to feel everything that was still the same that I cried."

"That's great," he said, "but you don't need a massage to do that. You can do that for yourself simply by bringing your awareness to all of those other body parts."

This was where she lost respect for him. Massage soothed her nervous system. Clearly, her nervous system needed to be soothed. And she had done her part to endure a lot, so what was wrong with getting help with this? Why was it better to do this herself? What was this obsession with independence in the culture?

They talked for a while, he offering to teach her mindful techniques to bring her more into the present moment and she telling him she'd already learned some of those in yoga classes . . . he trying to engage her in an exercise where he asked, "Why do you believe that?" after everything she said to lead her down a path to examining the roots of her beliefs, and she insisting she just wanted to know when most people felt better.

"Three months after the last surgery," he finally said.

She took a big breath. "Three months. Okay."

"If you don't feel better by July, come back and see me."

She thanked him, shook his hand, and left. July.

And until her second surgery, she really tried. She looked in the mirror and chanted, "I love my body, I love my body, I love my body. Heal, heal, heal," over and over at least once a day, and she said those words when she washed her chest in the shower—even if she was looking up.

But when the second surgery knocked her down again, she felt as if the noise in her own mind from trying to process all of these events was just too much. She just couldn't do it all at once. Enduring the physical discomfort of another recovery and trying to reach a deeper level of acceptance about the loss of her breasts at the same time was just too much. As she covered the bottom half of her bathroom mirror, she wondered whether she had made the right choice about not having reconstruction. Would having reconstructed breasts make her feel less of a loss—even if they had no nipples, even if she couldn't feel them, and even if the perky reconstructed breasts looked nothing like her original saggy ones? Or would the discomfort of the expanders under her chest muscles weaken her even more as they stretched out her muscles a little more each month for five months until they were finally stretched out enough to hold a silicone implant? She just didn't see how she still wouldn't feel profound loss even with reconstructed breasts, and she just couldn't imagine not wanting those uncomfortable objects out of her body. She had been through enough. Enough surgeries. Enough pain and discomfort. Enough. Just, enough.

When Amy had looked at her reflection in the top half of the mirror for the first time after the bottom half was safely covered with floral wrapping paper, what she saw were mostly the things that were the same—her face, her neck, her shoulders. Grateful, she exhaled. She no longer needed to look at the war zone. She no longer needed to look at the evidence of an experience she wanted to forget. On the wrapping paper, she taped positive affirmations she had cut out from the get well cards her friends had sent her. In one way, it was perhaps ironic to have any words about acceptance on the wrapping paper, but she didn't see it like that. She saw the wrapping paper as an act of kindness to herself that broke down the task of acceptance into more manageable pieces. Step one: Just see someone she recognized in the mirror. Just look at her own eyes and think, *I know you. I remember you. We're going to be okay.* Step two: Notice the parts of herself that were still very beautiful—her shoulders, her cheekbones, her ears. She didn't know what step three was yet, and she didn't know what step taking another look at all that had changed would be.

Now, in her motel room, she stripped off her clothes next to the main door out of view of the mirror and walked sideways into the bathroom with her back turned to the mirror, turned the water on, and stepped into the shower. *One day,* she told herself. *But not today.*

Promptly at six, Amy called Aunt Rae. Aunt Rae answered after just one ring.

"She's out feeding horses, so we have maybe ten minutes," Aunt Rae began. "First of all, how are you?"

"Getting better every day," Amy said. "You?"

"Glad to hear it. I'm fine. Your girl is fine too. Settling in. Even enjoying herself sometimes. She's a good worker."

"Thank you so much for doing this, Aunt Rae."

"My pleasure. So, what's this I hear about you taking off?"

"I know it looks strange. I thought I just wanted to return to a place that would make me feel more like me, but now that I'm here, I think I wanted to be in a place where I have so many memories of Mom."

"I understand. Paul was trying not to show it, but I could see he was concerned."

Amy deliberated and then spilled the beans about finding the divorce papers, ending the story by saying, "So, I left on the day he had planned to give them to me before he could just in case he actually went through with it. Just seemed smart to lose some attachment and see how the world felt out on my own." She thought her aunt would be outraged but was surprised to find she wasn't.

"I don't know whether you remember me talking about Sam, the young man I loved."

"Oh . . . yes, a little bit."

"Well, when he came home from the Vietnam War, I couldn't reach him. I mean, he could be in my arms and still I couldn't reach him. And then . . ." She didn't finish. "I don't know. I just know that ever since the bombing of the federal building, Paul's eyes have reminded me of Sam's when Sam came back from Vietnam. What I'm trying to say is that I don't think it's personal, Amy. I think he just couldn't be reached. What did he say when you confronted him about it?"

"I didn't. I needed him. I couldn't afford to rock the boat."

"Well, he stayed, you know? He saw you through it. That's better than a lot of men can do."

"So, no advice? You always have advice!"

"You can't make chicken soup out of chicken poop. Some things are bigger than us, kid."

Amy was quiet for a moment.

"Maybe he's had a change of heart," Aunt Rae said tenderly.

"Maybe it's me now that can't be reached."

In the background, Amy heard the door and Aunt Rae say,

"Just a sec," before redirecting her attention. "All fed? . . . Good job. Thank you. . . . Okay. Okay. Have a good bath." When Carly had gone upstairs, Rae spoke again. "Did you want to talk to her? I just thought it would be better to give her a little more time."

"I trust your judgment," Amy said, feeling the rejection and disappointment in her heart, even though she hadn't been foolish enough to actually believe her daughter would want to talk to her. The situation was just so sad.

"Don't worry, kid. I got this. It's going to be fine."

"Thank you so much," Amy said. "And thank you for always being there for me, Aunt Rae."

"Well, I sure love you, kid."

"I sure love you, too."

"Okay then, same time next week."

"Roger that. Good night."

A dial tone replaced her aunt's voice, and Amy felt pangs of loneliness, but when she imagined Paul in the room with her, she didn't feel any better.

There was still plenty of light out, so she walked outdoors to the large gravel parking lot. Walking up even the slightest hill hurt her abdomen, so the flat surface the parking lot offered was appealing. Along the perimeter she walked, listening to the sound of wind in the trees, breathing in the crisp scent of alpine fir, listening to a great horned owl call to another somewhere in the distance. She felt the wind on her face and on her hands and listened to the gravel crunch under her feet. Her walk was slow, so much slower than normal, but she was moving forward. That was the thing. She was moving forward.

Paul

Paul woke on Saturday with a desperate desire to go back in time, back to when he was happy, back before bombs and cancer. The best he could do was drive to Oklahoma State University in Stillwater.

He parked his car on Elm Street near Eskimo Joe's, where he had every intention of eating lunch later, and then walked to campus. It felt strange to him to do this backward. All those years ago, he would meet Amy at Bartlett Hall, the arts building, and walk from there to Eskimo Joe's. They usually walked through the small business district near campus on their way home, prolonging their sense of nightlife and of being grown-up enough to participate in it.

As he crossed Knoblock Street and stepped onto campus, a sense of overwhelming nostalgia hit him. The actual memories were a blur. It was a feeling, and the feeling was hope, the kind of hope that inflates a young man's chest like a hot-air balloon ready to lift off, the kind of hope that makes him feel bigger. When was the last time he had walked this path without holding Amy's hand? It seemed strange to walk here without the sensation of her hand in his. He remembered sitting under that tree right over there with her, holding her palm open, tracing the lines in it with the finger of his other hand, buying time by pretending to be a fortune-teller so he could admire the sheer femininity of it a little longer. Occasionally glancing up, he saw the muscles under her eyes twitch just a little when it tickled. What he mostly remembered was the excitement of the banter combined with the sexual tension. Yeah, she had laughed and scoffed at every outrageous thing he had said, but all in good spirit, of course. After all, everything Amy said and did was in good spirit. He recalled saying, "You will marry a very handsome man. . . . Oh! Look here! He's a musician. He will serenade you for the rest of your life! You're a very lucky girl."

Now, sadness hit him like a punch in the chest. He hadn't serenaded her the rest of her life—not even close. And he couldn't honestly say she had been a lucky girl either.

Wondering whether he might remember more if he sat under that tree, he walked over and did so, leaning back against the trunk. Sure enough, another memory fragment came to him and a big close-lipped smile spread across his face. It was a simple one—no words. Just him sitting right there like that, reading a history book, and Amy's head on his lap, eyes closed, sleeping, her abandoned textbook facedown next to her. He had looked down at her sweet face and thought, *That's the face I want to fall asleep and wake up next to for the rest of my life*. He had thought it with a level of certainty he'd never had about anything before.

Curious about what else he might remember, he walked on to the spot outside the window of the classroom where she used to paint.

"Keep that up and I'm going to fall in love with you!" she had called out to him one day right after he had finished a song that he had composed just for her. He hadn't told her that he had written it or that it was for her. He had been too shy for that. Could he even remember how it went now? The song could easily be lost forever. He wanted to look into the window and see her again, that

Amy, the one he knew when he was that Paul, but he didn't want to scare anyone who might be in that classroom, so he didn't. He did, however, walk from that spot to the door where he used to enter, his heart racing with anticipation, conditioned. Perhaps because it was summer, it was locked.

Continuing to walk the route backward, as if tracing his steps for something he had lost, he found himself at Theta Pond.

During the day, Amy had always been with him when he had gone to Theta Pond, but after getting a job with campus security in the evenings and early night, he had walked there alone. It was interesting to consider the duality of his experiences even then. In one life, he strolled in the sunshine with Amy, watching her as she delighted in something as simple as feeding ducks bits of old bread. He had amused himself by imagining her feeding their future children like that—throwing bits of bread at them in a swimming pool. And then there was this other life, the one where it was dark and he was without her. One where his apprehension ran high, anticipating a bad guy behind every tree, wondering what might happen and what might be demanded of him.

Looking back now, Paul tried to remember what he had been thinking when he went into law enforcement. He supposed he had been thinking about how best to support a family. It wasn't as if there were a ton of jobs out there for someone with a B.A. in history. And he supposed he had been thinking that this career choice would prove to his dad that he was, in fact, a man—a real man, as his dad defined it. Paul couldn't imagine how he would have done it differently if given a chance to do it again knowing what he knew now. There was no point in that kind of thinking, anyway. It was done.

Sitting on a bench, Paul remembered imagining a pool full of children, mouths open, catching bread. Then, the imaginary children disappeared and Carly was left alone in the pool. He hadn't wanted to bring more children into this world after the blast. This world, it had seemed to him then and maybe still did, was no place for children. And he had known then that he could no longer be the dad he had imagined he would be. But now, as he held this image in his head of Carly, sulking alone in the pool, back turned to Amy, who had just a fraction of an inch of hair all over her head, he wondered whether he had made a mistake back then, whether Carly might be different today if she'd had a sibling to commiserate with, a sibling to understand.

He picked up his phone and called John, who lived in Portland, Oregon, now. John answered on the second ring. "Paul? Everything okay?"

"Yeah. I was just thinking about that time I brought Amy home to meet the parents and when we left, how I could see how desperately you wanted me to take you with us, and I just wanted to say how sorry I am that I wasn't able to do better in that moment. I mean, I know Mom would have been devastated if you'd left with me, but I still feel so bad for leaving you alone in all of that. I think about it sometimes."

"Oh, brother, you've been carrying that around all these years?"

Yes, he could feel it like a brick in his chest. "I suppose I have."

"Well, you can lay that burden down. I lived. I turned out okay. I've got a good life."

"Jen and the kids are all good?"

"All good. Emma's at volleyball camp. Riley's flipping burgers. Jen's been rowing a dragon boat with some other teachers this summer. Work's been busy." He was a civil engineer who specialized in earthquake resistance in architectural plans. Paul worried about the big one a lot—the nine-point-something earthquake that was going to rock the Northwest at some point in the future, maybe in his brother's lifetime or maybe in his niece and nephew's lifetime. They were all so in denial. They didn't understand that it actually *could* happen to them. He desperately wished he could make them move but knew better than to try. "How about you? How's Amy?"

"Amy's good. Carly graduated a week ago. Lots of changes, you know."

"Yeah? What are Carly's plans?"

"I don't think she knows. This summer she's helping Amy's aunt with horse outfitting in New Mexico."

"Oh, that sounds like fun."

"Yeah." For a moment, Paul wondered what it would be like to be completely honest, to say it felt as if everything were wrong, that his daughter wasn't making good choices and not speaking to him, that Amy had left him for trees and he wasn't sure she was coming back, that he was on administrative leave at work and his whole world might be crumbling. He didn't want to tell all of those stories, though, and he didn't want his apology to get lost in all of that. "Well, listen. I know you've got things to do so I won't keep you. It was great to hear your voice. I need to get up there for a visit sometime this year." John had vowed never to return to Oklahoma, so it was all up to Paul.

"That would be great. And remember, I would gladly meet you somewhere in between, too. A weekend in Vegas. A Utah adventure odyssey. Or even California. Maybe after you retire, we can do something big . . . take a trip somewhere."

"That would be great." And then, in a moment of courage and honesty, he said, "I love you, brother," and his brother said it back.

Carly

After the guests left on Saturday, there had been plenty of work still to be done—unpacking, bathing horses, feeding horses, hosing the sweat off saddle blankets so they didn't get crusty and cause sores, taking saddle soap or oil to the tack so it didn't crack. There were dish towels and red bandannas that served as cloth napkins to launder. When Great-Aunt Rae asked her whether she wanted to go to the grocery store with her, Carly declined because her favorite part of the whole weekend was next on her list—the shower she had been looking forward to taking all week.

After her shower, she dressed and went outside to sit near the horses. T. Rex was lying on his side in the sun. Carly could not resist. She slid between the first and second rails on the fence, then talked to him softly as she approached his head so she wouldn't startle him. "Do you remember the time a little girl took a nap on you?" she asked him as she stroked his enormous face. "Do you remember how you held so still?" Squatting behind him, she slid her hands down his neck to his back and then up on his side. There, she rested her head on him, thinking about how it was that so incredibly much had changed since the last time she had done this and at the same time, nothing had changed. Trusting him more, she dropped to her knees.

The world around her seemed to hold still, as if time itself had stopped, and it was just such a relief—just such a blessed relief. She didn't need to react or respond to anything. She let her fingers burrow into T. Rex's fur as she had so long ago, feeling the warmth from his body and the warmth from the sun, wondering where one kind of warmth stopped and the other began. She watched a small purple butterfly land on a solitary buttercup nearby and stay there, still, supporting her idea that everything in the world had just stopped for a glorious time-out.

But then the sound of tires on gravel caused T. Rex to lift his head. Carly wasted no time moving out of the way. He rolled onto his back once, twice, and then with the momentum of that got his feet under him and stood.

When Great-Aunt Rae honked, all the horses made their way to the fence. It was part of her training, she explained, so that they wouldn't ever be afraid of any cars or trucks that honked at them, and if they ever got loose, she could call them back by honking and collect them easily.

Great-Aunt Rae was full of clever thoughts like that and some quirky ones as well. Earlier that day, she had taught Carly the finer points of trapping mice a number of different ways. The big takeaway had been that in most cases, it was best to put the mousetrap in a box, like one that had contained crackers or packets of oatmeal, so that if the trap failed to finish the job, a woman could take the box outside and bludgeon the mouse with the flat-nosed shovel she should always keep by her door. After all, a person never knew when she might need to grab it quickly and behead a rattlesnake. Yes, Great-Aunt Rae had used the word "bludgeoned" and had said it as if it were no big deal, though she had added that it was okay to cry and apologize while a person did this, so she wasn't totally heartless.

Carly walked over to the pickup to help Great-Aunt Rae unload groceries, but before she could pick up her first canvas grocery bag (Great-Aunt Rae had already explained it was important to use grocery bags that wouldn't break in her driveway because she didn't have the time or money to replace anything), Great-Aunt Rae handed Carly several postcards, all from her mom.

Carly wanted to pretend that she didn't care about them, but the pictures sparked her curiosity. "Mom and Dad just left me and went on a trip?"

"Just your mom. Your dad went home."

"Did she go with Aunt Alicia?"

"No, by herself."

Carly's brow furrowed. "That's not like her."

"I think cancer really shook her up."

Carly stared at the ground for a moment, then put the postcards in her back pocket and reached for a bag, but before she picked it up, Great-Aunt Rae asked, "How come you're so mad at her?"

Picking up the groceries, she replied, "I wasn't mad *at her*. I was just mad," and then walked away. She had never intended for it all to turn into something so big or so permanent. At the time, she hadn't known how to apologize to her mom for saying such awful things; she'd only known how to avoid her. She still didn't know how to apologize. But it never occurred to her that she would be abducted by her dad and dropped in the mountains of New Mexico and then her mom would take off and the whole situation would harden like concrete as time passed and that there would be no way to fix it. Anger had been draining out of her here with the horses, so she was rational enough for the first time in almost three months to see it all more clearly, and what she felt was immense regret. She didn't know when she'd have the chance to say anything to her mom now. It could be weeks. And what would she say then? "I'm sorry" would be way too small for that kind of damage.

Carly set the groceries down on the counter and pulled the cards out of her pocket and read them. Each of them said the same thing.

Dear Carly,
I love you.
Mom

Great-Aunt Rae was just a few steps behind her and set more bags down next to the others.

"All she said is that she loves me," Carly said, disappointed that there wasn't more information about what was really going on.

"Well, that's the right thing to say when you don't know what to say. Just distill it down to the part so pure that no bullshit can stick to it," Great-Aunt Rae replied. Then she walked back out to retrieve more groceries.

Later, when they were picking up the saddle blankets that had dried in the sun, Great-Aunt Rae said, "Your mom was only a couple years older than you when her mom died. Pancreatic cancer. My sister wanted to keep it a secret until the end so her girls would not drop out of college and everyone would remember her as she was, but in her final days she changed her mind and wanted to see us all one more time. It was such a shock to see her so frail and thin . . . dark circles under her eyes, you know. . . . My parents were there, and even though it had been twenty years, they were still mad at me for leaving like I had, but we met in an unspoken truce. Losing Catherine dwarfed the other bullshit. We simply hugged and said 'I love you.' We all took turns sitting with

Catherine, saying everything we wanted to say while she was still mostly conscious, but after a couple days we were all out of words and Catherine was mostly unconscious, waking with thirst but not the ability to drink much water. I got a squirt gun so we could shoot little bits of water into her mouth. Kind of messed up, but we chose not to overthink it. She would wake up and say, 'I'm still here?' as if that was a surprise even to her. Your mom and Alicia would lay on the bed near her and sometimes I squeezed in behind one of them, reaching over to hold Catherine's hand. Amy had been the little spoon in front of me when Catherine passed and I held on to that girl as if I was holding her here in the land of the living. I sat next to her at Catherine's funeral, too, and I thought of all the milestones these girls would have to go through without their mother, trying to think of practical ways I could fill in—do, say, teach all the things my sister would have wanted to do. The day after the service, everyone scattered. Jack put the camper on his pickup and drove to the national parks of California and Alicia returned to the University of Oklahoma. Your mom supposedly returned to Oklahoma State University, only she didn't. She drove to Chama with me and we rode horses bareback in spring snow . . . flakes falling all around us as if we were in a snow globe, isolated from the rest of the world but together. Grief can be so isolating. We made stews and chili . . . foods that could sit in a Crock-Pot and be picked at in manageable amounts when you didn't want to eat but knew you should try. And we made cornbread, which I cut into tiny pieces, tiny enough to slip into the tiny, tiny spaces not taken up by grief in our bellies. Your mom used to write her mom long letters every night. She'd put them in envelopes and address them 'Mom, Heaven,' and I'd put stamps on them and mail them for her. After five days, she packed up and returned to college to take her quarter finals or try to get them postponed. I remember watching her drive away, just feeling this severing.

"So, know that. Know that about your mom. If you want to talk to her, we can make that happen tonight. If you'd prefer to write to her, we can send it to general delivery up in Packwood and I can let her know it will be there. Just let me know how I can support you. Your mom is pretty special to me, and I know she'd love to hear that you love her."

Carly only nodded, not even looking Great-Aunt Rae in the eyes. It had been so close, such a close call. She'd almost lost her. She couldn't imagine what she would've done without her mother or would do if the cancer came back. It was always there—this uncertainty she could not unknow, leaving her just a tiny girl under a big, dark sky that was about to fall.

Great-Aunt Rae went back inside, with Violet trotting along behind her.

T. Rex nickered just then, as if answering the desperate cry in her heart. Carly crawled through the fence and walked quickly out to him, threw her arms around him, buried her face in his fuzzy neck, and cried the kind of tears that racked her whole body on their way out. She was just a girl. Just a girl.

That night, when Carly brought a basket of laundry into her room to fold on her bed, she noticed that on top of the stack of books were two packages of stationery from the Family Dollar store judging from the big one dollar printed at the top of the package. One set was pink with spirals and the other set blue with pictures of picnic tables and umbrellas at the beach.

She packed her clothes for the week into a bag and tossed two books, the blue package of stationery, and a pen on top.

Paul

The following Monday morning after his interview with the independent panel, Captain Lopez called him on the phone and cut right to the chase. "Bergstrom, the department is suspending you for a month."

"A month. Wow." He let that sink in. "So, they believed a woman that was lying about why she had a bloody nose over an officer with twenty-five years on the force and a good record."

"I don't think that's it, Bergstrom. I think they're just covering their asses."

"Okay. Thanks, Captain."

Hanging up, Paul felt demoralized. Day after day, he showed up and did his best. And despite his best efforts, all of the crime never stopped. People didn't stop hurting one another. People didn't stop stealing from one another. He kept trying to make the world a better place, and it never became one. Between meth and the internet, it had arguably gotten worse.

He held the phone in his hand, wondering whether to call Amy. On the one hand, that would be appropriate. News of this magnitude was widely expected to be shared with a spouse. On the other hand, if Amy could take one more thing, she wouldn't have left. And even though getting suspended from work for a month was big news, it wasn't cancer. It wasn't months of chemo. It wasn't amputation and then even more surgery. It wasn't of that magnitude. Compassion for her swelled in his heart, and in the spirit of wanting to protect her from his ugly world, he decided not to call her. If she called him, he wouldn't lie, but he didn't need to intrude on her healing. He could handle it. Even the loss of pay for a month after all the unexpected medical bills of the last year and with a kid he hoped would go to college—he would handle it.

Bergstrom, the department is suspending you for a month. Unbelievable. *Screw it,* he thought, not wasting one more minute before packing his tools into the trunk of his car along with some work clothes and work gloves. Even with a stop at Home Depot, he could still make it to Rae's by midnight. He had put his key in the ignition before he remembered that he hadn't packed his old work shoes. When he went back for them, he noticed the guitar case that had become so much simply part of the landscape of his closet that he usually didn't even see it anymore. He reached in and took it too.

"When I don't have mammary glands, will I still be a mammal?" Amy had asked him as they waited in an exam room for her presurgical consultation.

"Of course," he said.

"Fur is another defining characteristic of mammals. I don't have that either."

"You were born live—not from an egg. And you're warm-blooded."

She nodded. Silence followed. Then she asked, "When I don't have breasts, ovaries, fallopian tubes, and a uterus, will I still be a woman, or will I be an androgynous being with a vagina?"

"Oh, Amy, of course you will still be a woman." He reached over and took her delicate hand.

"I suppose. I mean, if you were castrated, you would still be a man."

Whether it was the same thing or not, he did not know. He just knew his wife felt like she was being castrated. "All that matters is that you're going to live."

"Live *longer*," she corrected, looking down at her shoes. "Sometimes people phrase it like you either live or die, but it turns out we're all going to die. It's just some people live longer." She was quiet a little longer and then she said, "I get to live longer, but there are children at St. Jude's that won't. That makes no sense to me . . . why some people get miracles and others don't. I mean why would an innocent, deserving child not get a miracle?"

"I stopped believing in an intervening God a long time ago," he answered. *Seventeen years ago, to be exact*, he thought.

"I wonder how it all works . . . like, is our homecoming to heaven a predestined date? I mean, people talk about it being someone's 'time,' you know? What if this is the time God and I agreed I would come home? Am I messing anything up by living longer? Or is this like a 'buy one, get one free' deal on life? Like everything after this health crisis is my super-bonus lifetime? Or was this medical intervention part of my destiny? I mean, if it wasn't a part of my DNA, I could see it more as something that just happened to me, but what if DNA contains our very agreements with God—because so much of what we experience here is dictated by DNA. Did God and I agree that I would have cancer before I came here and so that agreement was put into my DNA? Is that what happened? Is this the lifetime where I pay for something I did in a previous lifetime? Is that what this is about? I'm just trying to figure out what happened. I'm just trying to make sense of this."

"Oh, Amy, don't do that to yourself. Those are harmful stories. If stories comfort a person and don't hurt anyone else, that's one thing. I don't want to take comfort from anyone. But if stories are harmful, stop telling them. One day when this life is over, all of it might make sense, but until then, all we've got is stories. I don't believe in destiny." His mind flashed back to a particular child he had uncovered, one with no breath and no pulse. He had put his mouth over the child's and forced some of his breath into the child's body in case there was any chance at all of reviving him, and then he gently handed the little body to be carried down the line so he could keep digging. There was no way he could believe that was that child's destiny. "This is an extremely imperfect world. Sometimes our will is effective, and sometimes we're at the mercy of luck. Life is an imperfect experience."

They sat in silence until the surgeon entered, Paul pondering how all of these words could tumble out of Amy, all of her deepest thoughts, and still she felt so far away, so deep inside of herself that he could hold her hand and not touch her at all . . . how they could sit right next to each other and still be so alone.

Paul picked up his cell phone and dialed. Amy's phone rang, but she did not answer. He figured she was out of range. "Hey, Amy, due to a situation at work, I'm going to be in Chama for the next month working on the house there. Uh . . . I just wanted you to know. I hope you're having a good time. Say hi to the big trees for me. I . . . uh . . ." He considered saying he missed her, but he didn't want to sound desperate. "I went to OSU yesterday and walked around our old stomping grounds. Good memories. Okay. Love you. Bye."

Bye. Bye could mean so many things. He hoped it was a normal bye and not a really big one.

Amy

All around her, fir trees had the bright green tips of new growth at the end of every little branch, and vine maples glowed in an even brighter shade of chartreuse. A slight breeze shook some needles loose, and when they landed on her backpack, they made a sound she had completely forgotten—not a remarkable sound by any means, but one that made her feel home.

She started off on the trail that went past the hot springs where she had sat a few days ago and continued on to Silver Falls. It was a loop that she and Alicia had often taken once they were old enough to be allowed to venture that far. In an opening in the forest, hot springs water trickled out of a large brown formation uphill on her right, leaving green streaks as it ran down the sides. There, the trail turned to a boardwalk under which the hot water flowed through a trench someone had dug. Beyond that, a statuesque grove of maples grew, neither young nor ancient, moss covering their crooked trunks.

Walking on, she came to a pool of the clearest water she had seen in decades just a couple of steps downhill. Crouching down, she ran her fingers across the top of the surface, watching the little waves they made. Then, she wiped the water on her forehead as she prayed to be cleared of all suffering, all despair, all fear, all hopelessness, all pain, and of the intensity of fresh bad memories. She dipped her cupped hand in the water, lifted it above her head, and poured it on herself, praying that she be cleared of all attachments to how her body used to be and accept deeply how it was now. She prayed she would come to find beauty in it. Instead of feeling better, she felt a surge of grief for her body as it had been back when it was whole, back when it felt pleasure instead of pain. Staring into the pool, she fixated on the reflection of her face, her sad, sad eyes as tears dropped into the pool, sending concentric ripples that distorted the image of herself. Sadness did that. This time she cupped both hands, dipped and raised them, and splashed the water all over her face, praying to be washed clean of all negativity and to be returned to her true essence. She prayed to see it clearly.

Visitors walked by on the trail above her, disturbing her. Normally, she would have looked up and smiled, but she kept her back turned and waited for them to pass. After allowing a few minutes for some space between them on the trail, she walked on.

She came to a bridge over a cascading creek where fungus grew on nearby trees like shelves. One tree had a huge knob growing out of its trunk. She vaguely recalled hearing that was caused by a fungal infection but couldn't be sure.

Sometimes as she walked, she caught herself simply thinking, *Cancer, cancer, cancer, cancer.* She had caught herself doing that throughout the winter and at that time simply told herself to stop it. But now, she replaced the thought with, *I am healthy. I am strong. I am full of vitality.* This she repeated to herself over and over as she walked the next mile. The trail led past the big rock, over a log bridge, and past another creek, this one with moss-covered boulders and big fallen logs, past the Oregon grape, the kinnikinnick, the one tiny wild rose, past the tiny pine cones that littered the trail. All the while, she repeated her affirmations over and over and over.

After crossing the tall bridge over Laughingwater Creek, she followed a path under it, sitting along the river's edge, midway on the steep hill that it tumbled down. Despite her best efforts, she couldn't hear the laughter. She used to hear it. There was a time when she and Denny used to stand on the bridge and shout their best jokes to the water, cracking each other up and laughing with the stream after each one. *What did the train conductor say to the pumpkin? All a-gourd!* But now, all she heard was a force of nature, a force so much stronger than her, a force that could knock her down and pin her down if she happened to be unlucky. She stood and walked away from all the tumult and back into the peace of the forest, noticing lichen and the prolonged two-tone note of the varied thrush singing like a Mongolian throat singer.

Alongside the trail, she noticed a tree that grew out of the ground at an angle and then had righted itself to grow up straight and tall. If she were a tree, would she look like that one day, or could trees correct themselves like that only if they nearly fell over when they were young? Suddenly she noticed all the trees that didn't make it, the ones that fell and lay dead or dying on the forest floor, where they would become part of the earth again, nourishment for plants, then part of the animals that ate those plants. Other dead trees still stood, full of holes from woodpeckers and other birds that ate insects. Everything died and became part of everything else. Rationally, she knew this and had known it for a long time. But it was different now . . . now that she knew about suffering, now that she'd had a little taste of the in-between, the space between life and death that was kind to no one. It was all just so much more real than it had ever been before, so acutely real. One day it would actually happen. She would likely suffer in her physical body far more than she already had, and then she would actually leave her daughter behind, leave this beautiful earth behind, leave her body behind. And unlike the trees, her body would not become part of everything. This disturbed her every bit as much as the idea of decomposing disturbed other people. She wanted her body to become part of everything, to go back to the elements that had made it. Even if she did live to be elderly, which she might not because recurrence happened . . . it happened all the time . . . but even if it didn't happen and she had another thirty or forty years in her, she still felt the clock ticking, running out of time. Life was finite. It was hard to accept at the depth that she now knew it to be true. It terrified her. How was she supposed to enjoy the rest of her life with this knowledge? She looked at the mossy forest floor and wanted to lie on it, to sink right into it, to let it swallow her and make her part of everything. She wanted to just get it over with, because she had no idea how to live with this level of terror over an ultimate outcome that could not be avoided. Religion couldn't help her. It wasn't the fear of the afterlife. It was the fear of her transition there.

I am alive now. I am alive now. I am alive now, she repeated over and over as she walked on, and she listened to the songs of birds, of robins and hermit thrushes, and this combination made each second more tolerable, even though it didn't solve the problem of her mortality.

Eventually she passed a fork in the trail, rounded a corner, and saw Silver Falls. It was bigger than she remembered. In front of her stood a young, lean kayaker in a dry suit. His brown hair was wet, and a spray skirt hung around his waist. His camera sat on a tripod, and he stood behind it, waiting. Something about his mannerisms and expression struck her as cocky, which made more sense when, to her horror, his friend came down the roiling upper part of the river, which was riddled with boulders, and soared over the cliff, plunging forty feet into the base of the waterfall below. Anxiously, Amy waited for him to resurface, and he did. On a large boulder on the other side of the Ohanapecosh River, his two other friends who had waited for him cheered, and they all went on thinking they were immortal and that nothing bad would ever happen to them, or that if it did, they could handle it. She simultaneously envied this operating paradigm, resentful that they had it and she didn't, and felt deep gratitude not to be any of their mothers. She wanted to ask them what their secret was, but since she didn't see any kayakers her age going over the falls, she figured their secret was surely the ignorance of youth. God, she missed that . . . missed believing she would live forever.

Carly

Carly's second week on the job was so much easier in some ways and so much more difficult in other ways. It felt good to know what to expect and to have more confidence driving Frank and Drake, but this time, their guests were a family of four from Washington, D.C., and she could tell right away that they lacked harmony.

It appeared this trip had been the mother's idea. Carly guessed she was in her late thirties. She was thin and fit, as if she did nothing but yoga and Pilates all day. With her blond-highlighted hair swept back in a ponytail, Carly could read more of her face, and her face meant business. This was a woman determined to have some family fun. She turned to her little girl and asked, "Which horse do you want, Bella?"

There were two things wrong with that question, as Carly saw it. One, that she thought it was going to be a little girl's choice, as if there were nothing more to matching a person and a horse than determining which horse a girl thought was prettiest. Two, that the girl was given a term of endearment as a name, as if she were destined to be an incorrigible princess from the moment she was born.

"I want that one!" she said, pointing to T. Rex.

No, Carly thought, dreading the mere possibility that Great-Aunt Rae would placate the obnoxious girl.

"This is going to be your horse," Great-Aunt Rae said firmly but with enthusiasm. Then she bent down and whispered, "I saved the best one for you." She introduced Bella to Tea for Two.

"That's a weird name," Bella said, unimpressed.

"Yeah, horse names are weird. All of these horses came out of a black sire with white feathers—the fluffy fur on his legs—and a white spot on his chest. He looked like he was wearing a tuxedo, so someone had named him 'Dressed to a T.' It's customary for horse names to have something in common with their parents' names, so all of these horses have 'T' in their name somewhere—Mister T, Tee Time, Black Tea, T. Rex."

The girl laughed at the last name. "I like that name. I want that one."

"Well, fortunately for you, you've got me to make a better choice for you. I know these horses really well and I know which one you will have the best time on. Trust me."

About that time, the sullen boy, about twelve years old, slinked over near Carly and said with disgust, "She always gets what she wants. Just watch." He rolled his eyes under his long blue bangs that hung in his face. Every few seconds, he shook his head as if to try to get his hair out of his face, but it never worked. Whatever horse he rode was going to hate that.

Great-Aunt Rae looked up at the mom to solicit her backup, but the mom only looked scared of the reaction the little girl was about to have, and then sure enough, the little girl began to howl.

"It's okay to be disappointed," said Great-Aunt Rae, "or even scared to let go of some of the control that you usually have when it comes to calling the shots. But crying that loudly right here is upsetting the horses, so go over to that tree over there and have a good cry if that's what you need to do, and then come back and apologize to your horse because you hurt his feelings."

The girl looked at the mom, and the mom walked her to the tree and then bent down to comfort the little brat.

While all of that was going on, the dad walked all over the perimeter of the area where they had gathered, frantically trying to get cell reception, clearly as stressed out as he was well manicured.

It was going to be a long week.

On the second morning, while they prepared breakfast, Great-Aunt Rae said, "If you had been at this long enough to know where to go, I'd let you lead, and I'd be the distractor, but sadly, I'm the only one who can lead. That means today your job is to ride along in the back and keep asking the kids questions—especially the girl."

Carly nodded begrudgingly.

"Hey, Carly? I want you to know that this is really important. These are the kind of people who write online reviews. A lot is at stake. This week can be good advertising or bad advertising, but it's going to be advertising, so stay professional no matter what. It doesn't appear possible to please them, but we can try our best to preserve my reputation. As long as business is good, I can feed all the horses for the year. If reservations drop next year, I might have to sell one or two."

That was as unthinkable as selling a member of her own family. They *were* Great-Aunt Rae's family. Carly looked right at her and nodded. "Understood."

"Thanks."

So, later that day, Carly asked Bella about all the things she

did—ballet and hip-hop dance, yoga for kids, and children's the-
ater. Then she made herself listen to all of the seemingly endless
details about how much better Bella was than the other kids in
those activities.

Carly didn't think it could get more painful than that until
Bella began to question her about the activities she did or, rather,
didn't do. No, she did not go to dance classes or act in stage
productions—Bella actually used that term instead of plays. No,
she wasn't in student government. She wasn't an athlete or a
cheerleader. She did not say that she took care of her very sick
mother last winter. Instead, she offered, "I was a lifeguard last
summer."

"That's cool," Bella said, but not in a way that reflected she
was very impressed at all.

"I don't do anything either," said Jon without an "h"—Jon,
not John. He had been clear about that earlier.

Then Bella asked, "Where are you going to college?"

"I was given a scholarship to Oklahoma State. That's where
my parents went." She did not say that the scholarship would
probably be revoked after the school saw that her grades had
dropped fourth quarter and that Carly no longer intended to at-
tend college at all. She did not say that everything about the future terrified her.

"I'm going to go to an Ivy League college," said Bella.

"Good for you," Carly said, hiding all of the sarcasm. This
was torture.

"I'm not going to go to college," said Jon.

"Yes, you are!" shouted his mom from the front of the line.

From his place third in line, he looked back at Carly, smiled,
and shook his head, as if to say, *No, I most definitely am not.* He
was going to make all the wrong choices just to piss his parents

off, just to make them pay attention to him, just to have some control.

And then it hit her and her stomach sank. She knew all of that about him because she was more or less just the same.

On the fourth morning, the mother woke early and joined Great-Aunt Rae for a cup of coffee while Carly started cracking eggs and grating potatoes. Carly was far enough away to appear as if she couldn't hear but close enough to hear most words and piece together what was being said when she couldn't.

"I'm sorry," the mom said. "I thought this trip was a good idea. I thought it would save my family."

"Oh?"

"My husband doesn't know that I know that he's sleeping with his secretary. I've been trying to hold it together most of the last year for the kids, hoping it would change . . . thinking that if I just worked out more or was a good enough mom, maybe he'd look up and appreciate me. I thought if I got him out here away from his phone, he'd have to pay attention to us, but he's still in another world. All he can think about is her. He doesn't say so. He doesn't say anything at all." She looked up at the sky and shook her head. "No one else is into it. Bella maybe. I'd like for us to go back one day early."

Great-Aunt Rae looked to the sky. "The sky is full of moisture this morning. It's possible we're going to have wicked thunderstorms by one. Let's wake the others and hurry to get on the trail. If it storms before we get back, the horses will spook and the chuck wagon may get stuck. It will be very bad. So, if you want to do this, you have my full support. I think it would be wise to opt out of the storms today has in store for us. But we need to hustle."

"Thank you," the mom said. "I'm grateful for one last day of riding together as a family before I blow this family apart."

Great-Aunt Rae nodded solemnly and silently, and then she stood and called over to Carly, "Let's kick it into high gear, kiddo!"

Carly put down the food and helped Great-Aunt Rae saddle the horses while the guests woke and packed. Then, together, she and Great-Aunt Rae whipped up oatmeal and eggs and washed the dishes.

The bratty kids were about to have a bomb dropped on them. Carly wondered whether they would even care, whether they would even notice the absence of their dad.

The family rode mostly in silence that day—everyone out of things to say to each other, everyone just waiting for the trip to be over. Everyone except the mom, who was feeling, Carly knew. Feeling the others around her. Feeling the landscape of her life. She was drinking in the last little bit of normal the way Carly would have the day before her mom was diagnosed, if she had just known. The kids had no clue that they should be drinking it in too. Even though they were not likable, she still felt sorry for them.

When they stopped for a very quick lunch, she wanted to sit next to Jon and tell him not to waste his energy and burn his bridges trying to piss everyone off . . . to use that energy to create the future he wanted instead, or at least try things he was curious about if he didn't yet know what he wanted to do. She wanted to give him all of that advice, but realizing she was a hypocrite, she remained silent.

As she stepped back up into the chuck wagon, she wondered how it was that she felt so much more emphatic about trying to save that sullen kid than she did about saving herself.

Paul

Last Monday, Paul's goal was to have the new fuse box in and the bathroom replumbed by the end of the week so that he could sleep upstairs in his bedroom at his own house when Rae and Carly returned.

He wasted no time removing the old fuse box and replacing it with the new circuit breaker box, then calling the power company to come and do their part. He unscrewed outlets, removed them from the brackets in the wall, and then removed what remained of the old, sketchy knob-and-tube wiring that had been attached. When the house was originally built, there had been no electricity at all. The knob-and-tube electrical wiring had been added later, and so it had mostly run under the floor, which was now gone. This was an opportunity, he reminded himself. The new wiring would be so much safer. He attached one outlet to the fuse box so that he'd have a place he could plug an extension cord into, since he would need an electric drill to drill holes through nearly all of the studs in the house in order to send wiring through the walls.

That afternoon while he waited for the electricity to be turned on, he repaired the burst pipe that had destroyed nearly the whole house. The momentum felt good. He found himself thinking less and less about the situation at work, about the uncertainty of his marriage and of his daughter's future, about all the ugliness he had ever seen, as he focused on just this task and then the next one. It felt good to be able to actually fix something in his life where everything else seemed broken.

Over the course of the next four days, he rebuilt just enough of the bathroom floors that he could reinstall the toilets and sinks. Then he called the water company and had the water turned back on. Upon discovering two more leaks, he fixed those as well.

Finally, the power company turned on the power. Then he used his electric drill to install new floorboards over much of the floor—enough to make walking throughout the house safer and easier.

At some point, he came to see working on the house as his meditation or form of prayer. It was all right there, like a to-do list for himself. First, he'd needed to fix the plumbing so that shit had somewhere to go and could be cleared away. Plumbing made it possible to shower, or purify. A person needed that for a new beginning. Next, he'd put in the floorboards like a foundation, because Amy's diagnosis definitely had pulled the rug out from beneath them. They needed to get their feet on solid ground. Then, he needed to rewire—both the house and his nervous system. He knew Amy did as well. When all of that was done, it would be time to put the walls back up—the boundaries, though thinking of walls in that way made Paul wonder how it might be possible to open up the inside of the house more.

As he began to drill holes through the studs in the walls on Friday morning, he remembered a psychologist who was leading one of their mandatory small-group sessions after the blast saying that when someone is traumatized, their three minds separate—the primal survival-oriented mind separates from the rational mind and begins to perceive everything as a threat to life. The limbic mind was a big piece of it too, giving emotion to that perception so that a person would take action to ensure their own survival. What he remembered most was when the man said that we weren't rational, thinking beings that have emotions, but emotional beings that have thoughts about their emotions. Paul vowed to read up more on this. Maybe new research in the last sixteen years had yielded new insights. Something about the house made all the things inside of him, all the things between him and Amy, tangible in a way that they had not been before, and that left him hopeful. He began to believe that if he could just fix up this house, everything would be okay.

The phone interrupted his thoughts. For the first two rings, Paul simply looked at it warily. He could not think of one possibility of a call that he would look forward to. If it was Amy, it might be to ask him for the divorce he had once wished for. If it was work, well, who knew? But he was sure it couldn't be good.

He set down his drill, picked up the phone, and looked at the number. It wasn't anyone he knew, but it was from Oklahoma City. Torn between his suspicion that it was a telemarketer and concern that it was someone from work, he caved to the latter and answered, "Hello," less like a question and more like someone preparing to be annoyed.

"Bergstrom. It's Lamar Green, your union rep. I've got some good news for you. I did a little investigating of my own and found two neighbors who had watched your arrest of Mr. Miller. One was from a window and could not hear anything, but she did give the same account that you did. The other was peering through a fence, and he did not hear you say, 'Take that!' I confronted Mrs. Miller about her accusation and reminded her that witness statements are done under the penalty of perjury and that she could be charged for a false statement, and then I asked her whether she would like to change her statement now before it got to that point. She took the opportunity to clear your name. She was just trying to get her husband's charges dismissed because she loves him don't you know and she needs his paycheck to keep their house." He sighed. They had all heard victims lie to protect their abusers countless times. "So, bottom line, the investigative team will reexamine the evidence Monday and I expect you'll get a call before the end of the day informing you that you've been cleared, and that you will be compensated for the leave you were put on."

Paul looked all around him, at the exposed beams in the shell of this house. It was empty enough to hold a lot of dreams. It felt like a new beginning. But now he was being sent back to the world where all day long he put out spot fires in the larger arena of hell. Everything in him recoiled at the thought. But the only correct thing to say was, "Thank you, Green," because his union rep had cared enough about the truth to find it and clear his name.

The turkeys in the neighbor's backyard gobbled when Paul stepped onto the porch and cursed, almost as if they were laughing at his predicament. A breeze caused the leaves to quake in a large elm in the corner of the yard.

He heard the sound of raking leaves before he saw his elderly neighbor, who caught his eye and waved. She was short, and her silver hair blew in different directions. Seven months ago, he would have thought of her hair as short, but now that he compared it with Amy's, it seemed long. He waved back, noticing the clouds building near the mountains.

"There's supposed to be thunderstorms today!" called the neighbor.

"I suppose I should check the roof, then," Paul called back.

"Don't mess around up there once the thunder starts. You get down," she told Paul.

Paul walked over to a gap in the old wire fence and extended his hand. "I'm Paul Bergstrom," he said.

"Rae's nephew-in-law. I'm Cleo Ramirez." Her strong features showed her Spanish ancestry, and her eyes were perceptive and kind. She wore jeans and a flannel shirt, perfect for working in the yard. "A bear crashed through here. They like the fruit trees in our yards this time of year. There's no sense in fixing it until they hibernate."

Looking down, Paul noticed a large pile of what appeared to be poop, but he wasn't sure. It was about the size of cow poop, but much more colorful and textured with nuts, seeds, and fruits that hadn't been chewed well enough.

"This one has been hanging around for a few weeks now. Lots of people get dogs to chase them out of their yards. Do you have a dog?"

"No," he said.

"Well, maybe you'll get a dog."

Paul smiled but didn't reply. There was too much to explain and he really didn't want to.

"We'll have to fix this if you get a dog, though, because I've got chickens back there. The turkeys will only be around for another month or so, but the chickens lay eggs all year. Say, I've been noticing some changes in that tree," she said, pointing to the elm. "It could be that it's sick or it could be that it's just lived as long as these trees generally do."

Paul looked at the tree, considering it. He shook his head. "It looks fine to me."

"I played in that tree when I was a child," said Cleo. "I love that tree. I wouldn't say anything bad about it if I wasn't concerned about safety."

Just to appease her, Paul said, "I'll have an arborist come look at it," but he intentionally did not say when. There were many more urgent things to deal with.

"Well, I better get back at it," Paul said. "Looks like I'll be needing to head back to Oklahoma City tomorrow or the next day. I was hoping to stay longer and make more progress, but something came up."

"Oh," said Cleo. "Well, it makes me glad to see you making it beautiful again. That was once my grandmother's house." Then she gestured toward her own home. It was a small house that had seen at least three additions. In her front yard, she had an altar to the Virgin Mary and a statue of St. Francis. In the bird pen in the backyard, there was another statue of St. Francis. At the moment, a turkey stood on either side of it, about the same height. "My parents built a house here, next door. It was nice growing up next to my grandma. I kept hoping someone new would love that house. It's been empty a long time now."

Paul nodded, feeling bad that she'd had to see it sit in disrepair. "I dreamed of fixing it up and retiring here. Life got a little busy and then the leak . . ."

"I heard about your wife," she said. "I'm glad she's okay now."

"Thanks."

"Well, when you finally move in, let me know if you need help finding a dog to adopt or some chickens."

"Thanks," he said again, and added, "Well, back to work."

"Get to it," she said, waving him off.

Paul had begun to settle into the patterns of sounds around him. The neighbor behind him put his border collie outside each morning around seven thirty. For the rest of the day, it barked at anything that walked by the fence. Around nine o'clock, two old steam engines whistled at one another, the first usually pitched higher than the second. In the morning, the trains simply sounded ready, but twelve hours later when all was dark and they whistled again, they sounded like lonely ghosts with their long, shrill, haunting notes. Just before noon, two moms with a gaggle of small children between them walked to the library and later passed by again with a bag of new storybooks. One mom pushed a stroller, and one young girl pushed a toy stroller with a doll in it. Just as he was wondering what time it was, they walked by, and he knew.

By two in the afternoon, the tall, white cauliflower-like columnar clouds had leveled off and darkened the sky as they spread. High winds slapped branches against the roof, the sky flashed and rumbled, and then a torrent of rain fell like a wall of water.

Not being a fan of thunder, Paul unplugged the extension cord from the outlet and retreated to the first-story bathroom to contemplate what kind of flooring he should buy when he returned to Oklahoma City—linoleum or tile? He needed to put the flooring in before he could bring the old claw-foot bathtub back in from where it had been sitting on the back porch for the last eight months. As much as he hated anything that would slow him down, he knew he would kick himself for a long time if he didn't install tile. Tile it would be, he decided.

Just then, a clap of thunder exploded above the house, shaking the earth and reminding him of the blast. Big claps nearby did that, and he had survived plenty. Despite his racing heart and memories, he knew he would survive this one too. That is, until the elm, its roots shaken loose in the soft, moist earth, came crashing through the roof.

Sudden explosive event
Loud noise
Debris falling from above

"Oh my God! Oh my God!" Paul screamed, and after the crashing, he paced furiously along the edges of the floorboards where there were still open spaces in all the spots that needed custom cuts. He looked into the gaps for people under the house, his rational mind knowing he was in a house in Chama, his limbic and primal minds panicked and desperately searching for survivors, especially the children. "Goddammit!" he yelled. "Goddammit!"

In his mind, he saw it and smelled it and heard it: debris falling from the higher floors of the nine-story building. All the anger he still held for Timothy McVeigh bubbled up to the surface. All the anger he had for this tragic world. All the anger he had for a God that had not intervened to prevent that big tragedy and a million smaller ones from happening. All the anger he had for himself for being no more than just one man buckling under the weight of the world on his shoulders. He knew that he had just been transported back to the site of the Oklahoma City bombing, and he was mad as hell about that too. That was a place to which he never, ever wanted to return.

Debris fell down as they sifted. It killed a nurse and injured other people who were trying to help, but still none of them, including Paul, could leave the muffled voices they heard under their feet—not even after they were ordered out.

They dug through rubble, still smoking.

Papers from the upper floors floated down, a reminder that just moments ago, people had been there working . . . working as if everything weren't about to change, as if they weren't about to die.

The voices under their feet grew quieter as the hours passed. They saved some. And they failed to save others.

Above where Paul searched had been the headquarters for the Bureau of Alcohol, Tobacco, and Firearms. He had been there only three days prior to get help on a case. He had friends there. Now, they were somewhere in the pile of smoking debris.

There was a moment pretty early on when someone had shouted, "There was a day care here!" and Paul had walked over to the vicinity, wondering whom he might be stepping on, and began to dig through to the layer with the stuffed animals and the blocks. The officer next to him found a tiny, lifeless body, one of the fifteen children who perished that day. Someone else found a child who was miraculously still alive, but for how long was anyone's guess. . . . The whole time, all of them trying to make sense of something so senseless, trying to comprehend that a member of their own species had done this, wondering how that was possible, how anyone could . . . all of them understanding something terrible about this world they lived in and the people who walked among them, something terrible they'd had the luxury of pretending wasn't true until that moment.

Paul remembered looking around at those toys, looking up at what remained of that grand building, knowing there was no way justice could ever be done. There would be no justice. There would be no forgiveness. There would be no forgetting. All of those who remained would simply have to come to accept something none of them could comprehend.

Shaking still, Paul walked out of the back door into the rain, hoping the drops on his face would remind him several times a second that he was here, in Chama, where no one locked their doors.

"Are you okay?" It was the old man who lived behind him with the border collie.

Paul snapped out of it enough to say, "I'm okay."

Then, Cleo called out from the other direction, "Dear Lord! Are you all right?" She peered over the wire fence from the backyard, since the tree had taken down power lines in the front.

He gave her a thumbs-up with minimal eye contact.

"Come over! I'll make you cocoa and cookies!"

"Thanks—another time!" he called back over the loud wind.

Satisfied that he was all right, Cleo ran back into her house.

Paul was relieved. He did not want to be seen by her.

His other neighbor was on Paul's porch now, looking at him carefully. "Were you a soldier?"

"No. Police officer. Oklahoma City PD."

"Well, come on. Come to my house."

"But I should . . ." Paul looked back.

Another clap of thunder burst nearby. The old man startled and shouted, "Come on!" grabbed his sleeve, and started to run. The only polite thing to do was follow.

Once inside, his neighbor introduced himself, Ramiro Martinez. When Paul complimented him on a large black-and-white photo of a train rounding a bend, mountains in the background, and conductor waving, Mr. Martinez said, "That's me."

Paul studied it for another moment, finding it calming to look at the image of Mr. Martinez's smiling face and of the nature behind it. He felt his heart slow and his breathing deepen.

Mr. Martinez said, "Trains are the Grateful Dead of machinery. People come from all over to photograph our trains. I let one train groupie come aboard and sit up front with me once—right after he took this photo, in fact. I wasn't supposed to do that, but I could tell he was a vet and I knew he was long overdue for something good to happen. He sent me this print as a thank-you." Smiling, he continued, "Those were good days. Hey, I want to show you something."

They passed through a covered passageway out his back door

to his wood shop. There, he nodded at two very large pieces of wood, both standing vertically. "It's a train door. This old one is rotten, so I was asked to make a replica."

"Wow," Paul said, smiling his approval. Then he noticed a half-finished guitar. "You're a luthier too?"

"Oh, I wouldn't call myself that yet. I'm still learning. Self-taught for the most part. I read books and watch videos and try to figure it out. I've got one in the house I made." He then led the way out of the shop, shutting the door behind him. "Do you play?" he asked as they entered the house again.

"I used to. Just a little. Nothing like you. I heard you play once from my yard. I thought it was a recording at first. You're really good!"

He led Paul over to the corner of his living room where three guitars sat in stands—two classical and one steel string. "Here," he said, handing Paul one. "Remember, it was my first guitar-making attempt."

Paul took a seat so that he wouldn't accidentally drop it and paused, unsure of what to play. "It's been a really long time," he said.

"Can you play G—E minor—D—A minor?"

Paul strummed those chords, while Mr. Martinez picked up the other classical guitar and played an improvisational solo. The notes, it seemed, filled Paul up, filled places that had felt empty for a long time. For the first time in recent memory, he felt truly happy. So focused was he on the music, he didn't notice the thunder move off to the west and he didn't think about the blast. "I always wondered how people did that—how they knew what notes would work and what notes wouldn't work," Paul said.

"Oh, you've got to know your scales. No one likes learning scales, but it's like eating your vegetables and taking your vitamins. You've got to do it!"

Paul laughed. "One day when I move here, will you teach me?"

"Sure." Then Mr. Martinez looked outside. "Storm's passed. Thank you."

"Why are you thanking me?" Paul asked. "You're the one that did me a favor."

"I don't like thunder and lightning. Reminds me of bombs."

Paul winced as he looked down and nodded.

"I could tell it reminded you of bombs too. And I knew what you would do if you went back into that house by yourself because I've done it. Here is what I've figured out: music. And I don't mean writing songs about it or anything like that, although that might work for some people. What works for me is losing myself in a difficult piece of music—something that requires all of my concentration. I had to learn to be gentle with myself at first when I couldn't concentrate well—just keep asking myself to try this little part one more time, just this little part. But eventually my capacity to concentrate increased. Being able to play beautiful music was really just a great side effect. The main goal was simply to harness my mind."

Paul listened intently. He needed to hear this—every word.

"Your eyes look better now—not so shell-shocked. You haven't been sleeping over there, have you?"

"No. Tomorrow was going to be my first night. I've been sleeping at Rae's. She's employing my daughter this summer and I didn't want to infringe on her autonomy when they come back from this week's trip, but it doesn't matter now. I have to go back to work sooner than expected. If I go tomorrow, I'll have a little time to prepare for the week ahead."

Mr. Martinez scribbled out a name and number of someone and handed it to him. "That's my son. He's a carpenter. He does good work. Hey, do you need to borrow a chain saw?"

Paul took him up on it and returned to the house to cut the large branches that pierced the roof, hoping he could tarp the roof before returning to work; but in the meantime, he put a call in to a tree service.

Parts of the ceiling hung down, still attached but barely. Looking at those pieces made him shake. Still, he pulled the cord to start the chain saw's motor. He held the saw in his trembling hands for a moment before making his first cut. As the moments ticked on, he found himself conflicted by the chain saw—the way it vibrated in his hands, the smell of the two-stroke engine and sawdust, its loud noise. All of that was different from the scene at the federal building, which was comforting, but still, it was too much for his nerves. At some point, he realized this task was pointless anyway, because finishing the job would require standing on a ladder with a chain saw, and he no longer thought he was a superhero who could take those risks.

He turned off the chain saw and returned it to Mr. Martinez.

"If it seems like a war zone in there and takes you back, play music. Play it really loud. I've got CDs you can borrow. Andrés Segovia. You would like him. Most incredible guitarist of our time."

"That sounds like good advice. Thanks," Paul said on his way out.

Only when he was prepared to leave did he notice a wire draped over his car. A utility truck from the power company was just pulling up, but he didn't want to wait inside the house. Instead, he returned to the house for his flashlight and started walking the mile or so up to Rae's house.

The scent of rain on hot sagebrush rose up and filled the air with bright, astringent notes. Underneath it was the smell of wet, hot pavement, a smell he didn't much care for, but if he smelled a little longer, he picked up the scent of pine needles, bark, and earth. The air smelled different here than in Oklahoma City, and he liked it.

In the distance, one train whistled and the other one answered, the pitches of their whistles different for some reason. He wanted to call out to Amy like that and longed to hear her answer back.

When he reached Rae's house, he noticed the horses. Most were huddled under a lean-to shelter, but one stood on the edge of the fence, looking in his direction and sniffing the air. They had come back a day early. He had not picked up his things as he had intended to do the next day in an attempt to leave no trace. Evidence of his presence was there. He stood in the rain on the gravel driveway at the edge of the trees, wondering what to do. If he turned around and walked back to a motel, he would be stuck with wet clothes. And Rae would worry.

Just then, he noticed Rae walking down the driveway toward him. He was going to have to act normal—even though it was weird to just stand in the rain the way he was.

"Hey, Paul," she said, much the way she might talk to someone on a bridge, ready to jump. "What's going on?"

"A big tree fell on my house. So, I'm a little . . . uh, rattled."

She walked a little closer to him and, studying him, said, "Yeah, I've seen that in your eyes before." She slowly reached out and put her hand on his elbow. "Come on. How about a hot bath? You can get warm again. Wouldn't that feel good?"

And so, he followed her to the house. Carly was upstairs in her room, so he slipped into the bathroom, grateful to be unseen by her.

Carly

With the needy guests that week, Carly hadn't had time to write her mom a letter. Now, she sat on her bed, a piece of stationery positioned on the back of a book, pen in hand, at a complete loss of what to say.

There was a gentle knock on her door, and then Great-Aunt Rae walked in and shut the door behind her. "Hey, I want to tell you something," she said quietly. "Your dad is here."

Her stomach clenched. Had he come to take her home already? She didn't want to go.

"I don't know the whole story. I just know I found him in the driveway pretty shook up. I haven't seen that look in his eyes since you were a baby." She waited for Carly to understand. Almost whispering, she asked, "How much do you know about that?"

Carly shook her head. "Not much. Mom said he helped people. Dad doesn't ever talk about it."

"I'll never forget when I saw him for the first time after that and saw the expression in his eyes. Oh, I thought we'd lost him. I'd seen it once before, but not him. . . ." As she searched for the right words, she studied the raindrops hitting the window. "I'm going to tell you the rest of my Sam story because I want you to understand something about your dad. It won't mean anything to you if I tell you that your dad was like Sam when Sam came home if you don't know what he was like before, so I have to start there."

Carly put the book, paper, and pen down on the bedside table, then crossed her legs where she sat on her bed, settling in to listen.

"After the summer we met, during a little break between summer tourist season and fall hunting season, Sam and I set off on our own private packing trip for four days. We went up this secluded river valley to the end of a box canyon where there was a waterfall. I was riding this big trusty bay named Winston, and wearing a duster that Sam had outgrown a few years ago. He had loaned it to me for the season and it still smelled like him. I was so happy, just listening to the sound of horse hooves and the sound that sprinkles of rain made when it hit the duster as I rode. Sam rode in front on Marty, a young bay that was almost black. That horse was so funny because he would swing his head back and forth whenever Sam sang."

Carly laughed. "Really?"

"The ranch guests loved it." Great-Aunt Rae smiled and then looked down at her hands. "It was so nice just being by ourselves, not having to pretend we didn't love each other. And the low clouds made the world appear very small, as if we were the only ones in it. Time nearly stood still in the very best, most peaceful way.

"When we got to where we were going to camp, we tied the horses and walked up the narrow river to the little falls, and there Sam said my name and then, unable to find more words, simply dropped to his knee and offered me a ring. In that moment, everything made sense—everything. The reason I'd had such a strong compulsion to run from home into the wilderness of Montana. The reason I'd always been drawn to horses. Everything.

My whole life made sense for that perfect moment. I kissed him and put that ring on and I just couldn't stop smiling. Sam stood and squeezed me as if he never intended to let go. Later, I would realize that was a clue, but I'd missed it.

"For four days we were in paradise. I will leave out all the really juicy parts."

Carly swore she saw her great-aunt blush just then.

"Sam made a sweat lodge for two by lashing a small tent frame together with sticks and twine, and laying a canvas tarp over it. While the rocks were heating on the edge of our campfire, he got a bucket of water from the stream and put it inside. Then, with two long sticks, he carried in the rocks. We crawled inside in our birthday suits and tossed handfuls of water onto the hot rocks so that the sweat lodge filled with steam."

"Wait. I thought you said you were going to leave out the really juicy parts."

"Oh, I have, kid," Great-Aunt Rae said with a naughty smile, and then looked out the window again. "I remember we just stared at each other like we knew we were experiencing a miracle. That's what true love feels like—like a miracle unfolding. It was beautiful. And then . . . Okay, this part is going to seem like too much information, but I want you to understand how profoundly tender he was. With soap and a washcloth, he bathed me. He was so tender and utterly devoted. That's the part I want you to get. The part where he was able to connect with me so deeply." She paused to shake her head. "I remember he had said, 'I am etching this into my memory. I never want to forget how beautiful you are right now.' And you know, that had been another clue, but I missed that one too because I felt the same way. I never wanted to forget that moment either. When it was my turn to bathe him, what I remember feeling was pure reverence."

Carly knew silence was the only response.

"That was such a phenomenal trip. When the sun had come out one afternoon, we braved the icy waterfall, standing under it for only seconds at a time"—Great-Aunt Rae closed her eyes and leaned her head back—"letting the falls massage our scalps and our shoulders, then we warmed each other up. We were in Eden.

"Well, we were until the final morning. As we were packing to go, Sam took me in his arms and said, 'Rae, there's something I need to tell you. I don't want you to feel like I was keeping a secret from you. I just wanted these days with you to be pure . . . without any cloud hanging over us.' He took a big breath and I hoped to God he wasn't going to say what I thought he was going to say, but he said, 'Rae, my number's been drawn.'

"He was talking about Vietnam. I remember looking in his eyes as my heart shattered, and then I looked off into the distance behind him for a path we might take to just disappear until it was safe to come back. But I knew that wasn't who he was. It was as good as done. He held me and promised to come back, telling me all the reasons he would be okay—he had spent his whole life in the woods and had been hunting since he was a kid. He kept assuring me that he would be okay. But you have to understand how many men my age did not come back. So many men. I tried to be brave about it all, but I cried the whole way back.

"For two years we wrote letters, and then one day, it was his time to come home. It was a miracle that he lived—that anyone did. It really was. I have no idea how he survived every minute of every hour of every day for those years. I can't imagine the things he witnessed and was asked to do. I just can't imagine.

"But I'll tell you this. I knew the first time I saw Sam again. I knew even before he said anything. When I greeted him and hugged him . . . when I sat next to him in the back of his parents' car, I knew for sure. But I don't think I knew that it wasn't temporary.

"For those two years, he often wrote about how he wanted to go back into the mountains on horses with me . . . how he was going to find peace there . . . so, we set out on horseback—the same horses, but this time Marty didn't sway to Sam's singing. Instead of peacefully plodding down the trail like he always had, Marty was distracted, agitated, and jumpy . . . as if he thought every stump was a bear, every large rock a wolf, and every fallen tree a cougar . . . or, maybe he didn't think those things at all. Maybe he could see Sam's memories or knew what Sam was anticipating. I don't know. Maybe he simply smelled Sam's anxiety and stress. Sometimes Sam would break out in sweat. But either way, Marty undeniably knew as well as me—and maybe even more than me— that Sam was different. And Sam knew that Marty knew.

"We rode up to the top of a ridge, intending to follow it to the top of a taller ridge, but Sam was understandably tired from the trip and tired from fighting his anxious horse, so we stopped and dismounted. I noticed that instead of standing out in the middle of the open clearing where the view was best, like most people would, Sam stood near tree trunks along the edge, scanning his surroundings constantly. He jumped toward me when a pine cone dropped off a tree as if to shield me from its imaginary explosion. Then he tried to pretend he hadn't."

Carly rested a hand on her great-aunt's back as she continued.

"He untied a canvas tarp and a blanket from the back of his saddle and laid it down under a tree, and I knew that he had imagined this very moment for two years and that he was trying his best to follow his own script. None of it felt natural. It all felt forced and awkward. In his letters, he wrote about wanting to ride into the places that were ours and made him feel like himself . . . how he just wanted to hold me there and listen to the songs of familiar birds instead of exotic ones and smell the earth . . . how he just wanted to feel the peace he could only feel there and only feel with me. But we were both realizing he couldn't feel peace anymore—not anywhere, not with anyone. I think he had really thought that when he flew away from Vietnam and came back home, he would leave it all behind. And I guess that's what you have to believe when you're fighting a war. I think it was a real shocker to him the day he came home to find he was haunted. I remember lying down next to him, resting my head on his chest, hoping love poured out of me and into him like medicine. I mean, my love for him was so immense . . . I was sure that it alone could heal him. But as the days passed and I saw no effect, I began to lose faith and I questioned whether he still loved me."

Now, Carly rested her head on Great-Aunt Rae's shoulder and reached for her hand.

"One day, he pushed me away completely, telling me he was not the same man, that he was a different man now, that he didn't want to be, but he was. And he told me I couldn't keep waiting for him to come back because he was never going to be like he was. I told him I loved him just the same, but he said that I couldn't possibly because even he didn't like who he was now.

"I told him I would never leave him. In that moment, I completely understood how dogs stayed with the people who kicked them . . . that kind of devotion. But . . . he just shrugged and said, 'Okay. I'll leave then.' And then he drove off. And I knew. I could feel it. Something very bad was about to happen.

"I ran up to his parents' door, begging his dad to go look for him and bring him back, but his dad thought he needed space. He said that soldiers usually didn't come home all at once—that often their body led the way and their mind caught up later. He didn't

say that sometimes their minds never made it completely home."
Great-Aunt Rae bit her lip. "I still wonder about that . . . about
what happens to hearts when minds don't come home . . . whether
hearts die or simply go into a deep coma when minds cannot make
sense of the darkest aspects of what human beings can be.

"Anyway, that night, Sam got drunk and drove off of a mountain road. I don't know whether it was an accident. I suspect it was
on purpose. I think he wanted to set me free so I wouldn't waste
my life tethered to such sadness. I wonder whether he looks down
from heaven and sees that I never fell in love again. I wonder
whether he's been up there, all healed and peaceful, just waiting
for me. Sometimes in my sleep, even after all these years, I have
dreams where we're back in that steamy lean-to or standing in the
small waterfall, and that ring is back on my finger. I don't know
whether that's his way of visiting me and fulfilling the destiny he
left behind, or whether they're just the cruel effect of memory. I
sure hope that there's a place where all the parts of broken people
come back together again, back into something whole and happy,
and that they have the opportunity to reclaim their destiny somehow, but I don't know how it all works."

Great-Aunt Rae had been speaking quietly so her dad wouldn't
overhear, but then she lowered her voice even more. "Anyway.
Your dad's experience was a little different. Two weeks instead
of two years. But two weeks is a long time to dig through rubble
and find dead people. During the first day, he found a few that
were still alive, but as the days went on . . ." She didn't need to
finish. "You weren't old enough to remember your dad before
the Oklahoma City bombing, but your mom told me once that
he used to play his guitar and sing her songs when she sat in the
bathtub. And here's the thing about your dad's case. It wasn't
like he could get on a plane and leave it all behind. It happened

in his home. And all the horrible crime scenes he's seen in all the years before and since, all that happened in his home. How do you come home when all of that happened where you live? So, I know you've probably spent the last few months thinking of your dad as this big, mean authoritarian, but appreciate that he's a soldier that can't come home from war. And appreciate that seeing your mom go through what she went through wasn't likely easy for him either. Be gentle with him, because even though you think he's indestructible, he's actually quite fragile."

"Okay," Carly whispered.

Great-Aunt Rae put her arm around Carly and gave her a squeeze before she stood. "I wish you had known him before," she said quietly before opening the door, walking out, and shutting it behind her.

Paul

Lying in Rae's guest bed, Paul replayed the thunder and the tree crashing through the roof in his mind. A new shot of adrenaline coursed through his veins. The comfort he craved to calm himself down was the same thing that had eventually worked after his days of work at the site of the Oklahoma City bombing—holding Amy in his arms. Since he couldn't have that, he tried calling her, but she did not pick up, and when her voice mail message came on and then beeped, he froze. Every word was too small to represent this feeling. All the words together were still too small. Too small and mixed up. He didn't know where to start and was certain he would fail to truly communicate what was going on inside of him. It was just easier to hang up.

His mind floated back to the sifting, the digging, trying to find pieces that would move and could be removed to get to what and who was underneath, wondering whether he was standing on anyone, pushing them over the edge and into death. Panic surged through his veins and sped up his heart. He remembered looking up at the other officers who were searching, occasionally meeting eyes, the sense of despair he saw in theirs mirroring what he felt.

He tried fast-forwarding his memory, to the part where he drove home. It smelled like apple pie, like another world. The toxic smoldering still lingered in his nose, but the smell of the pie got through anyway. Amy greeted him in sympathetic tears or maybe tears of relief or both, embraced him, took his hand, and led him to the shower. She started the water, undressed them both, and, when the water was hot enough, guided him in. Exhausted, he just stood there as she lovingly lathered him with sweet-smelling soap, massaged his back, massaged his scalp as she worked suds through his hair, touched his face so tenderly as she washed it as well. Amy never had the ability to hide what she was thinking or feeling. It had always been on her face for the world to see. In that moment, he saw the odd mix of concern, gratitude, and respect. *I'm just in awe of you,* she used to say in those moments when she saw a tiny hint of the ugliness he had dealt with. On that day, when she had seen far more than just a tiny hint, when she had seen the full live coverage on the news, she just said it with her eyes . . . *I'm just in awe of you.* She knew he could not have a normal conversation, and so she did not ask that of him. She just loved him. She pressed her beautiful body against his and embraced him, nuzzling her face into his neck. He closed his eyes and tried to fathom how he had come from the lowest level of hell all the way up to this level of heaven in the space of less than an hour.

Just thinking of it now calmed him and slowed his heart.

She had turned the water off, pulled a towel from the rack, and dried him off and then herself. After she held up his robe for him to slip his arms into, she stepped into him and pulled the sides of the robe around her back, looked up at him with the purest love he had ever seen in his life, and said, "You're home with me now."

And that was when he finally broke down and cried, cried for all of those children buried, all those living people who were still buried, cried for all the children who had been orphaned that day, cried for all the people who had lost someone they had loved. As he cried for all of the tragedy and suffering, he felt guilty that it had not been him. He did not know why. It seemed unfair that in hundreds of households that very night, people were crying for the ones they would never get back in this lifetime, and here he was with his beautiful wife wrapped in the safe cocoon of his bathrobe with him. How could that be? How was that fair? Her love poured over him like heavy rain on clay. He could not begin to absorb it all. Most rolled right off of him because he felt he did not deserve it.

After putting on her own robe, she led him to the kitchen. He peeked into Carly's room as he followed her down the hall. There she was, sleeping, and the small noises of her breathing filled him with gratitude and relief beyond measure and, again, the irrational guilt.

Amy pulled roast, mashed potatoes, and gravy out of the oven where she had been keeping it warm. He touched the crisscrossed stripes of crust on top of the pie that sat on the stove. It was still warm. He guessed she had made it just for him after Carly had gone to sleep.

She dished him up hefty servings and slipped in behind him on his chair, resting her cheek on his back as he ate, her arms around his belly as if they were riding a motorcycle. She loved him so much.

Only when he looked back now from Rae's guest room did he see with pristine clarity the survivor's guilt, the walls that went up, the love rolling off of him. Surviving had been no reason to feel guilty. It was okay to survive. His girl deserved a dad. His wife deserved a husband. And true, "deserve" was a pointless word because so many people did not get what they deserved—whether that be bad or good. But in his moment of pristine clarity, he watched the memory of himself as he would watch a movie, eating roast at the dining room table, and he felt immense compassion for Amy, loving him so, and immense compassion for himself, picking through that wreckage, seeing things that would haunt him the rest of his life, yet somehow functioning every single day that followed. One hundred sixty-eight dead, fifteen of whom were babies. More than six hundred eighty injured survivors, six of whom were babies. Babies no different from his own. It really was a miracle, he thought, that someone could dig through that horrific destruction and somehow function every single day that followed.

He reached for the pillow next to him and, imagining it was Amy, held it tightly.

Amy

Judging by the pain in her abdomen, Amy had overdone it on her little hike on Monday. She resigned herself to spending the day in or near the campground. Other campers had mostly left for the day to explore other places in the park, leaving Amy and a handful of others to listen to the breeze in the trees while they read books, sat by the river, or took peaceful naps in their reclining lawn chairs or on blankets.

Unable to concentrate on anything she attempted to read, Amy simply listened. She listened to the wind. She listened to the birds. She listened to the river. She listened for an answer to the question that she could not extract from her heart: Why?

And after she cycled through all of the possible stories *again*, she stopped herself, simply noticing everything around her—all of the living things. And then it struck her that maybe there was just nature, where things were born and reproduced, and sometimes cell division went according to plan and sometimes it went rogue, where sometimes mutations were an evolutionary advantage and sometimes they were a disadvantage, where survival was a species-wide effort as much as it was an individual effort and being part of the genetic variation was just part of the deal. Maybe that was all there was to it. In that moment, it gave her peace of mind to believe that, to believe she hadn't been forsaken by God or done anything wrong . . . to just observe that despite the societal belief that somehow humans were above or apart from nature and that this whole planet was created just for humans, it turned out that human beings were very much just a part of nature. And in nature, living things were born with mutations. Living things suffered and died. And it didn't mean they did anything wrong. It didn't mean they failed. It just happened. It was the most sense she could make of her experience.

Listening as hard as she could for the voice of God, she heard only the wind, the birds, and the river.

The next day, after another unsuccessful attempt at reading, she found herself wishing for a sketchbook and colored pencils, and so she took a trip into Packwood to find and purchase them.

While she was in town, she checked her messages. When she listened to Paul's voice mail about being in Chama for a while because of a situation at work, she could not make sense of it and knew something wasn't right. Her finger was poised to hit "Call back," but he hadn't asked her to, and she didn't want to. It sounded like there was a problem and she had no capacity to take on any more. There had been another call from him, this time with no message at all.

Alicia had sent an email with links to articles on the virtues of hyperbaric oxygen chambers in cancer treatment as well as UV treatments, all prefaced with lots of statements about how Big Pharma didn't want anyone to know about these things. She read about the oxygen chamber and then did an internet search for information to the contrary. What she found was an article out of the United Kingdom that said in fact some cancers had been cured by this, however others had been made worse because some cancers grew in an anaerobic environment and others in an aerobic one. Not all cancers were the same. People had trouble grasping that.

Opting not to reply, she wondered how she was going to preserve her relationship with Alicia if she didn't knock this off. Her sister loved her so much. She did. But good intentions did not mean they had positive impact. Alicia thought she was saving Amy. It was the same as if Alicia belonged to a different church or different religion and believed she had to convince Amy to see the light her way in order to save her soul. This perpetual breach of her boundaries was maddening and exhausting.

Back at camp, she found a pretty spot near the river and sat, leaning back against a big cedar. She began to draw the little things she saw, a meditation on the tiniest details—the veins that ran through petals and leaves, every curl of a bit of lichen, the wings of a beetle. As long as she drew, she did not obsess about the things she often obsessed about. Thoughts of them crossed her mind but didn't stick. They couldn't when she was noticing this shadow and that curve and where the color lowered in intensity.

A junco scratched the forest floor nearby, and she tried drawing it as quickly as she could, but it flew away before she finished. A black moth whose wings had fuzzy edges flitted by too quickly to draw, but she stopped and admired it anyway.

Days passed this way, lying back, enjoying the sweet songs of birds and the cool air filling her lungs . . . sleeping when she felt tired—at least until the next hot flash woke her . . . going for little walks among the big trees when she felt strong or simply restless . . . drawing small miracles when she needed help emptying her mind. It was exactly what she had come for.

When she went back to the visitor center for more postcards, she noticed the large slice of a log where different years were labeled. It had been there since she had been a kid. Out of all of those years, only one ring was blackened. Just one two-hundredth of its whole life. She thought about how her cancer treatment was in actuality less than half of a year. One ninety-fourth of her whole life. That was all. Who defined herself by something that was such a small fraction of her life? She supposed Olympic athletes and lottery winners did, but she didn't want to. It was true that she would live the rest of her life without breast tissue and nipples, but that didn't have to define her. After all, Nick Orem from high school lost part of his finger in a lawn mower, but to the best of her knowledge, he hadn't spent the rest of his life identifying himself as a lawn mower survivor. He was just Nick who made his friends laugh, rode his bicycle down the Pacific Coast Highway, was modestly successful in business, was a good father and husband, and—oh yeah, decades ago lost a finger in a lawn mower.

By Thursday, she was ready to walk to the falls again, hoping this time that stopping to sketch what she noticed would slow her down, allow her to rest, and prevent her from overdoing it. On her way to the falls, she sketched a red flower bud that hung on the end of a cane-like stem. It had long, slender, whorled leaves, somewhat leathery and serrated along the edges. It was not a plant she knew. She could identify it later, along with another she had sketched, one with just a single heart-shaped leaf.

She noticed black spots on many trees and wondered if they were in fact colonies of fungus, but she didn't choose to sketch those. Instead, she simply walked by the sickness and continued on down the trail.

She crossed the bridge over the Ohanapecosh River and walked up to an overlook. There, she noticed tiny plants clinging to the cliff next to the falls and found them both tenacious and elegant.

Voices caught her attention, and looking up the riverside, she spotted the kayakers on a rock. One began to walk away from the group with his kayak over his shoulder, back up from where he had already paddled. She did not particularly want to watch him go over the falls as she had a few days prior. Something about watching a person be so careless with his life when she had endured so much to keep hers was a bit upsetting to her, so she walked on. The trail went farther upstream before turning back toward camp, though, and as she followed it, there were times when she could see him below her. She watched him for a moment as he prepared, turning her back when he peed before stepping into his boat. He cracked his neck, put on his spray skirt, then pushed himself back into the little inlet tucked behind a boulder several times before blowing his whistle to signal readiness and finally going out into the giant aqua streak of frothing, churning water, into the force so much greater than him. Immediately he tipped, rolled, and continued on. She waited to hear cheers, but the river was too loud.

Moving on, she noticed how fresh the air was, the trill of birds, a small spider hanging from a tree.

The kayaker's roll played over in her mind as she walked, and it occurred to her that he could perform at that level only because of that ability to roll, that ability to bounce back from a moment of imbalance, that ability to let go of the mistake and let go of the past instead of replaying it over and over in his mind. He had to completely turn his attention to the present moment and the future in order to be immediately ready for the next obstacle. She needed to be more like that.

"I am healthy, I am strong, I am full of vitality," she whispered to herself. "I am alive. It is good to be alive. I am alive. It is good to be alive. I am alive. I am happy. I am alive. I am happy." She tried different affirmations until she found one that worked and repeated that to herself softly over and over as she hiked.

She noticed the medium-sized Douglas fir cones and the structures between seed scales that looked like the forked tongues of snakes. Since she was ready to rest, she stopped to sketch the pine cone, trying to capture all of the tiny shadows in its form.

Just then, clouds rolled in and everything but the vine maples went dark. They glowed, as if lit from within.

At the rock overhang, Amy paused to appreciate the little maidenhair ferns that grew out of it, the Oregon grape above and below, and the vanilla leaf, a three-leaved plant that looked a little like a moose's head complete with antlers. She leaned in and studied moss closely.

With each breath, she tried to inhale all of this life that was around her, all of this green. She imagined a forest like this living in her heart, in her core, in her head, imagined that those spaces were rich and teeming with purity and life instead of looking and feeling like wastelands where nuclear bombs had been tested.

A wren sang. A tree trunk squeaked as it bent. She passed a stagnant pond, walked down a hill, and crossed over a land bridge between two swamps filled with tall grasses, skunk cabbage, and fallen logs. In the distance, a dog barked. The overwhelming scent of roasting marshmallows filled the air, and she wondered how every bear in a two-hundred-mile radius did not find its way here.

Descending into the campground, she smiled at a very old couple wearing matching sun hats and carrying trekking poles and exchanged pleasantries with them as they passed. Unlike her, they had no chance of living thirty or forty more years. Their future was more certain. Their time was running out. She turned around and watched them walk on behind her. They were here. Together. Smiling. They were living. Today. They were living today. Yes, they had today and each other, and apparently, it was enough.

She wanted that. That peace. That grace. That acceptance. And the love between them. She wanted that too. For the first time since she left, she had a pang of missing Paul, although it wasn't really missing him as much as it was grieving for him, grieving for how things had been decades ago.

Back at her car, she noticed the progress she'd made in accepting things exactly as they were—particularly Paul. She reached in the little paper sack of postcards and drew one out at random. On it, she wrote,

Dear Paul,
What I couldn't tell you before I left was that I found the file
last November when I was looking for my insurance policy.
THE file. With THE papers. I haven't known what to say
or do. And no matter how hard I've tried, I haven't been able
to unsee it. I think I've been holding very still, just hoping it
would pass and we would both forget it. But I can't forget it.
You get full credit for helping me this winter instead of leaving
then. But when you text me that you're thinking of me, I don't
know what to do with that because, well, you were thinking of
me when you tallied up our assets and filled out those papers.

Not knowing whether to sign it "Love, Amy" or just "Amy," she did neither. She affixed a stamp to the card but then realized she didn't know how to send it. Paul was back in Chama, where mail came only to P.O. boxes, and they didn't have one. She didn't dare send the postcard to Aunt Rae to deliver. It was far too personal for that. So, she put the card back in the bag for the time being.

On Friday, when it was time to leave Ohanapecosh Campground again, she found a spot at White River Campground. It was only twelve miles away from Sunrise, a part of the park where they had lived during one of their many summers up here. It remained covered with snow until July and had large patches even then, but she couldn't wait any longer. Tomorrow would be her day.

The campground had showers that were in little stalls with no mirrors. Prior to this year she would have never dreamed that would make her so happy. Even though the wrapping paper had been kind, it had also been a reminder that something was wrong. It was like using earplugs to cope with Paul's snoring. It made the noise manageable, but the adaptation wasn't something she could lose awareness of. She saw it, and even though he never said anything, Paul saw it. Her inner struggle was right there on the mirror for him to see. The first time Paul used the bathroom after she had put up the paper, she felt extremely exposed, but after that, she didn't care as much.

But here in the shower stall at the campground, she was quite happy. There were no mirrors at all, no signs that anything was wrong. If she looked at the spider in the corner of the ceiling, she could sometimes believe that she was simply in some alternative reality, one where her body was still whole.

The warm water rinsed off days' worth of sunblock and dirt, splattering the concrete under the flip-flops that she wore in the public shower. It was easy to shampoo and condition her short hair in very little time, leaving extra time to just enjoy the water beating on her shoulders before her five minutes ended and the coin-operated shower automatically turned off. Scanning the ceiling for more spiders, she actually felt happy.

No mirrors in the spaces where she was naked. No magazines or television telling her what she should look like or how important boobs were. None of that. Just big trees and wide-open spaces. Just a sleeping bag that felt like a hug or maybe being wrapped tightly as a baby. No one to consider. No one to let down. No one to scare. Just anonymity and friendly strangers.

She put on her warmest pajamas and then brushed her teeth at the sink where there was a mirror. Looking in it, she noticed her eyebrows growing back.

After she'd lost them, Alicia tried convincing her the answer was to have fun with eyebrow pencils, as if it were possible to have fun at all when she felt that sick. "Think Mr. Potato Head!" she said, having no idea that for the next three months, that's exactly what Amy would see when she looked in the mirror—just a head that looked like a plain potato. When Amy didn't respond, Alicia called her on the phone to tell her how she had found eyebrow wigs online.

"Stop," Amy said. "Please just stop. I'm begging you to stop. Look at my skin. Look at the rashes all over my skin. You have no idea how much it hurts. Putting anything on this skin is not the answer, but putting glue on this skin is definitely not the answer. I know you're trying to make my world kinder by helping me to conform to all the societal norms and expectations, but stop. Make my world kinder by telling me none of that bullshit matters, because right now it doesn't." Anger rose up and came out as tears. "Tell me you still see me in here somewhere, that you look in my eyes and you still see me. That's the kindest thing you could say. For the love of God, don't mention Mr. Potato Head because I know I look just like him. You know? Just . . ." Amy clenched her fists as she started to shake in that way she did when she felt she was surely going to explode.

"I'm sorry, Amy. I was just trying to make you laugh."

"Don't. Just stop that too. There is nothing funny about this. Nothing. This is terrifying. This is miserable. This is not some fucking joke, so please stop acting like it is. It doesn't make me feel better."

"I'm sorry, Amy. I don't know what to do."

"Just sit with me. Read a book or something. Don't feel like you have to say anything. I like it when you're quiet. I can't listen to all of the words in my head and listen to you at the same time too. It's too much. But I like it when you sit with me because I'm so scared and I don't want to be alone. If you absolutely have to say something, just tell me you love me and that you're here for me. That's all I want to hear." She sobbed and Alicia was silent for a moment before she said she loved her and was here for her.

A woman walked into the campground restroom and said hi as she took out her toothbrush.

Amy was grateful for the distraction because she really did hate getting sucked into memories like that.

Back at her car, she crawled into her sleeping bag. Then her scalp began to prickle, and she felt an acute pang of ambiguous anxiety. Finally catching on to the new patterns of her body, she knew what was coming next. She unzipped the sleeping bag, then opened the car door and sprang out into the cool evening air, hoping she would sweat less and stay drier. She thought about this feeling, this uneasy feeling she had so much of the time now. It was a feeling she used to know each month in the three days before her period. She found herself wondering how to untangle what feelings were in her soul and what feelings were actually her body reeling from suddenly having its estrogen supply cut off. *There is nothing wrong. There is nothing to fix,* she told herself. *My body is finding balance.* That thought calmed her somewhat and made her more patient with the emotional discomfort as her sweat dried.

Once back in her sleeping bag, she turned her attention to the crisp mountain air. In her body, it felt almost effervescent, like the air equivalent of sparkling water, chilled, and infused with the sweet fragrance of alpine firs, a scent so distinct from other conifers, she could pick it out anywhere. She breathed it in and out, in and out, calming herself until at last she slept.

Paul

The next morning, Carly prepared breakfast for the three of them and then sat next to him as if everything were normal again. He could see that she didn't know what to say. He really didn't either. It was enough, he supposed, that she simply said that things were going well. After all, that had been his greatest hope at this point. It was more important than remorse and apologies. When they were all done eating, he said good-bye, and she gave him a really big hug, a hug that seemed to say all the things she could not.

Carly stayed behind to do dishes and farm chores while Rae drove him back to the house with the intention of staying to hold the ladder while he tarped the roof—something he needed to do before he left.

When they reached the house, though, it turned out the worst of the work had been done by the power company in his absence. It appeared that to get the power lines off the ground, they'd had to cut the elm a little bit and, fearing their cuts would damage his house more, had taken care to cut the branch that pierced his roof before doing the rest. They still left him large segments of log in his front yard to deal with, and the branch that pierced the second floor of his house had fallen all the way through.

He didn't like it up there on the roof, looking down into the hole. He hated holes. But he listened to Rae and Cleo visit from down below and their conversation kept him in the here and now.

Once done, he profusely thanked her for everything and then started on home. After checking the time, he thought it unlikely that he would make it all the way home tonight.

Hours later, when he was out of the mountains and back on the plains, his phone rang. Not wanting to miss a call from Amy, he pulled over. It wasn't her. It was his boss.

"Lieutenant Bergstrom, Captain Lopez here. Look, uh, I'm sorry to ask anything of you while you're enduring your own poop storm. I understand Green cleared your name yesterday and now we just have a little paperwork to do to reverse your suspension. So, this isn't a professional call. It's a personal one. We have a bit of a situation here. One of your sergeants—Robinson—fell off the wagon last night, beat up his wife and teenage son, and then fled the scene in his car when his wife called 911. There ensued a high-speed chase through town, ending with a fiery crash in front of a vacant elementary school."

With one hand, Paul rubbed his forehead. Robinson. Dammit. Robinson had been there after the bombing too and turned to the bottle to help him sleep at night. He'd about lost his job on the force not six months later, but Paul had intervened back then, getting Robinson to agree to let Paul take him to a residence program for twenty-one days. Paul had never known him to be violent with anyone. What happened?

"Oh, no," Paul said, assuming the worst. Fiery crashes usually didn't have survivors. And Annie. Paul had met Annie, Robinson's wife, a few times over the years, and she always struck him as pure goodness. She had hung in there with him through all of the rough times. Paul felt sick and winced, imagining her and their son being savagely attacked. They would never be the same. Something was broken now that could never be fixed—at least not by Robinson. Well, if Robinson had lived, his whole life would be more or less ruined—family, career, probably health . . . all of the things that offered a man the opportunity to be happy.

The choice of words in his own mind did not go unnoticed by Paul. *Offered a man the opportunity to be happy*. Family, career . . . in that order.

"Remarkably, Robinson survived. He's in the Trauma One Center at OU Hospital and is in critical condition. Looks like he'll make it, but it's not a given. Plenty of internal injuries."

"Okay," Paul simply said matter-of-factly, because what was the appropriate response? Both he and the captain knew this man's life as he had known it was over.

"I thought you might want to check in on him."

"Yeah," Paul agreed.

They discussed the details of Paul returning to work, then Paul drove farther away from the mountains and farther out into the vast, flat land. He passed a deserted house, a solitary tree by its side, a windmill just a little farther away, and then he drove on into the void, closer and closer back to hell. He didn't want to return, but it wasn't as though people had stopped committing crimes or ever would. Sometimes he imagined himself as a sheepdog, keeping wolves at bay but never really making a difference in their population. There would always be wolves. And there would always be sheep—defenseless innocents who couldn't save themselves if and when their lives depended on it. Being a sheepdog wasn't glorious, but it was better than being a wolf or a sheep.

Hours later, as the evening turned to night and Paul's own eyes became heavy, he considered the markings above the eyes of many sheepdogs, light spots meant to look like eyes open when a sheepdog slept. Humans didn't have that advantage. They just had to sleep and hope other sheepdogs would cover them.

He found a dumpy motel in a tiny town and pulled over.

Soon thereafter, he lay in bed with the blue light from the TV news flickering on his face as he caught up on all the terrible things human beings had done to one another just that very day. The noise of the news dominated the quiet memory of Mr. Martinez's music. Paul took note of this but did not change it. It was part of the process of deadening himself like the calloused bottom of a foot in summertime.

After turning off the television, he rolled over onto his side and faced an empty pillow. Old motels like this one reminded him of his honeymoon with Amy, a trip they took on a shoestring down to the Gulf Coast. He peeled one layer of white lace off of her to find another. She stood before him, trying not to act as awkward as she felt, but he already could read her too well, and somehow, he knew to just hold her . . . just hold her and wait until she took a deep breath and her tense muscles softened. He knew to simply tell her that she was beautiful, and he loved her so much and was so happy that she was his wife forever. She peeled her face off of his shoulder, looked up into his eyes, and said, "God, I love you," more emphatically than anyone before or anyone since. When he tried to remember feeling joy, that was one of his most recent memories. It was a memory like a worn-out nine-millimeter movie, something that became a little scratchier each time he played it back, until he could see it but not really feel it as he had the first time. He looked at the empty pillow and tried to remember how Amy had looked lying in bed when he woke up the next morning. But then the other memories slipped in through the wall like rats or raccoons into a secret garden, and instead of seeing Amy lying on the pillow, he saw four different homicide victims in motels after housekeeping staff had found them and called the police. Three of them had been raped first. Another time, he had seen a woman in a wedding gown, stabbed by a new husband who had gotten drunk and jealous at their wedding reception when she had danced with his brother. She lived, though Paul had not thought she would. Other disturbing images resurfaced in his mind . . . pictures that a sexual predator had posted online just prior to Paul arresting him, photographs of twelve- and thirteen-year-old girls in white lace lingerie. This world was so ugly, so inconceivably ugly.

He got out of bed and walked to his car just outside the door and retrieved his guitar. If only he could erase those ugly things and save only the beautiful—tucking in his daughter, teaching her to throw a ball and play catch, leaning over for a good-bye kiss from Amy before he left for work early in the morning or a hello kiss when he came home so late that Amy had already gone to bed. She had kissed him pretty much every single morning, and she had greeted him with a kiss pretty much every single day he had come home. While tuning the guitar, he tried to remember one of the songs he used to play for her. It took him a few tries, but eventually he did.

God, I love you so much, she said in his memory again, and this time it was Amy that was brighter and louder than all of the ugliness. He closed his eyes and fell asleep.

He woke in the morning after having a police dream, the one where he runs through city streets knowing he must find a killer on the loose, panicking at each intersection where he has only a one-in-three chance of guessing correctly. He runs circles around blocks, listening for screams. Sometimes it's night and sometimes it's day. He yells at innocent bystanders to go inside and lock the door because a killer is on the loose, but they don't hear him. They keep walking, often visiting in pairs or small groups as they do, and he doesn't know how he will ever keep all of these people safe from harm. As he always did when waking from these dreams, he put his hand on his heart as if to tell it to slow down and waited then while it did.

Stepping into the shower, he remembered three dead people he documented who were found hanging in motel showers just like this one and wondered whether anyone had ever hung himself in this particular shower or in this particular room. Sometimes it seemed like the whole damn world was haunted. His career had been long and he had seen so much . . . too much. Far too much. Far more than a human brain was ever meant to hold, he was sure.

He waited until the next morning to visit Robinson. Although conscious now and out of critical condition, Robinson was understandably despondent when Paul took a seat next to his bed. He turned his head so as not to make eye contact.

Paul sat in silence for a bit because he suspected just being there counted. "I care about you, buddy," he finally said. "We've been through a lot together. We've had experiences most people don't understand."

Looking over, Paul could see Robinson purse his lips and shut his eyes, as if he were determined to keep words and emotions hidden behind his face . . . as if his face were a dam.

"I want to say that I'm glad you're still with us here on earth because I know you still have good deeds to do. You had a really bad, really destructive day. But you've had thousands and thousands of good days, days where you did so much good in this world, and they still count. I just . . . I just want you to know I haven't forgotten that. And even though your way forward right now is not clear, I want you to know that I do believe it exists, and I do believe you'll find it, and I do believe you will experience some degree of redemption that will bring the intensity of this memory down to something tolerable. When you find your way out of this very low place you're in now, I have no doubt you will help others out of their low places as well, because that's what you were born to do, Robinson—help others."

These were perhaps the most words Paul had ever strung together, and he sat in amazement of how they had all tumbled out of his mouth. They were kinder words than Paul had ever said to himself.

Robinson turned his head and looked up at the ceiling. "Last week, I was sent out to respond to the tornado in Verden. I stopped to check on this couple that were sifting through the wreckage of their house. Their daughter's doll was poking out of some debris. I tried not to look at it. I tried to stay focused on the people. But I couldn't stop looking at it."

"I always hated Carly's dolls," Paul said. "They looked like dead babies. I used to have nightmares about them sometimes. And I used to wish she had been a boy so I wouldn't have had to have those dolls in my house."

Some degree of relief showed on Robinson's face.

"A tree landed on my house in New Mexico three days ago. Roofing was hanging down." Paul didn't need to say more. Robinson understood.

Paul sat with Robinson for another half hour, a half hour of silence, a half hour of self-reflection. He thought about his own father, his anger, his edginess, the way he teetered between harsh and abusive. Surely his father had perceived himself as strong— stronger than most men. And even though Paul had acted differently than his dad, perhaps he perceived this about himself as well. Robinson was evidence that they weren't. They hadn't gotten tougher and better able to handle trauma; they had only gotten closer to the breaking point. Robinson was evidence that pieces of glass stuck in the bottom of a foot might stay there for decades before finally abscessing, but things that went in eventually came out. It could be fast and clean or slow and messy, but harmful things eventually came out.

"If a miracle is offered to you, receive it," Paul said in a moment of uncharacteristic faith. "Don't think you don't deserve it and turn your back on it. You've done a lot of good in this world."

Paul stood, looked at his friend, who shut his eyes instead of looking back, and walked out the door.

Amy

As Amy reached the end of the long, winding road to the second place in the park she had called home, she found herself stunned again at the sheer size of Mt. Rainier as it completely dwarfed the massive Sunrise Lodge. How many things were actually bigger than a person remembered them as a kid? Off to the left a little way from the mountain's mostly round top was a small sharp peak called Little Tahoma that pointed up in the same way her grandfather's index finger had next to his face when he had an idea. That was what the whole mountain seemed to say—*I have an idea!* These ideas included run around for the pure joy of it, carve channels for snow runoff to follow, watch a bird, a chipmunk, a marmot, or an elk . . . climb to the top of the ridge and let the clouds caress you as they whip by, imitate birdsongs, or simply find a soft place and take a nap.

She could not say when exactly she had begun to think of this mountain as her grandfather—perhaps when she was seven or eight, about the time her real grandfather had died. This mountain had watched over her the way he had—quietly and ever present. Seeing the mountain up close again filled her with inexplicable relief, as if she could just fall into his arms again, rest her head on his shoulder, and tell him, *I have been* through *something*. And he, this mountain anthropomorphized with characteristics of her grandfather, would anchor her back down to the earth, inviting roots to grow from her feet so that she would stay with him this time, here in the home where a big part of her spirit had continued to dwell all of these years.

Behind the block house her family had called home that summer had been a picnic area used from the thirties to the sixties. In the fifties and sixties, there had been some drive-in campsites neighboring it, and the picnic area had been used for campfire programs. A big outdoor fireplace with a chimney had been built, perhaps to keep the smoke from blowing in the eyes of the visitors who attended the programs. However, by the late seventies, the campsite and picnic area had been closed for enough years that trees had grown up around it and enclosed it, and those who had ever known about it had forgotten about it—except her dad. They used to follow a trail until it appeared to dead-end at a bunch of trees, and that was when they would slip into the secret place.

Amy parked and searched for it. The fragment of trail they used to follow was gone now. Since it was so early in the morning and the Sunrise Lodge wouldn't open for another week, Amy ignored the signs instructing visitors to stay on the trail, looked all around her, and then ran straight for the outstretched arms of the trees.

She pushed her way through them as if they were a revolving bookcase on *Scooby-Doo*. Inside the secret world she had shared with her family, time had allowed the earth to reclaim more. Still, she found a spot near the old stone fireplace and lay down the way she used to. Inhaling deeply, she let the scent of alpine firs transport her the rest of the way back in time. She could almost feel a Nancy Drew book in her hand and the presence of her dad nearby.

Nights had been the most magical of all here. When the moon

was dark and new, stars shone so brightly at this high elevation—6,664 feet, to be exact. Free of light pollution from Seattle and particulates in the atmosphere, the starry sky had taken on dimension, as if she could really see which ones were closest, as if she could pick her way right through them to any star she wanted to visit. Her dad used to call in short-eared owls for them with a squeak that didn't sound particularly owl-like, but invariably the owls would come, fluttering like big moths. Amy had soaked in the songs of the nocturnal birds on those nights, and on full-moon nights diurnal birds joined the choir, robins and sparrows tricked into singing by the brightness of the moon.

Oh, this place. How could she have let so many years slip by without visiting this place? Rolling over onto her tender chest, she spread her arms wide and hugged the earth as she lay on it. She imagined her arms growing roots into the earth the way branches of subalpine firs did when they touched the ground . . . imagined lying there long enough to be reclaimed by the earth the way dead trees were. Baby trees and huckleberries would grow out of her back, mosses and lichens would cover the rest of her, and she would just lie there, content to be part of the way that nature takes broken things and makes them whole. The earth would take her pain and her memories of the hospital and compost them into life force.

Overcome with the emotion of both being home and her keen awareness of the passage of time, she found herself watering the earth with her eyes, hoping the salt wouldn't harm the small plants below her. If only her dad were nearby. If only she were still seven or eight and just beginning this life, fresh and whole and charged up with the energy of life like a brand-new battery. If only she could go back in time to those moments when she didn't really know loneliness—not really, not like the loneliness she knew now.

Growing increasingly uncomfortable on her chest, she rolled back over, and looked at the window of sky framed by fragrant firs. She had never brought Carly here, never shown her this magic. Perhaps if she had, Carly would have weathered last winter better. Perhaps she would know something deeper about the cycles of seasons. If, God forbid, Carly ever developed cancer, where would she go to heal? *Stop it, stop it, stop it,* Amy commanded her thoughts. *I am breathing. I am healing. I am breathing. I am healing. I am breathing. I am healing,* she recited in her mind, calming herself again, returning to a place where she was supported by the earth and lulled into peace by birdsongs. After all, it was true. She *was* still breathing, because that's what living things did, and she *was* healing.

"Hey, Amy," said Aunt Rae, who picked up on the first ring.

"Hi, Aunt Rae. How are things going?"

"Well, your daughter's doing a great job. We had a family with some real brats last week, so she got to take a look in the mirror. I believe she was feeling pretty sorry about what happened before, but having to tolerate the brats turned the volume way up on that. She's been trying to write you a letter, but having trouble finding the words. I was asking her about it and she said she feels like she let it sit too long and now that's a whole other offense. She didn't use those words, but that's what she was trying to say. She seems to think it has permanence."

"Oh." Amy sighed. "I really do understand."

"Well, check the Packwood Post Office in a few days in case she gets one done tonight. She might not. I don't know. But I know she loves you very much. And this is good news—she and Paul had a civil breakfast this morning. Even warm."

"Really?" That was a shocker.

"Well, Carly felt sorry for him. He was pretty shook up. A tree fell on the house during a storm. It rocked him. Reminded him of the bombing. I found him in my driveway in the rain kind of disoriented or out of it . . . traumatized, I guess. He was traumatized."

"Oh my God, is he okay?"

"I think so. I helped him patch the roof this morning, so he could go back to work. His work situation's apparently been cleared up."

She considered asking for details about it but then realized she really didn't want to know. Whatever it was, was fine now. "Oh. Well, that's good."

"I thought he'd be happier about it, but he wasn't really himself."

"Geez, it sounds like I should come home."

"I'd say no. Oklahoma City is full of therapists and you're not one of them. Paul will bounce back regardless. Carly's on a good trajectory. Your voice sounds good. I can hear your strength coming back. I think you can help everyone best if you just keep healing out there."

"It's been so good to be here. It really has."

She told Aunt Rae about her hikes and about rediscovering the secret place today—not because there was any chance Aunt Rae could picture it but because it just felt so good to be connected for the length of their conversation. It was so nice to hear a friendly, loving voice—her voice. Sometimes it sounded a little bit like her mother's.

Carly

Carly brought down the package of pink stationery to the laundry room, where Great-Aunt Rae was folding clothes. "I don't mean to be rude or ungrateful, but Mom and I hate pink so much. It reminds me of breast cancer every time I see it. I thought maybe you could use it or give it to someone else."

"Oh. Okay. Yeah, I can do that."

"Thanks."

"Did you write to her?"

Carly shook her head. "I just sit there with the pen in my hand."

Great-Aunt Rae pursed her lips and nodded. "Can you tell me about what happened? Maybe I can help. I mean, what started it all? What changed?"

"I couldn't figure out why she needed the second surgery so I asked and then she told me about the gene mutation and I started putting two and two together and I completely freaked out and told her that I was nothing like her."

"Well, I bet she understood."

Carly shrugged and looked at the ground. "Maybe. But then it just went on too long. I was busy being mad at the whole world and the argument never got resolved—as if mean words like that can get resolved, you know? I mean, once they're out there, they're kind of out there. You can't really take them back."

"Want to take a walk or a drive-by to see your parents' house? Your dad patched the roof this morning. Sometimes a walk clears the mind."

"No," she said. The very last thing she wanted to think about was how she almost lost her mom last winter and she almost lost her dad yesterday. The world was an unfathomably uncertain place. It was too much.

Carly tried to sleep but couldn't. She turned on the bedside lamp, sat up, and tried one more time. This time, the words came. Regret and remorse poured out of her heart through her hand and onto the paper, and when she was done, her heart felt empty in a good way, like her stomach after a night of the flu.

She slipped the letter into an envelope, addressed it to General Delivery, Packwood, WA 98361, just like Great-Aunt Rae had written down for her, and then took it downstairs, wishing she could slip it in the mail tonight. It felt good to get it out of her room, at least.

Violet descended the stairs, the nails on her paws clicking on each step, to check on Carly and tried to herd her back up to the second floor where she belonged, but the summer night beckoned to Carly, so Violet had no choice but to surrender and follow her outside. Carly found a spot at the edge of the porch and sat down, mesmerized at how clear the stars were so far from the city and at this elevation. A person could get lost in the depth of all those stars. Violet turned a circle and then sat down and leaned into Carly. From the corral, one of the horses nickered. Carly wanted to imagine that it was T. Rex telling her to stay.

She was supposed to want to go to college. That had been the goal. But she didn't feel ready for all of that, for being around all of those people, for having her thoughts occupied with things on a syllabus. This was what she wanted. This space. Space in her physical environment. Space in her mind. Horses and a dog and stars.

Amy

Driving to Sunrise in the dark and missing all the anticipatory views the next morning was a price to pay for watching the sunrise from the top of Sourdough Ridge. There was a reason this place was named for this event. Relaxed and enjoying the blessed warmth of the car heater, she let her mind drift back to the early summer mornings when her dad would gently wake her and Alicia.

"It's going to be a good one," he would say if the sky was clear or mostly clear. On cloudy days, their parents let them catch up on sleep, enjoying the silence and stillness.

It had always been a struggle to get out of bed on the mornings her dad had summoned them, but the two times she had lost the battle her first summer there, she had to listen to her sister and her dad talk about how utterly magnificent it had been for the rest of the day and, in the case of one, even months and years later. During her second summer there, she made herself get up each and every time. She did not want to miss a single one.

On this day, she was the first guest to arrive. Since no camping was allowed at Sunrise, it felt as if she had the park to herself. After zipping her coat all the way up and donning a scarf and hat, she slipped her backpack on. Setting off, she walked behind the majestic old lodge, four stories high and covered with shingles, a sloping roofline over the giant dormer that took up a third of the roof on each side. Then she started up the ridge on the exact same path she and her family had walked long ago.

Her body felt so different now from the way it had then, no longer light and springy and not used to the altitude either. She remembered what she used to think about to distract her from this uphill climb back when she was seven and eight—wanting a mystery to solve like Nancy Drew. Somehow the park would be jeopardized by greedy developers disguised as park officials, but by virtue of her own sleuthing skills, she alone would expose their sinister plan and save the park. The plot was vague and changed with the "clues" she would find as she went about her day. When she found tracks, she imagined tracking the evil developers to the spot they intended to build a hotel on. Once, she found a pen someone had dropped and imagined the villains had used it to formulate their evil plan. Amy smiled now, wondering whether all children created stories like that.

She paused to think about her writing career and how unfortunate it was that she could not imagine writing one more book, because once she was divorced, she would probably need to work. Either way, she just didn't have it in her. Didn't have the mental clarity, didn't have the drive or desire. Words seemed like clutter now. Like litter. Like all of it was the opposite of what she wanted now.

Looking down toward the massive meadows called Yakima Park, she remembered, too, being fascinated with the Native Americans who used to convene in this very place to pick berries and trade with other tribes. Now, she had an even deeper appreciation for how these gatherings had been a convergence of Plains tribes and Coast Salish tribes—people of the wind and people of the water.

Oh, it's going to be a good one! her dad's voice echoed in her head, and she imagined him and Alicia walking in front of her now, the anticipation on his face as he turned around, motivating them to keep the pace up so they would reach the top of the ridge before the big moment.

"Let's climb Mt. Rainier when I'm sixteen," she had said to her sister, afraid that if she waited longer than that, her sister would be entangled in the world in a way in which she could not free herself for such an endeavor.

"Okay. And then let's hike the Wonderland Trail," her sister had said.

Amy supposed they had been seven and nine when this conversation had taken place, the last summer before her sister began to grow into a really big girl and then a young woman, leaving Amy behind for a few years. That summer, they had been particularly fascinated with the Wonderland Trail hikers who came through Sunrise and into the lodge for a meal. At one point, their mom even carved backpack frames for them out of an old box with a box knife, and the girls had tied their pillows to them with twine and then hiked around the area nearest the employee housing with exaggerated fatigue.

The fabric of her shirt rubbing against her chest made her feel as if she were wearing a shirt full of fiberglass slivers and leaning against a low-current electric fence, and she wondered how long it would be before all of these freshly cut nerves would calm down. A stabbing pain on the left side jolted her the rest of the way out of her memory and back into the present, but she kept walking, one foot in front of the other, because that was all she could do in this moment—just walk through it.

She wished Alicia could be here with her and that things could be as simple as they were when they were kids, back before Alicia became an AMA conspiracy theory zealot. How nice it would be to simply take this hike with her sister and reminisce together, maybe even remember things they had forgotten. Amy missed her. Now the likelihood of Alicia saying the wrong thing was somewhere between very high and certain, and Amy didn't want to invite disaster. Wanting to preserve this relationship until she was less likely to overreact and destroy it, Amy thought it best to step back and hope that one day Alicia's ignorant suggestions and conspiracy theories wouldn't rile her at all. She loved her sister so much. She did. And she was grateful for how Alicia had been there for her when it counted, going not just the extra mile but many extra miles—literally.

In the days that followed each chemo infusion, Alicia brought food to Amy's house, hoping something would sound good. Chicken soup. Vegetable soup. Scalloped potatoes. Mac and cheese. Fettuccine Alfredo. As time went on, the food became plainer and plainer. Rice Krispies. Steamed potatoes. White rice. Canned peaches. Lemons to squeeze in water.

The things that worked when she had the flu didn't work with chemo. "You know the smell of the ink in a ballpoint pen?" Amy asked her. "It's like my belly is full of that ink. I just keep burping it up."

Neither of them knew what to do.

Day four, the third day after infusion day, was the worst, the day Amy would wake up and cry, feverish and nauseated, her skin in an itchy rash, her feet burning and blistered, the extremely tender skin on her cold, bald head unable to tolerate anything but the softest fleece hat, her tongue so swollen it seemed to barely fit in her painful, sore mouth. Sometimes Alicia would cry with her.

"I hate this," said Amy.

"I know," replied her sister, lying next to her in bed, only on top of the covers, a look of such deep concern and empathy in her eyes.

And so, after the first round, Alicia drove eight hours to a pot shop in Trinidad, Colorado, to buy something to help her sister. The woman who worked there was very helpful, explaining the difference between indica and sativa, Alicia told Amy. Indica, she joked, was short for "in the couch," the kind of effect it had on people—a deep, relaxing body high. Sativa was more of the head high people thought of when they thought of pot. Both, she said, would help with appetite. Alicia left with indica ginger candies, indica chocolates, indica-blend mints, and two packages of tiny indica-blend raspberry-lemon drops, which she suspected would be the winner. While Paul was at work, Alicia offered them all to Amy. Ginger and chocolate had been unthinkable with her nausea, despite the fact that ginger was supposed to help with that. And mint had been unthinkable with her sore mouth. But the lemon drops were a miracle. As per the saleslady's suggestion, Amy sucked on only one—just a half dose. And although she never felt high, her stomach relaxed, and the ink smell in her belly reduced to something manageable. She stopped crying, ate some fettuccine and a little salad, watched TV, and shouted out *Jeopardy!* answers with Alicia. And after that, she had fallen into a blissful sleep.

Enough of a waxing moon lit her way that she didn't need a flashlight as she walked along the ridge, its sharp edge just a few steps to her right as she passed through the saddles between small peaks. Eventually, she reached the top of Dege Peak, where she perched herself on a rock and dug into her backpack for a granola bar and a crisp apple.

A sliver of green light over the eastern horizon hinted at the arrival of the sun. Slowly, it grew and grew until there was pink . . . until the pink and gold spread across the sky like a promise and lit up the mountain with alpenglow. She chose to believe the sky was hearkening a new day for her after her long night of the soul.

From farther down the trail, Amy watched an elk turn his head and work his antlers into an impossibly thick cluster of trees and then slip the rest of his body through it.

Many, many years ago, she had watched the same thing with her dad. The next day, they had returned to the same spot and pushed their way between the trees and through the branches just as the elk had. What they discovered was a sanctuary inside a fortress.

Her dad had explained that once there had been an old tree right in the middle where they were standing now. Subalpine firs could regenerate and reproduce asexually when their branches touched the soil, and all of the old tree's branches had done just that, creating new trees in a circle around it. Then, the old tree died and decayed while the others matured, and that was how these circles of trees were formed.

Not wanting to disturb the elk, she walked on farther. Further down the trail, she noticed another cluster of trees and wandered over to it. It appeared impenetrable, and as she stood there looking up at the wall of green branches, it felt like a metaphor for this very moment in her life, where she could not see a path forward or a way to the other side. Taking a big breath, she considered that both likely needed to be approached in the same way—one day at a time or one branch at a time . . . even when it seemed no progress was being made, even when she was only going on faith that the other side of this was a better place to be, even when it seemed impossible. Both would take some determination.

Lifting a branch, she slid under it and then pushed her body through some smaller branches until it hit one that wouldn't give. She slid under that one as well and found herself wedged between two tree trunks, spaced marginally farther apart than pickets on a picket fence. Her body protested. There were just so many parts that were tender after her two surgeries, and she realized this had probably been a stupid idea. But here she was. She could go forward or go back. So, despite the resistance of branches, she pushed one leg up and over, where the gap was a little larger, then pivoted and pulled the other leg through. Closing her eyes and covering her face and chest, she pushed her way through the rest of the branches.

Inside the circle grew huckleberries, Indian paintbrush, and lupine. She found a spot to sit and listened to sparrow songs for a moment before lying back. The ground was soft from frost heaves, the process by which moisture in the ground expands with freezing temperatures and then melts, leaving the soil fluffy and ready for new life.

She rolled over onto her side, curling up and holding her legs. It still wasn't completely comfortable to lie like that, her chest squished together in a way that felt as if the skin could pucker and tear off the tissues below. The outside edges of her boob stumps felt bruised still. She hated how the region felt tingly, like a foot that had fallen asleep, and wondered to what degree the nerves would regenerate and to what degree they would not. Remembering the first times Paul had touched her breasts, or taken off her shirt and kissed them, she shut her eyes as if she could block out the grief. So many people thought breast reconstruction was the answer, but she didn't want reconstructed boobs. She wanted *her* boobs—the ones she could feel. That was the loss. A nipple tattoo wasn't going to do it. She wanted her real nipples, the ones she could feel. No, reconstructed boobs weren't going to trick her into thinking nothing had been stolen from her. An erogenous zone had been stolen.

She remembered the early days, before the bombing, before parenthood, when Paul used to bring a kitchen chair into the bathroom while she soaked in a candlelit bath and play his guitar for her. Eventually, he would set it down, take off his clothes, and slide in behind her. She leaned back on his chest, and his hands always found their way to her breasts. She would never have that again.

Sitting up, filled with sadness, she surveyed her surroundings. What had seemed like a sanctuary now felt isolating, and she wanted to leave. Slowly, she stood, reaching out to a nearby branch for support. She missed having a body that didn't feel fragile and unfamiliar. Then she began to pick her way out of the subalpine atoll.

For a moment, inside the labyrinth of greenery, the back of her coat became hung up on a branch. Unable to reach it, she momentarily gave up and simply cried.

When she was done, she pushed back just a little instead of forward and, with a twist, freed herself. She stepped over the place where two trunks touched, slipped through the gap, and climbed under or pushed her way through the rest of the branches back to the outside world.

Paul

He paused before he opened his truck door, stepped out, and walked across the parking lot and into the station . . . into the place where people were questioned—people who had been beaten and robbed or raped, people whose kids had run away or simply disappeared, people who appeared to have a mental illness and no treatment, people who had made the biggest mistake of their lives in some way . . . getting behind the wheel after too many and killing someone . . . getting mad and hitting someone over the head with a beer bottle the way they did in movies . . . playing with their dad's gun. Yes, he sucked it up and walked into the hell where people suffered. But a voice inside of him, his heart, implored him not to.

He had three more years until retirement. Just three sounded like so little, but two hundred fifty days times three was seven hundred and fifty days. It was an unthinkable number of days. And yes, if he stayed, he might get promoted and get a raise and that would factor into the amount of money he would receive from his pension for the rest of his life. The rest of his life. That seemed uncertain in this line of work.

Years ago, he'd had something to prove to his dad. Now, he no longer did.

He looked around the precinct, at his captain's office, the office he thought might be his one day, and the things that had mattered and didn't seem to now. He just wanted to go back to Chama and finish his house and make it nice for his wife. He wanted to be near his girl. He wanted to walk in the wilderness.

However, just then Captain Lopez waved him over and so he walked back into that sad world as if he were walking down a slope into water that would eventually cover his head.

Later that week, Paul stood at the crime—a woman, eye blackened and swollen, boyfriend dead in the doorway, shot three times in the chest. In a back room, a baby cried. It was only the wee hours of Thursday morning.

"My baby," said the woman to Paul as two officers led her out to a car to take her to the station. He nodded to let her know he would take care of the baby. She had made the call to 911, saying only that she needed help. Two hours earlier, officers had responded to a concerned neighbor's call to their home for possible domestic violence. At that time, she had insisted that everything was okay. Paul remembered a similar call at the beginning of his career. He responded to a neighbor's complaint but could do nothing in the face of the woman's insistence that everything was okay. He knew it wasn't. The next morning, she was dead. Paul carried the weight of that to this day. He didn't know what he could have done differently, but he knew that there had been a fork in the road there—an opportunity to intervene and save her life. She hadn't chosen it. No one should have expected her to be brave enough to. It was an imperfect system for an imperfect world.

Paul called CPS as he walked into the back room to pick up

the crying child, leaving the detectives who had begun collecting evidence. Her diaper was dirty, so Paul changed it and hoped a greater degree of comfort would help her stop crying, but she sensed that something was very wrong, and she wanted her mother, so all Paul could do was rock her, coo reassurances, and quietly sing. The room seemed like a normal baby's room in a normal house, pink like the color of love and happiness. Her little brown curls tickled his jaw as he held her.

He remembered coming home from the federal building and holding Carly like this, just holding her and holding her, marveling that she was alive when danger was ever present, wondering why he had ever thought bringing a child into this horrible world was a good idea or kind in any way, wondering how he was going to protect her from everything.

In his arms, the baby began to give in to the exhaustion from crying so hard for so long. He sat in a rocking chair with her and wondered what would become of this little one.

After the bombing, not wanting his supervisors to doubt his fitness for the job, he had gone to a therapist not provided by the department and paid not with insurance but with cash. He had been so desperate for respite from his nightly nightmares. She asked him to hold a doll, symbolic for his child-self, and to allow her to guide him through a meditation of sorts, a review of his life, where he would show his child-self significant scenes from his life and say to his child-self, "It's okay, I'm here, I'm holding you, I won't let anything happen to you, I love you unconditionally." But Paul could not get over the doll. He held it for a moment, as he had held one of the dead children from the day care in the federal building, then stood up and gave it to the therapist. "This is making it worse," he said simply, and walked out, certain that no one knew how to help him because it simply couldn't be done. To the extent possible, he would have to help himself, and to the extent it wasn't possible, he'd have to figure out how to simply live with it.

Now, he held this baby and wanted to protect her from seeing anything tragic. She had likely already seen and heard too much. What he wanted to do was take her out of this house, out of the madness of this "civilized" world, out into nature. It was not possible to do that for this baby.

He thought again of that therapy session and realized that if he held his baby-self the way he was holding this baby, he would also not show him tragedy and assure him that he would take care of him. As he would for this baby, he would get his baby-self out of here. It was a moment of pristine clarity. As of today, he had officially seen enough. He held the child in his arms, rocked her back and forth, and thought, *Yes, I think I am done.*

Immediately he felt weight lifting off of his chest, weight he had once thought was Amy. He paused for a moment just to feel it continuing to lighten as his decision sank deeper and deeper into his consciousness. The baby in his arms stopped crying, sputtered a little bit, and then fell asleep. Paul kept rocking, lulling both of them into deeper levels of peace.

After the social worker came and took the baby from him, Paul checked on his detectives. Then, instead of walking through the bloody crime scene, he walked through the house to the back door and stepped out and into the sunshine.

Back at the office, he talked with Captain Lopez. At first, his captain wanted to talk about the stressors in Paul's life—his wife's cancer and cancer treatment, the accusation and investigation, seeing Robinson in the hospital, and he tried to caution Paul against making such an important decision that was a reaction to any of these things. But Paul explained that Robinson's situation was an involuntary reaction to these things and that every day at work was a little like lead or mercury poisoning—slow, drop by drop, where a person could take it until the day it killed him, and the thing was, no one knew exactly which drop was the one that would put them over the limit. He wanted to leave with integrity, he explained, but he really had reached his limit. Still, the captain wanted him to consider all of his options—a leave of absence, light duty in the office for a time, transfer from homicide to a different department—parking, maybe . . . all the ways to try to hang on until his official retirement age. Paul closed his eyes to hide his distress. And then Captain Lopez looked at staffing and at the amount of Paul's leave he had banked, and they determined Paul could use up his remaining leave to fulfill the courtesy of two weeks' notice and remain in good standing.

He put his firearm and his radio on the table. That was it. He was free.

Paul wasted no time returning to Chama. For almost three days, he felt good about his progress. He had repaired the roof, but not the ceiling. He needed to route new wires to the light fixtures first.

He had even taken a guitar lesson from Mr. Martinez to begin learning scales.

Since it was now Saturday, he left a note by Rae's phone, thanking her and letting her know he was in town, then he left her house. It was no surprise, then, that later that day she stopped by on her way to the grocery store.

"Wow! You accomplished a lot in just a few days!"

"Thanks!" he said. "I hope Amy will love it."

"Oh." Rae seemed surprised by that, which made no sense to him since that had always been the plan. "I wasn't sure whether you were still thinking of moving here after you retired or whether you were thinking of selling."

He could tell there was something she wasn't saying. "Why would I sell?"

She deliberated and then spoke. "Well, Amy told me about the divorce papers."

"I didn't give Amy any divorce papers."

"No, you didn't. . . . She found them. She asked me not to say anything."

He looked at Rae, the gravity of the situation hitting him like a wrecking ball. "Oh God," he said with his face in his hands. "When?"

"On the day she learned she probably had cancer. She was looking for her insurance policy."

Paul shut his eyes and exhaled a deeply regretful, "Oh." He shook his head in disbelief at how badly he had screwed up. "Oh my God." How could a person possibly apologize for making the most horrifying moment of a person's life exponentially worse?

"Have you heard from her?"

"No." He rubbed his forehead. "I thought, well, surely she was out of reception . . . and she clearly needed space . . ."

"Well, she calls me at seven my time, six hers, on Saturday nights, so you might want to try calling her around seven thirty . . . see what you can straighten out over the phone. . . ."

He considered that and shook his head. "It's a way too important conversation to have over the phone." He thought for a moment and then asked, "Do I go up there uninvited and find her?"

"Well, you know, tomorrow *is* her birthday, so you have an excuse. If you wait for her to come home, she might be the one with divorce papers."

"Do you really think she'd do that?"

Rae shrugged. "She's not quite herself. Anything is possible. Did you get her a good present?"

"Uh . . ."

"Oh, buddy," said Rae, shaking her head, "get down to Antoinette's store before it closes today and buy her a piece of jewelry." She looked at her watch. "Go. Go right now. Then go to Albuquerque and get yourself a ticket for an early flight tomorrow. Go!"

Carly

The week's guests had been two grown sisters with one daughter each. One of the sisters was married to a U.S. diplomat who had recently been transferred from Zimbabwe to Georgia—the country, not the state, which up until that week Carly had no idea existed. Her daughter, Isabella, was thirteen and loved being in nature with horses. The other grown sister was an attorney along with her husband in Florida. Her daughter, Sydney, was fifteen and went to a private boarding school for rich kids and was a competitive swimmer and horse jumper. She was competitive about everything else too.

On days that Carly rode with them, Isabella liked to ride in the back and ask Carly questions about what a normal childhood was like, and Carly liked asking Isabella about hers. Isabella used to ride horses among zebras and giraffes in Zimbabwe—an experience that was nearly inconceivable to Carly.

All of this made Sydney jealous and more competitive. She would talk about the fancy horses at the stables she rode, and her riding coach who had been in the Olympics, vacations all over Europe and the Caribbean her family had taken, and how it looked like she was going to get a swimming scholarship to some elite private college Carly had never heard of. It had been annoying, to say the least. But since Sydney was a guest, Carly politely asked questions about her life too so that she would feel important and have a good time.

Sydney would then ask Carly questions intended to make her feel inadequate, but since no part of Carly wanted to be like Sydney, it didn't get under her skin too much. After a couple of days, Carly began to give answers that would throw Sydney, like how she used to believe it was important to be excellent, but now it was more important to her to be kind and happy than excellent. Still, Sydney kept at it.

"So, Oklahoma State, huh?" Sydney said, disdain evident in her voice.

"Maybe," Carly replied. "I don't know. I'm reevaluating my life."

"Aren't you a little young for that?" Sydney's mom called back.

"Yep," Carly agreed. "It's just . . . I used to care about my grades so much. I was at the top of my class. And then my mom got cancer and none of it mattered to me anymore. So, I'm just trying to figure out what does matter."

That seemed to send a silent shock wave through the group.

"Did she live?" Isabella asked after a moment. It didn't surprise Carly that she was the one who would be brave enough to ask.

"Yes."

"Is she okay now?" asked Sydney's mom.

"Pretty much."

For a little while, they rode in blessed silence, and then normal conversation resumed again. This time, Sydney and Isabella left Carly out of the conversation, and Carly was glad.

That night, while Carly was prep cooking, Sydney's mom approached her. "I want to apologize for saying you were a little young to be reevaluating your life. I was making assumptions, and you know what they say about making assumptions."

Carly didn't, and her expression gave it away.

"When you assume, you make an ass out of u and me. You've never heard that? It's an idiom that breaks the word apart."

"Oh."

"And I want to tell you something else. My whole life I've been an achiever. I became a lawyer because it's one of two jobs considered the pinnacle of success, but you know what? It's miserable. I work sixty or seventy hours a week—sometimes even more. And yes, it feels good to do a good job for someone, to win their case, to succeed . . . but am I happy?" She shrugged as if to say she didn't think so. "I was thinking about your mom today and about how if something like that happened to me, I sure would have regretted not spending far more time with my daughter. So . . . I just wanted to say that I think you're smart to figure out what really makes you happy, because you're right—it is more important to be happy and kind than excellent. I wish I had known that twenty years ago."

Carly didn't know how to reply, so she just said thanks, and Sydney's mom joined the others at the table, where Great-Aunt Rae was teaching them how to play BS before leaving them to cook dinner.

Carly passed the solitary days that week reading the books Great-Aunt Rae had left for her, sometimes while lying on T. Rex's back and sometimes with her feet in the cool creek. She looked up birds and flowers in the field guides, and other times just lay back and watched clouds drift by. Despite Sydney's presence, Carly felt more peaceful this week than she had during the others.

When Saturday afternoon came and they all were saying goodbye, Sydney's mom said, "I want to thank you for being a role model to Sydney. She would never say so, but I could tell that she was watching you closely and listening to everything you said. I suspect she'll think about it for some time and that she might be a happier and kinder person for it."

Carly didn't know what to say, but before things became too much more awkward, Sydney's mom hugged her, and then the others hugged her, and then they piled into their rental car and drove off.

Great-Aunt Rae turned to her and said, "Sometimes this job makes me so glad to be who I am."

Carly thought about that as she untacked the horses, rinsed them off with the hose, and then wicked the excess water from their backs with a tool. She wanted to be able to say that when she was Great-Aunt Rae's age and every age in between—that she was glad to be who she was. She wasn't there yet. She had a ways to go.

Usually Saturday nights were a time when everything was pretty much done, so Carly was mystified when Great-Aunt Rae insisted that she go with her on a special errand. First, Great-Aunt Rae had already been gone at the store for a good long time, and second, she turned left instead of right, going out into the national forest instead of to town. She bumped along a dirt road for a bit and then pulled over in a well-worn turnout. There was nothing remarkable about the spot—no panoramic views, no water . . . just little bits of garbage . . . a beer can with holes in it, bullet casings.

Great-Aunt Rae told her to face in the other direction and close her eyes, and after Carly did, she could hear her lift the tarp off the bed of her truck and move it to a spot not so terribly far away. She heard a big thud, followed by the crinkling of the tarp, and then another. After that, she heard her great-aunt make several trips between the truck and that spot. Finally, she heard the truck door open and close and then her great-aunt say, "Okay, you can open them now."

Great-Aunt Rae stood with a revolver in her hand, barrel down pointing to the ground. Behind her, Carly could see that Great-Aunt Rae had moved two log segments onto the tarp and piled several pink objects on them—a pink mailbox, a pink decorative bottle, a small pink metal pail, a pink ceramic mug, two pink ceramic salt and pepper shakers shaped like roses, and a small pink lamp.

From inside her pocket, Great-Aunt Rae pulled out bullets and loaded the revolver, pointed out the safety before taking it off, and handed it to Carly. "I tried getting stuff that would shatter. When you're ready, pull back the hammer with your thumb until it clicks, and then hold it like this"—she put her arms straight out in front of her—"two hands, and pull the trigger. Try not to hit the tarp. We don't want holes in it when we collect all the broken glass in it later. Look at your target through that little V on the top. Don't forget to breathe."

On the first try, she aimed too high, but on the second, Carly shot the pink mug, shattering it to bits, and it felt good—really good. Then she shot the bottle, which exploded into a million pieces.

"Do you have it?" Carly asked.

"Have what?" asked Great-Aunt Rae.

"The BRCA2 gene mutation."

"Uh . . . I guess I don't know. I never thought about it."

"Your sister died of pancreatic cancer at age forty-three, so it seems likely she had it. That's one of the other cancers people with this gene mutation are more likely to get. So, if she did, you would have a fifty percent chance of having it too. A lot of the breast cancer happens to women around fifty, but a lot of the ovarian cancer happens to women in their sixties. You should get tested and then get your ovaries out if you're positive so you don't die early. I mean, your odds of getting ovarian cancer would only be twenty percent so the surgery would either be completely unnecessary or absolutely life extending. It's either one or the other and you'll never know which one it was for you. So, it comes down to peace of mind, right? Like if you just have them removed, you don't have to live the rest of your life feeling like you're being stalked by a cancer cougar."

"Is that how you feel?"

"Pretty much. I mean, I don't know whether I inherited it or not, but fifty percent odds are pretty high, so what do I do with that?" Carly held up the gun and lined up one of the salt and pepper shakers through the little V on the top of the gun, then blew it away. "I mean, say I have it. Is it ethical to have children when there is a fifty percent chance of passing this gene mutation on to my children? Is it ethical to create kids that are destined to get cancer? That's not something people have had to think about before."

"I suppose not. Back in my day, people had to get their blood type identified before getting a marriage license . . . and there was sickle cell anemia . . . but people knew whether they had that or not. . . ."

Carly fired another two shots at the other salt and pepper shaker that sat on top of the mailbox. She hit the mailbox instead and it flew off the stump. Great-Aunt Rae took the gun from her, double-checked it was empty, and put the safety on. Then she trotted over to the pink junk, put the mailbox and salt and pepper shakers back up on the stump, trotted back, and reloaded the gun.

"If I have it, it could stop right here with me. But if I decide that I'm entitled to live the life I would have had if I had been able to live it in ignorance, not just my kids, but hundreds of more people, mostly women, down the family line could go through what my mom went through. And if it's not ethical for me to have children, is it ethical for me to date guys who want to have children without telling them that I shouldn't? Am I obligated to tell all the guys I date that I am flawed and that half of all the children we would have would likely get cancer, possibly significantly earlier in life, and die of it?" She pulled the trigger and shot the remaining shaker and then shot at the lamp, missing the base but getting the shade. Firing again, she hit the base. "Do I tell him that I might? That I might leave him with a bunch of children to raise on his own because my odds of dying early are greater than average? Who is going to want that? So, what's my plan now? Because my plan was to go to college, meet someone nice, graduate, get a career, and marry that someone nice and have a family, and now I don't really see that happening. I mean, I could twist the truth. As long as I don't get the test, I can claim I didn't know. But that feels like lying. And bringing children into this world that are pretty much destined to get cancer just seems wrong to me."

"Well, what about adoption?" Great-Aunt Rae asked.

Carly shrugged. "I still might leave them orphans."

"I think if you knew you had it for sure, you could have frequent enough checkups so that any problems would be found early and your survival would be fairly certain."

"*Fairly* certain."

"Look, kid, none of us get certainty. We drive in cars. We get the flu. We ride horses—big ones. People see cougar walk through my property, so I just stick a shovel down the back of my shirt when I chop wood, hoping the blade would protect the back of my head if a cougar bit into it. I painted eyeballs on it so that the cougar might think it's my face. That's nuts, right? But we just live with it."

"And you can . . . because no one is telling you that you have a ten percent chance of getting attacked by a cougar in the next twenty years, or a five percent chance of dying in a horse accident. You don't have those numbers floating in your head, where you try to manipulate them into something you can handle. You get to live your life in ignorant bliss about all the odds. I looked it up on the internet. If I have this gene mutation, I have a sixty to seventy percent chance of getting breast cancer, a twenty percent chance of getting ovarian cancer, a five percent chance of getting pancreatic cancer, and chances of getting lung, brain, peritoneal, and skin cancer that are less than that but still many times higher than most people. If you add all of those up, that's maybe a hundred percent chance of getting cancer. How do I live a normal life knowing that? Because it feels like being stalked by something that intends to kill me." She shot the mailbox with all the remaining bullets in the chamber.

"Seems to me, you could needlessly wreck the rest of your life thinking about all of this when there's a fifty percent chance you *don't* have it."

"Yeah," Carly said, unimpressed, because the possibility still loomed so large.

"And again, if you do, you can increase the odds of your survival by having more frequent screenings."

"Say I do. Do I run right out and replace my boobs with fake ones like Angelina Jolie? Do I have my ovaries out like Mom? That has risks and side effects, too."

"I suppose you could, but there's a thirty to forty percent chance you will never develop breast cancer and an eighty percent chance you'll never develop ovarian cancer. So, I would say . . . if it were me . . . I would say no. At least not for twenty or thirty years. I would say just show up and do your screenings whenever they want to see you."

Great-Aunt Rae reloaded the gun two more times and Carly obliterated everything that was left.

"Well, I'll tell you what, kid. Whenever you're ready, I'll go with you. I'll get tested, too. We'll do it together. You won't be alone. And whatever the results . . . well, we'll either celebrate them or we'll face them together. We'll figure it out together. Because you're right. All of this is a lot."

"Yeah," Carly said, not as if she were saying yes to taking a genetic test together but as if she were simply agreeing that yeah, this is a lot.

Amy

Waking up on her birthday, Amy had a recollection of hiking to two lakes as a child and swimming in the second one. It was in a deep cirque just below Little Tahoma, the small peak on the side of Mt. Rainier, and a field of snow led down steep cliffs and right into the water on the opposite side. Yes, finding this lake would be the perfect way to spend her birthday. She felt strangely excited about this one. She'd made it to forty-seven. It was a privilege not everyone got.

Of course, it could be argued that going home to heaven early was a privilege not everyone got, and that likely was true too. It served no purpose to see one as success and one as failure. She had no clue how it all worked. She simply had to trust that it was all good. Even when it was scary. Especially when it was scary.

She felt grateful for more time to be in nature here on earth and intended to make the most of it. Studying the topo map she'd bought at the visitor center, she figured out that the lakes she remembered might be Bench Lake and Snow Lake and that if she and Alicia had hiked it when they were little, it was probably within her ability even now. Ready for a little change of scenery, she set off, driving first for several miles on the road to Paradise before parking and beginning her hike.

Along the trail, bear grass bloomed nearly waist high, and she giggled, remembering a long-ago conversation with Alicia, who must have been about fifteen or sixteen at the time.

"I don't like these," Alicia said. "They remind me of penises."

The word "penis" alone was enough to get Amy laughing, but as she looked around at all the thousands of creamy white blossoms and knew her sister was imagining they were all penises, well, that just sent her over the edge. "Is that what penises really look like?" she asked. "I thought they were longer."

"Yeah, they are. These just look like the tips."

"How do you know what penises look like?"

"Tina's mom subscribes to *Playgirl*."

Satisfied with that answer, Amy slowly turned around and took in a three-hundred-and-sixty-degree view of the flowers. "That sure is a lot of penises."

"I kind of feel like they're out to get me," said Alicia.

"Quick! Put your knees together and run!" Amy shouted jokingly, attempting to do just that.

Awkwardly, Alicia joined in, their little bodies turning with each stride to compensate for the lack of movement in their hips, laughing hysterically until they were out of the meadow and back in the woods.

"That was close!" Amy joked, tears streaming down her face, hands clutching her sore sides.

Alicia, laughing just as hard, agreed, "So close! Way too close!"

When their parents caught up to them, they asked what was so funny, and instead of telling the truth, Alicia said, "Amy just blew a really big snot bubble out of her nose."

Left with no choice, Amy said, "I didn't mean to. Sometimes

I'm just really disgusting," and this set both of them off into a fit of giggles again.

Amy stopped with her sketchbook and sketched a close-up of three bear grass blooms with the alpine meadow in the background. Later, she would cut it to the size of a postcard to send to her sister, writing nothing except, "Thinking of you!" or maybe, "Wish you were here!" It would surely give Alicia a laugh.

It wasn't long before she reached the shore of Bench Lake. The opposite shore dropped off steeply, making the lake seem not quite believable and more like something that had been photoshopped poorly. Behind it sat majestic Mt. Rainier. Being in no particular hurry, Amy stopped to sketch it as well.

As she walked on, she thought about all the parts of her body that were relatively the same. Her arms and legs still worked, and her hands and feet too. Her heart, lungs, kidneys, liver, pancreas, gallbladder, thyroid . . . they all worked. They even worked without her doing a thing, without her telling them what to do, without her thinking about them at all. Her digestive system still worked. After chemo, she knew what a big deal that was. She could still smell and taste things. She still had all of her teeth, and they were in decent shape. Her eyes and ears still worked. Her wonderful brain still worked. Gratitude filled her. Most of her body was normal now. Sure, some things were different, but most things were the same. If she had to lose a body part, breasts were a pretty good one to lose, really. Sure, they had played a lovely role in lovemaking. That was a loss. And sure, they filled out women's clothes. But mostly they were pretty nonfunctional. She hadn't needed to feed a baby with them in a very long time. She wasn't ever going to feed any more babies with them again. She didn't use her breasts to walk or lift things or even float. Having them didn't make any activity easier. They didn't make her smarter. They didn't make her a better friend. And yeah, if given a choice, she would have kept them, but life was going to be okay without them. It was. If she lived to be in her late eighties, she would live as many of her adult years without them as she had with them. That was plenty of time to solidly get used to this changed body.

The changes in her abdomen were harder to grasp. She had been using her ovaries and had hoped for more time before menopause. Up until now, she had no idea what a big role estrogen played in so much of what went on in her body—the suppleness of her tissues, including her circulatory system and her skin, thermoregulation, even the clarity of her thoughts. Estrogen replacement wasn't an option for her because her tumor had been estrogen positive—fueled by estrogen. Replacing estrogen would make her far more likely to have a recurrence or a new cancer. This was how it was, and not having to deal with periods was pretty darn nice, so . . . onward, she supposed.

Along the trail stood a grand old tree, too large for her to put her arms around. No one judged it as less desirable in any way because of its age. Trees did not judge themselves for changing, for getting wrinkles in their bark, for getting larger. They were simply part of nature. Putting her arms as far around the tree as she could, she rested her cheek against its bark.

Just a little farther on down the trail, she found herself at the shore of Snow Lake, and sure enough, it was the one she remembered. On the other side of the lake was a curved cliff, carved like a bowl by a glacier. Snow still covered most of the talus slope that interrupted the forest. Behind the cliff, Unicorn Peak protruded like a breast, complete with a nipple. Behind it was another small peak, giving the illusion of looking at a woman's chest from the side. Ugh, she thought. Boobs were everywhere. Just when she was feeling good, there they were again.

Nearby, a family of five was collecting their things and putting them back in their backpacks after a picnic lunch, preparing to go. It seemed as if in a few minutes, she would have the whole lake to herself.

Walking farther down the trail, she scouted for a good swimming spot. When she finally found one, she looked around for people, saw none, listened, and then, hearing none, shrugged off her backpack, took the towel out of it, and stripped. She didn't look at her chest, but she didn't look away from it either.

Carefully, she took a step onto two not particularly user-friendly rocks submerged just a few inches below the surface of the aqua glacier water. Squatting, she put her arms out in front of her, hands together, tucked her chin, and launched herself into the freezing water with the intention of washing away all the horrible experiences from the past year.

Surfacing, she wicked the water off her face and out of her short hair. She reached and stretched with each informal stroke, feeling the cold water on all of her skin, all of her skin that was the same. She hadn't anticipated that—the extreme awareness of all the parts of her body that were not numb and had not changed.

She rolled over on her back and, keeping her head out of the freezing water, kicked for shore. Normally, this would have made her boobs jiggle back and forth on the surface of the water. She noticed the difference, but before she could dwell on it, she noticed that the water was so cold she was losing feeling in her arms. In just a few strokes, she reached shore and crawled out up onto the rocks.

For just a moment, she stood there rather victoriously, having taken another step into acceptance. The sun warmed her skin and the gentle breeze dried it. Reaching her arms up to the sky, she smiled. She felt alive—not just alive as in not dead, but truly alive.

Seven years ago, on Amy's fortieth birthday, she had wanted just one thing. To her, it had seemed such a small thing to ask of Paul. That year, her birthday happened to fall on a Sunday, a sign that it was written in the stars, because that's when it happened—summer concerts in the Myriad Botanical Gardens. To her, this idea seemed like the pinnacle of romance—her husband sitting with her on a blanket, with a picnic in a basket in such a beautiful setting, and the Leftover Cuties onstage. She hadn't known who they were and discovered on YouTube that they were unlike anything she had heard in her daily life. They had a vintage jazz style, and Amy couldn't have been more excited that they were the band that was going to play on her birthday.

She planned out every detail. Carly was staying at a friend's house overnight, so if the mood overtook her and Paul, their romantic evening didn't have to stop at the botanical gardens. For a full week ahead of time, she collected the perfect picnic—Brie cheese, bruschetta, a baguette, grapes, white wine discreetly hidden in a green 7Up bottle with a screw top, sweets from her favorite bakery. She even bought a new dress for the occasion, one with big flowers on it that reminded her of things she had seen Frenchwomen wear in movies. Her birthday date reminded her of footage she had seen of French people picnicking in parks while watching a movie. This picnic seemed a little French to her, as did the jazz. It was going to be the trip to Europe she had never taken.

The concert started at seven thirty, so Amy wanted to leave at six thirty to get a great spot to set out their blanket and just visit a little bit with her husband before the music began. On the morning of her birthday, she left Paul a note on the counter saying that she'd meet him back here by or before six thirty for her birthday date.

Some days, it was easy to forget that terrible things happen. It was easy to believe that no one committed unspeakable horrors on her birthday. It seemed perfectly acceptable to expect that just one day out of the whole year—well, two with Christmas—she might just be a normal woman married to a normal man, instead of a woman married to a man who dealt with all of those horrible things. And so, when Paul called around five o'clock to say something came up and there was no way he was going to make it home in time, Amy was sure her initial tone of voice reflected her disappointment and not her understanding when she said that she understood.

She put on her new dress, packed up her perfect picnic and blanket, and set off, determined to have a good time.

What she remembered most was sitting on her blanket, looking at a sea of couples and families in front of her and all around her. She concluded that she was the only person there alone. She thought it would not have bothered her quite so much if it hadn't been so divergent from the fantasy she'd had about that night. She felt the disappointment and deflation in her stomach, in her chest, behind her nose where latent tears threatened to surface. From time to time, an acquaintance would walk by with his or her spouse—someone Amy had chatted with at her daughter's school, a neighbor, perhaps. She had acted like Paul was coming but running late—she didn't know why. In retrospect, maybe she wanted to assure people that she was loved, because she needed to assure herself that she was. When it came to Paul, Amy wasn't feeling it. She was feeling his sense of duty but not his love.

She kept thinking that once the music started, it would be better, but it wasn't. Couples moved closer to one another. Some danced. And the music was so intoxicating that it seemed such a deep shame not to be sharing the moment.

Amy never did know what happened that day. Paul didn't talk about it. Someone may have beaten their own kid to death, or someone may have been robbing and beating people in wheelchairs. She sometimes read the newspaper just to find out what Paul might have been working on and knew these things happened. It was safe to assume that someone dangerous was at large and Paul needed to figure out who it was so the perpetrator could be caught before more people were hurt. And so, it wasn't Paul that Amy was mad at so much as simply her experience with him in life where it felt like she never came first. Someone else's need was always more urgent and someone else's pain was always more severe. That was just a fact.

When Amy got home, Paul was sitting in his easy chair, a glass of something hard in his hand, a ritual she had come to understand he indulged in only on the very worst days. Sometimes he talked in his sleep on those nights.

"How was the concert?" he asked. It seemed to Amy that he often hoped that if he acted as though something weren't a big deal, she would forget that it was. Maybe that's just how it came off.

"I missed you there," she said. "I'm sorry you couldn't make it." She gave him a little smile.

He nodded, his face showing no emotion at all. "I had planned to pick up a gift for you on my way home from work, but by the time I left, everything was closed. I'm sorry, Amy. I'll make it up to you."

But any man who thought that a meaningful birthday present could be picked out in ten minutes on his way home from work would not know how to make it up to her even if it was possible.

"Okay," she said, resigned. She put her leftovers in the fridge before she walked down the hall to take a bath and go to bed. There would be no love. There would be no romance. He would avoid coming to bed as long as he could, avoid facing her and her disappointment, avoid her and her desires, avoid the simple act of shutting his eyes and seeing his day replay.

There was nothing to forgive, really. No one should have to apologize for serving his community in one of the most difficult ways or for simply being who he was. Amy didn't want to poison what was left of their love with unnecessary resentment. She could have chosen the narrative that he had disappointed her, but she chose to simply say that she was disappointed. He couldn't help it. She couldn't help it. It was over. She survived. She survived feeling unbearably unimportant to him. She survived feeling unbearably alone. Tomorrow was a new day, and each new day brought hope—a little less hope than the day before, but still, hope.

After she had dressed and eaten a snack, she sketched the lake and its surroundings. It was so peaceful, so quiet, except for the happy chirping sounds of birds, and she was grateful to no longer be tethered to that hope. Instead of always longing for more, she felt deeply content.

When she was done, she packed up and started back down the trail. This birthday was extra-special. It was absolutely an accomplishment. She had earned it—not for battling cancer and winning but for enduring treatment while her doctors battled it and won.

After all, before her doctors showed up, she wasn't winning at all. She had earned it by simply enduring.

Paul and Carly had endured a lot this year too. They played an important role in her survival. It would have been nice to celebrate this day together as a collective accomplishment. But that wasn't what was happening, and she didn't waste the time and mental energy that she used to wishing things were different. It was up to her to make sure the rest of her day was celebratory.

This day felt sacred. The first day of a new year. She'd had cancer when she was forty-six and that was over. She was forty-seven now. A new beginning.

Paul

When Amy finally arrived back in the campground, Paul was so relieved. He had been waiting for a couple of hours, imagining all the worst-case scenarios, talking himself out of believing each one but not completely able to dismiss any of those possibilities either.

It had been a long trip with several legs to get here, and although minutes ago he had been feeling tired from his travels and from the effort of tracking her down, now the gravity of what was at stake hit him with full force. In a little while, he would return to the small cabin he had reserved at Whistlin' Jack's forty miles away, but whether he would return with Amy or alone was yet to be determined.

He'd left his rental car in the day-use area and walked to the spot the ranger told him was hers, and there he had waited at her picnic table for what seemed like an eternity. Now, as she pulled in, he stood and smiled hopefully. On her face he saw surprise, but he wasn't sure it was necessarily a good surprise.

Still, she'd stepped out of her car and greeted him with a courteous hug and peck, saying, "Paul! I didn't expect to see you here!" It was a neutral statement—not *Paul! I'm so happy to see you!* or *Paul! What a wonderful surprise!* That was not lost on him.

He wanted to hug her for so much longer, but when she stepped back, he let her go.

"Happy birthday," he said.

"Thank you."

"I hope I'm not intruding. It's just . . ." He had rehearsed what he was going to say in his head countless times in the last twenty-four hours, and now it was all scrambled. "I was telling Rae how much I missed you, and about all my hopes for the Chama house—you know, living a peaceful life there with you—and I guess she felt sorry for me or maybe she just wanted what was best for both of us, so, please forgive her, but she told me that you found the papers back in November, and . . . my heart just sank. My heart just sank, Amy. I am so sorry. I wish I could go back in time and undo all of that."

Amy

So many emotions ran through her mind and coursed through her blood, and she paused to see which one would step forward and present itself first. Feeling the stinging behind the bridge of her nose, she knew she was about to cry, so she was surprised when it was anger that beat the other emotions to the finish line. "Yeah, but you can't," she began, too loudly, she realized too late. She didn't want to make a big scene in the campground, so she lowered her voice, spitting the words out as if they were teeth that he had knocked out with a punch. "You can't take away that moment for me and all the moments that followed. The moment when I realized there was a giant hole in my safety net. The moment I realized that while my love was unwavering and deep and true, yours was fake. Critical moments when you acted loving toward me, like when the nurse first pierced my arm for the infusion and it was so real. It was so real that all this was happening, and I would have given anything to believe your love was real, but I knew it was all an act. I knew your true feelings and your intentions, and I felt so alone—alone and terrified. You want to show up on my birthday, say you're sorry, and take that all back? You can't. You can't undo it with some magic words. You love me? No, you don't. You feel sorry for me—too sorry for me to leave. I know you and

I know your sense of duty. It's what kept our family together as long as it was."

"I know that all of that is how it must have looked." His eyes began to water and then spilled over in tears as he searched for words. She didn't know if they were tears of guilt or the tears of a man who just realized he had made an irreversible mistake that would take his life in a direction he no longer wanted to go, so she simply waited. Maybe he would redeem himself, but more likely he would simply say all he had to say before she ended it. He had cared for her faithfully when she needed him most. He had provided for her and Carly all these years. Even though sense of duty was not the same thing as love, she owed him some respect for all that his sense of duty had done for her. He lifted his head as he readied himself to speak and she saw the anguish on his face. "I know that all of that is how it must have looked," he began again, "but what I remember feeling all those months ago was that I was unworthy of you because you loved me so deeply and I didn't have the same capacity. Like all the bad stuff I've seen and dealt with—I had to become numb in order to cope, and when you do that, you don't just block out the bad; you block out the good, too. And I just felt that you deserved more than that."

She broke from his gaze and dropped her eyes, then looked back up at him and said, "I did."

"Amy, I feel like a part of me has been in a coma for all of the years since the bombing, but I am finally waking up. Please don't give up on me. You and Carly are by far the two best things to ever happen to me. And I would give anything to go back in time and not have brought those papers into our home, not to have filled them out, not to have even considered them. In all our years together, it was the only time I ever lost faith. And even then, I didn't lose faith in you. I only lost faith in me. Please forgive me,

Amy. I made such a big mistake and I regret it so much. Please forgive me. I love you with all my heart, Amy. I do, and I need you in my life."

Studying the ground, the fir needles and small pieces of moss that had fallen, she considered his words. They actually made sense to her. "You know, the interesting thing about this moment is that I understand things I didn't understand eight months ago . . . like what you were just saying about feeling like I deserved more because you didn't have the capacity to love me like I loved you." Taking a big breath, she dragged her foot through the needles and the moss that would never return to the branches above. "The good news is that I understand that now. I actually do understand how you surely felt shell-shocked and numb and like you had nothing to offer me or at least not enough." For a moment relief washed over Paul's face, and then he realized she wasn't done. "The bad news is that I understand it because that's how I feel now." She shrugged helplessly. "I don't know what to do."

"Well, how about we go for a little walk to the river, and then you let me take you out for a nice birthday dinner? Because this isn't a good moment to make any major life decisions, Amy. It's not. Give it time. Give it a lot of time. And know that I love you and I'm going to see you through it."

Why she started to cry she wasn't clear, but she covered her face with her hands. Paul stepped forward and embraced her and she rested her head on his shoulder. Maybe it was relief. Relief that Paul really did love her and her whole life had not been a lie. Relief that they just might somehow make it and she would not have to figure out how to live the second half of her life in a new way. But none of that seemed to feel like the reason for her tears. Her attachment to the past or the future was no longer great enough to elicit that kind of response in her. No, she realized it was simply the beauty of Paul willing to love her through her moment of faithlessness, resolute to love her even if she couldn't love him back. Such a generous love, agape love, the kind of love that came straight from heaven.

Over dinner, Amy told Paul about her time in nature, and Paul told Amy about problems—problems at work, problems with the Chama house, problems with his mind, and more problems at work. She felt herself weaken with every word. Thank goodness she had driven her own car, she thought, ready to escape. She realized she had been sucked back into what felt like home. Paul felt like home. And that was the thing. People and situations that felt like home could be really comforting, but they weren't always what was best for a person.

"Paul, I have to stop you. It's not that I don't care. It's just that I can't handle negativity right now. I feel like my head is barely above water and you're pushing it back under again. These days I'm so keenly aware of what is strengthening and what is weakening, and this is definitely the latter." The waitress came to clear their dinner plates, interrupting her, and then left. Feeling as if her birthday had been hijacked and had taken an ugly turn, she said, "Look, I really appreciate you coming all the way out here, but I think I'll just skip dessert and go back to the campground. It's been a long day."

But then Paul said something that stopped her in her tracks. "Amy, I retired. Well, not really retired because I can't start collecting for a few more years. I'll have to figure out something else to do in the meantime. That's where I was going with all of this. I know retiring is something married people should talk about, but

I just couldn't take anymore. That's what I was trying to explain. I wasn't trying to bring you down or make it all about me. I just wanted you to understand why I did what I did . . . why I couldn't take it anymore."

Immense compassion washed over her. "Oh Paul, good for you. No one should have to see all the things you've seen."

He looked at her with such gratitude, and she wondered what he had been expecting. How could he have expected anything else from her besides mercy? And then she dared to wonder how this might change him. He would never change back into exactly who he'd been decades ago. A person couldn't undo their life experiences, but she wondered whether he might change into a truer version of himself, a version more alive, more aware, a version with a greater capacity for love.

And so, she ordered dessert and when it arrived with a lit candle, she wished for the best for each of them, with no idea what that looked like, only knowing it involved profound healing. Already he had solved several of the problems he had talked about over dinner.

Her mind began to race with all the things that needed figuring out now—how to ensure she continued to have health insurance, what his travel plans were, Carly's college tuition if she chose to go . . . all of the things. She looked up and saw his mind racing with all of the things too. "I know," he said, reading her mind. "But, one thing at a time."

He handed her a little gift-wrapped box, and she opened it. Inside was a necklace and earrings all made from small green stone beads and a silver ring with a stone that matched.

"The lady I bought it from said it's aventurine. I thought it was appropriate because it has the word 'adventure' in it and it's green like the trees you love. She said it's good for healing, growth, and renewal, but since I'm from Oklahoma and not California, I just thought it would bring out your beautiful green eyes."

She laughed and said thank you, hardly able to believe that he had, for the first time in their marriage, gotten her a thoughtful gift.

As they walked out of the restaurant, she still hadn't made up her mind about where she wanted to sleep.

"I wrote you a song," he said.

She was stunned.

"If you want to come back to my cabin and take a bath, I'll play it for you. No pressure. No expectations. But if you'd let me, I'd love to hold you all night."

When she looked into his eyes, she saw glimmers of the man she married. She said yes.

Amy didn't know why she felt so exposed sitting in a bath without bubbles. After all, Paul had changed her drains each day the week following her mastectomy. She had stood near the bathroom sink, unbuttoned her shirt, closed her eyes, and plugged her ears while Paul held one tube near where it was attached to her wound and, with the other hand, squeezed the tube and slid his fingers all the way down to a grenade-sized plastic bulb to prevent clots from building and clogging the drains. He lifted the bulb out of the flannel pouch she wore around her waist and emptied its contents in the sink, rinsed it, and reattached it. She was so grateful because all of it made her queasy—the tender wound, the goo that drained from it, the fact that a part of her had been amputated. And when she wanted to take a shower, he gently and ever so slowly removed her bandages and put new ones on after she was done. He had been so profoundly tender in those moments that she could not reconcile that in a desk drawer file sat divorce papers.

Sitting in the bath, she had an acute understanding of how something could happen to a person that would leave them feeling so unlike themselves that their capacity to feel love was far away, like something that was in a storage unit instead of in the house, something a long drive away.

Feeling awkward, she sat forward and embraced her knees to hide her chest, even though it wasn't as if he hadn't seen her changed body, as if he hadn't seen it up close and personal. This was different. This setting was romantic and the other setting had been clinical. As it turned out, it felt unbearably vulnerable to be seen with her changed body in a romantic setting. Unbearably. But if she was brave, if she was really, really brave, this moment could be an opportunity for another step—even if it could be only a baby step—toward acceptance, toward discovering a new way of being or an old way of being—she didn't know. She released her legs and sat back.

Paul walked in with a candle, but before he lit it and turned out the lights, she said, "I haven't figured out what to call these. I've been calling them my boob stumps, but I don't think that's really good for me."

He looked at her chest, considered it, and said, "They still sort of look like boobs. Like here"—he pointed to an area near his armpit—"that still looks like your boob."

"But breast tissue and nipples are pretty defining features of breasts, you know? I don't even qualify for indecent exposure anymore."

Looking at her as if it were no big deal, he said, "Yeah, still boobs."

After her oophore-hysterectomy, she'd had to stay out of the bath for eight weeks, and since she'd only taken one once it was okay to do so again, the experience was still novel.

He lit the candle, turned down the lights, picked up his guitar, played, and sang. It was a song about how she was his home, his heart, and the only girl he'd ever loved. His voice shook at times, endearing him to her more. He was really laying it all out there— all of it, things inside his heart she didn't know were there.

When he finished, she said, "That was beautiful, Paul. The best birthday present you could have gotten me."

"I was nervous," he confessed. "I haven't done that in a long time."

"Welcome back, Paul Bergstrom."

"Would it . . . ? Um, I don't want to pressure you or anything or make you feel like I'm putting the moves on you and if you say yes it's going to lead to something you're not ready for, but I'd really like to slide into that tub with you, like we used to. Would that be okay?"

She appreciated that. Although the surgeon who had done her oophore-hysterectomy had said it would be okay to have sex after eight weeks, she couldn't imagine it. Her body still hurt. But she knew Paul meant what he said, so with a little smile, she nodded. "Yeah."

She scooted forward so he could sit in the back and then she laid back against his chest. He wrapped his arms around her. "Either bathtubs have gotten smaller or I've gotten larger," he said, and laughed.

"Must be the bathtubs," Amy said.

He rested his hands at the base of her ribs. "Are my hands all right here, or do you want them somewhere else?" he asked. "I mean, I don't know the right thing to do. If I've always put them here before"—he lifted them up to her scars—"I don't want you to feel like I'm avoiding any part of you, but I don't want you to think I have attachment to what is no longer there either. And I sure don't want to hurt you or cause you any discomfort. So, just tell me what would feel good to you."

That was sweet, she thought. It was vulnerable. She could appreciate vulnerable. And she definitely appreciated listening.

"Where they were is good. My chest is a little nervy sometimes. Kind of electrical. That will probably change one day, but for now . . ."

He rested his hands on her lower ribs and leaned his head back against the wall. She rested her hands on his. Feeling his ribs rise and fall with each breath, she breathed with him, the space between them getting smaller with each breath.

Paul

It had been so nice waking up with Amy in his arms, feeling her stir and then lift her head off his chest. "Good morning," he said, kissing the top of her head.

"Good morning," she replied.

"So, listen. I have something I want you to think about. I have to return the rental car today. Then there's a choice. I can fly back to Chama and work on the house, or I can get in your car, let you show me your favorite spots, and then have an adventure with you driving back south. Or, if that's too big of a commitment, I could stay for a couple more days, let you show me your favorite places, and then you drive me back to the airport and I fly back."

"I have a lot of places I want to see after this . . . ," she said. "I'm not sure whether you really understand what you're asking to be a part of."

"If you need more time alone, Amy, that's okay. You can say so. I really didn't mean to barge in."

"It's not that. It's just . . . well, do you even enjoy this kind of thing? I'm worried you won't have a good time and then I'll feel like I should cut my great adventure short when I really don't want to. That's my hesitation. I mean, it's not like you've been begging me to go hiking with you for the last twenty-six years, you know? And you once said that since you spend all day driving around in a patrol car, the very last thing you wanted to do was drive for vacation. . . ."

"Fair enough. How about I spend a few days with you here and then we decide?"

"Okay," she agreed.

After they dropped the rental car off at Yakima Airport, they drove back up the pass in her car. They stopped in Packwood to see whether there was anything for Amy at the post office, and she was thrilled when the postal worker returned with a blue letter. She gave Paul a big smile and walked outside to read it.

Dear Mom,

I am so sorry. I said some terrible things and I wish I could take them all back—every last one of them. The one that haunts me the most is that I didn't want to be like you. You are so deeply loving, so kind to everyone . . . and you are so brave and so strong . . . of course I want to be like you. How could I not? I just was so scared, Mom. Scared I would have to go through what you went through. Scared you might get it again. And I was just so mad that of all the people in the world, it had happened to you, and that it could happen to me. There are all these bad people out there running around and they're fine, but us . . . ? It's wrong. You know? It's wrong. You didn't deserve it. I don't deserve it. Up until last April, I always tried to do everything right and I just felt like it bought me a whole bunch of nothing. I wasn't mad at you. I was just mad. And I'm so sorry that I took it out on you like that . . . took it out on you when you'd already been through so much and

were about to go through more. I was just so mad. And now I'm
just so sorry. I hope you can forgive me even though I'm sure you
will never be able to forget those horrible words I said.

Love, Carly

Amy handed Paul the letter. "She came around. Aunt Rae is magic."

Paul put his arm around her as he read it and squeezed her shoulder when he was done. "Thank goodness."

Carly

This week's guests were a crack-up—four brothers whose mother had named them alphabetically from oldest to youngest in the event she had so many children that she lost track. She'd stopped at four—Andy, Ben, Caleb, and Dale. Joking between them was nonstop. Carly's sides hurt from laughing at the things she had overheard in the last twenty-four hours.

They had grown up on a ranch in Texas together—that is, until it was foreclosed, and that was one thing they didn't joke about. Whenever that came up, the tone was somber. Anyone could tell that it was as if their hearts had been yanked out when they'd had to leave. Their parents had made them promise to not make the same mistake—to get city jobs. And so they had, but it seemed to Carly that Andy and Ben in particular regretted it. Usually, they met once a year for a dude ranch experience with all of their kids, but this year their kids were old enough to not want to go and their wives were pretty much over it as well, so the brothers had chosen something different—tents and wilderness and mammoth horses.

Black Tea had thrown a shoe and they had stopped so Great-Aunt Rae could nail it on.

"I should have done that—been a blacksmith," Ben said, watching Great-Aunt Rae nailing the shoe. "You don't have to own land to live the life. I could have worked with horses."

"What do you do now?" Great-Aunt Rae asked.

"I'm an electrician at Dell in Austin."

"That sounds interesting!"

"Yeah, I like it. I do. But I miss being out in all of this."

Andy chimed in, "If you'd been a farrier, your back would be so messed up by now. Can you imagine spending your days bent over like that? Trust me. My back is on its way out."

"He's got his own concrete company," said Ben.

"That's hard work," said Great-Aunt Rae.

"I'll say. Caleb and Dale got it right when they got desk jobs as far as I'm concerned. Caleb's a bank manager, and Dale's an engineer at HP. Great benefits."

"But bro, that's why they don't have all of this," Ben said, flexing his muscle and prompting all four brothers to get into a flexing contest and exchange insults.

Later, when they were back at camp and Ben had come to the chuck wagon for a lemonade refill, Carly asked Ben, "Did you mean it—when you said you wished you had become a farrier instead of an electrician? Because I'm trying to pick a career path."

"Oh, I don't know. I've really enjoyed being an electrician. If you're at all inclined, I'd sure encourage it. The thing about the trades is that they can't be outsourced. Dale's job could be sent to India. Mine won't be. Even if Dell went there, there's plenty of electrical work people need done here. It's a union job, so pay and benefits are good. I don't know what life as a farrier would have been like. I'm sure I'd make less money, but farriers get to visit with several nice people a day while they work on horses. There was one guy who used to shoe our horses that went to Alaska in the summer and shod the horses that pulled the wagon rides in

Denali National Park. That would have been some gig. I guess I just miss that life. That's all. Once you've had it, it's hard to settle for anything less. I would have loved to have grown up and worked the family ranch, but . . . you know . . . that's gone now. And it's not like ordinary people can buy ranches. How long have you been here?"

"It's only my fourth week. Rae is my mom's aunt. I grew up in Oklahoma City."

"So, you're wrecked now." He laughed. "Yeah, just try going back to the city after this. You'll go nuts. You'll think what good is money compared to this?" He gestured all around with his hands.

"I could be a farrier," she said.

"Some people apprentice, but there are farrier schools. Some community colleges even offer farrier programs. Sure, why not? Do it for a while and if you find you want to do something else, change. You don't have to stick with one thing your whole life. There's no rule that says you have to. Life shouldn't be nothing more than a race to retirement."

"Thanks."

"No problem." And with that, he joined his brothers for a raucous game of cards, where the bets became outrageous dares.

That night when Great-Aunt Rae settled into her sleeping bag on her cot, Carly said, "I think I want to be a farrier."

"Huh," Great-Aunt Rae replied. "I suppose I should have seen that coming, but I didn't."

"I want to work with horses."

"Well, that's a sensible choice then. Most young people think of becoming a vet, but that's a lot of school and a lot of student debt. Plus, farriers don't have to put horses down. I hate putting horses down. I could never be a vet."

"I thought the same thing," said Carly.

"The vet that does Drake's corrective shoeing went to Mesa Community College in Tucumcari. Corrective shoeing is quite a science. Anyway, you might want to look into that program."

Carly nodded. She liked this plan. Getting to work with horses while she went to college sounded all right. For the first time in months, she had an inkling of looking forward to her future.

"Carly, I don't know whether it's a disservice to you to float this possibility. A day is going to come when I can't do this anymore. Most of these old boys will be ready to retire when I do. I could sell Frank and Drake. So, there are a lot of ways to let this operation wind down. But if you decided to become a farrier and if you were interested in this business, there might be a way we could transition it to you so that it worked for both of us."

"Wow!" said Carly. This was a possibility that made her heart sing.

"Let's just chew on that for a while. You've got a lot of options in your life to consider."

Something else had been on Carly's mind for the last two days too. "Great-Aunt Rae? I've been thinking about it. I'd like to take you up on your offer to get genetically tested with me. I don't want to waste my life worrying about something that might not be."

"Right on, kid."

"And if I have it, well, you're right—I don't have to run out and have surgery. I could just make sure I get my checkups."

"That's right. You don't have to change your body or your life. You could simply take the opportunity to make sure any problems are found nice and early."

Carly nodded. "Yeah. And I don't have to figure out the whole thing with kids now either. Maybe I'll just have foals."

"Always an option, but not your only option, and you're right—you don't have to figure out any of that now."

"Thanks, Great-Aunt Rae . . . for understanding." Carly snuggled into her sleeping bag.

"You bet, kid. We're in this together. I sure love you."

"I sure love you, too."

Great-Aunt Rae turned out her battery-powered lantern, leaving Carly alone with her thoughts. And mostly those thoughts were that things were going to be okay. They might not always be easy, but they would probably be okay.

Paul

Paul had seen pictures of mountains before, but he had never quite conceived that someone had stood there to take them. Of course they had, he knew, but still, the mountain before him seemed like something he would see on a calendar instead of in real life.

Stepping out after Amy parked the car, he said, "I don't think I understood until right now why you had to come here."

That made her smile. "Come on! Wait until you walk on top of the ridge! You'll feel like you're walking on top of the world!"

All around him wildflowers of every color bloomed, and in a few places, there were even large patches of snow. "Snow!" he said.

"I know!"

She took his hand and together they walked up toward the sky and the light. It was the complete opposite feeling of when he had felt like he was walking into and then under water as he'd walked into the precinct. This was a new experience, and it made him feel very much alive and free.

"I can't believe I've wasted my life not doing this!" he said.

"You didn't waste your life," she replied seriously. "But I'm glad you're happy to be here."

He was wondering why she had never insisted he come here or even places like it that were closer, then remembered that in the early days she'd tried. "Remember that time we went to Carlsbad Caverns?"

"Yeah," she said, a smile crossing her face as she remembered.

"That was a good day."

"Yes, it was."

They rested for a moment when they reached the top. A small orange butterfly danced around them for a bit.

"It's a sign," she said. "Emergence. We're coming out of our cocoons."

Paul didn't believe in signs, but he believed in that one.

They walked along the ridge for a while and then she showed him the secret worlds inside circles of trees. Standing there in a world all their own, she reached up and put her hands behind his neck, and said, "I was here a week ago, and I missed you." Then she kissed him, and in that moment, he knew that they were going to be okay.

When they reached the lodge, he followed Amy in. She wanted to buy some postcards. Seeing a concession counter, he asked her what sounded good and then stood in line to order food. A park ranger, shorter and younger than Paul, walked in and stood in line behind him, and a thought crossed Paul's mind.

"Mind if I ask you about your job?" Paul asked.

And the ranger explained everything he wanted to know—about how there were law enforcement rangers and interpretive rangers, about how he had to go through federal law enforcement training to be a law enforcement officer, about how a lot of their job was patrolling traffic in the park, giving speeding tickets, and ticketing people for harassing wildlife, littering, picking flowers, and camping where no camping was allowed. Occasionally, they dealt with poachers or hunters that tried to herd elk or bear out of the park and onto forest service land, where they could legally shoot them during hunting season. Occasionally, a camper in Ohanapecosh Campground had a little too much to drink and a law enforcement officer had to respond. Sometimes there were car accidents. Sometimes there were missing people they searched for. There had been a murder or two in one of the parks in California quite a few years ago, so it was possible, but mostly, it was a job he liked.

Paul ordered and paid, and after the ranger did as well and they were both waiting for their food, Paul said, "I just left the homicide division of the Oklahoma City Police Department. Just too much tragedy, you know? Are these jobs hard to get?"

"You can usually find job openings if you're willing to go anywhere. Look online. Even after the season has started you can often find opportunities."

Paul thanked him for his time and picked up his food.

A few minutes later, as he and Amy ate lunch at a table, he asked her where she planned to stop on the way home, and she pulled out a little blue book and flipped to the page with a map of the Pacific Northwest states on it.

"Mount St. Helens National Volcanic Monument . . . then up to the beaches and the rain forest of Olympic National Park . . . Lewis and Clark National Historical Park . . . Crater Lake . . . Oregon Caves National Monument and Preserve . . ." Then she flipped to the page with the western region on it. "Redwoods, Lava Beds National Monument . . . Lassen Volcanic National Park . . . I'd like to see Yosemite, but I've heard nightmare stories about how backed up the road there gets in summer so I think I'll save it for another season. It's important to me, though."

He remembered a moment during her second chemo infusion when she was sitting in the large cushy chair, the first of two bags of chemo hanging above her shrinking as it traveled down a tube and into her arm. She had a *National Geographic Travel* magazine in her lap and had started to cry. He had asked her whether she was okay, whether it hurt. She had opened the magazine to show him a picture of Yosemite Valley and said, "I'm just so grateful that I'll still have time to see it," and he had told her that yes, she would.

"We'll make sure that happens," he'd said then, and he said it now too.

Her expression changed as she remembered, nodded, and, with tears in her eyes, smiled.

Sitting across the table from her now, he felt determined. "What if we went in the middle of the night under a full moon? No traffic. The whole park to ourselves."

"I like the way you think, Bergstrom!" she said, and even though she was trying to be light about it, he met her eyes when she glanced up and knew the solution he had just offered meant the world to her. If their eyes could have spoken out loud, they would have said:

- *Wow, you really do see me, don't you?*
- *Yes, I see you, precious one.*
- *Thank you for seeing me.*

Amy put her finger back on the map and continued. "Okay, after that, cut up here and over to Great Basin National Park . . . Zion, the North Rim of the Grand Canyon, then back up to Cedar

Breaks National Monument, and Bryce Canyon, of course. . . ." She flipped the page to show him pictures.

"Wow!"

"I know! Otherworldly, right? Okay, then Capitol Reef, Natural Bridges, skip up to Arches and Canyonlands, then back down to Hovenweep and Mesa Verde . . . have you seen this? Doesn't that look interesting?" She showed him a picture of massive ruins built into a cliff. "There are a whole bunch of national monuments nearby here. I don't know whether I will get to all of them. Chimney Rock looks really pretty, Chaco Canyon—I have to go to Chaco Canyon. . . . Maybe Bandelier National Monument or maybe I'll be exhausted by then. And that puts me back near Chama."

"Holy smokes! I was wondering whether you were ever going to come home!"

"Well, some of these places I might just spend a couple hours in and then move on to the next. But yes, there's so much to see and . . . you know, I can. I get to. It's just such a privilege to get to." Then she looked down at the table and quietly added, "Not everyone gets to."

He reached over and took her hand. "I really want to do this with you," he said boldly, and he hoped with all of his heart she would say yes.

"Okay," she said, smiling. "You're in."

He thought of avalanche lilies they had seen on their hike that day, buds that had poked through the melting snow after such a long winter. They faced the sun and bloomed. Against all odds, they bloomed again.

Amy

Dear Carly,

As far as I'm concerned, there is nothing you need to apologize for. You were being asked to deal with so much. That you didn't reach your breaking point earlier is remarkable to me. You were heroic last winter, Carly. You cared for me with profound tenderness. I will never forget it. But thank you for your letter. I was so glad to hear from you and I am so glad to know you are doing well. Your dad surprised me by showing up on my birthday. It was sweet.

Love, Mom

Dear Aunt Rae,

You are a miracle worker and a saint. A million thank-yous. Paul is here. Things are going well. Even though I asked for you not to tell him, I'm glad you did. Paul is going to adventure back with me, and then I guess we are going to move to Chama! Thank you for everything. I love you with all my heart.

Amy

Dear Alicia,

Everything here reminds me of you—trails, bear grass, the big rock, the river, the mountain itself. Someday I'd like to return with you and see what you remember. It's not too late, you know. We could still climb it or hike the Wonderland Trail. We'd have to train hard, but it's not too late. If you're ever in, I'm in. Maybe for my 50th birthday? I love you, sister. I don't always agree with you, but I sure do love you. Thank you for everything you did for me last winter. From the bottom of my heart, thank you.

Love, Amy

Dear Dad,

I found the secret place by Sunrise Lodge that used to be a campground—do you remember the spot? There was an old chimney and you used to call in owls for us. I hiked up Sourdough Ridge to watch the sunrise. The alpenglow made the mountain look like a giant strawberry ice-cream cone. I remembered you taking Alicia and me up there for the sunrise a few times, saying, "Oh! It's going to be a good one!" and it always was. You were the best dad. You were. You made my childhood pure magic. I love you from here to the sky.

Love, Amy

After she stamped them and dropped them in the collection box, she stamped her passport book and felt especially happy to see "Sunrise" stamped on the paper.

Before they left Mt. Rainier National Park, she had to make one more stop—to the Grove of the Patriarchs to pay homage to the truly ancient trees. She couldn't wait to show Paul. Nothing he had ever seen in Oklahoma had prepared him for what he was about to see.

Although it was possible to hike to there from Ohanapecosh Campground, she was still regaining strength, so they drove down the road to the place where the trail crossed it and started hiking there. The trail followed a river until at last a suspension bridge crossed it. A sign advised people to cross it one person at a time, so she went first. As she walked across it, it bounced, and she held on to the wires that served as handrails. Halfway across, she stopped and waited for the bridge to still before walking on.

"Do you want me to come to you and walk with you?" Paul called from where he waited.

"No," she called back, and then continued. *Sometimes,* she thought, *a person has to cross her bridge in her own time and no one can do anything more than love and encourage her while she does.*

When he caught up, they walked a short distance farther and then there they were, even bigger than she had remembered—firs and cedars six feet in diameter—maybe more. Wooden decks had been built around their base to protect their roots from the hordes of visitors.

"I can't believe this," Paul said.

Amy just smiled. "Aren't they wonderful?"

"They're taller than skyscrapers."

"And more beautiful."

After wandering down a boardwalk to a large cedar, they came upon two huge firs whose trunks had grown together, making them appear like an old married couple—one who had been together forever.

On a bench facing those trees, Amy and Paul sat for a spell. Amy had said she needed to rest, and she did, but mostly she wanted to sit there to listen. It seemed that after a thousand years of marriage, the trees might have some advice for her. She waited to hear something, and eventually what came to her was just this: *Stay.* That's why those trees were together. They had simply stayed.

When they were ready and had finished walking the rest of the loop through the ancient grove, they made their way back to the suspension bridge. "Let's go together this time," Paul said. "I promise I'll be graceful. Go ahead. I'm right behind you."

Although she wasn't sure it was a good idea, she ultimately trusted him and stepped off the solid ground and onto the far less certain surface of the bridge. True to his word, Paul was steady. And when she paused in the middle this time, looking down at the rushing river below, he slid his hands up the guardrail cables on either side of her, so that she was sandwiched between his arms.

"I got you. I won't let anything happen to you." She leaned back against his chest for just a second and then, with a little more courage, finished crossing.

On the deck of the Johnston Ridge Visitor Center in Mount St. Helens National Volcanic Monument, Amy and Paul saw their own reflection in the mountain.

"Look at that bulge in the center," said Paul.

"That's the lava dome. It's been building since 1980. Slowly, the mountain is building itself back."

"Did you watch it?" he asked.

"Only on TV. We came up to Mt. Rainier about a month later. Yakima was covered in ash. It looked like gray snow. It was messy and gross, and bad to breathe. I never dreamed anything would ever be able to grow here again."

Together they looked at the plant life that had begun to grow. "Life returns," he said. "Renewal. Slow, but certain."

"In my low times, I'd think about how everything in nature wants to grow . . . how strong the life force in living things is, really."

He put his arm around her, pulled her into his side, and kissed the top of her head. "Yep."

The next day, Amy and Paul walked downhill on the path from the little parking lot to Ruby Beach, one of several along the Pacific Coast in Olympic National Park just north of the Kalaloch Lodge, where they had stayed the night before and would again that night. A wide but shallow stream crossed the sandy beach where the trail through the forest came to an end. Enveloped in the misty fog, haystack rocks stood in the surf like memories of better days or giant ghosts. Amy found herself thinking about the love between mother and daughter in those terms, the rock being the mother and the surf being the daughter. That was how she wanted to be, anyway—strong like that. Unmoved on the most tumultuous days.

She bent to take off her shoes, more for the sake of keeping them dry than for any other reason. Paul followed suit.

"The sand is cold here!" Paul exclaimed.

"It is indeed!"

"Do people swim here?"

"I don't think so. At least not on purpose."

Hand in hand, shoes in the other, they strolled out to the place where the ocean kissed the land over and over with each wave that rolled in. Then they wandered south, toward where the sun seemed to be trying its hardest to break through the thick marine layer. After perhaps an hour, they stopped to rest on a log, one of many that had washed up on the beach, but before they sat, they paused to study a tide pool at its base.

"Sea stars!" Paul said.

"And urchins—look!" Amy pointed. They squatted to look more closely. Around them, the sand was relatively dry, a clue that the tide was coming in instead of going out.

"Barnacles."

"All these things just waiting for the tide to come back in. They've mastered the art of holding on."

Just then, the sun broke through the clouds, immediately warming them.

"It's a sign," said Paul. "Before John's wedding, his future mother-in-law came back to the room, where we were all waiting, to talk to him. I overheard her say that in marriage, you fall in and out of love several times, so when you fall out, just hang on and wait it out because you will fall back in. She said she had felt that she had been married three times, just all to the same man."

"Hm," Amy said, pursing her lips together in a small smile as she watched the waiting sea stars and twisted her new aventurine ring around her finger. She supposed it was happening. At the moment, she was still surviving in her tide pool, but anytime now the tide would be back in. The clouds were gone. The sun was back. Hope was all around them.

While driving over to the Olympic Peninsula, Amy had received an email from Alicia.

You wouldn't believe how much Dad loves your postcards. He had a lucid moment today and was emphatic that I tell you to visit the Maple Glade in some place that starts with a Q in Olympic National Park. He said it's just as magical as the Hoh, but you'll have it all to yourself.

That was how Amy and Paul found themselves there in the Maple Glade, wandering through an otherworldly landscape, one that was hard to place, a little Jurassic period with ferns, a little Louisiana bayou with the sheets of moss that draped down from branches. Below the canopy of the colossal maples and above the ferns and shrubs were wide-open spaces where birds flew. Amy and Paul found themselves silenced by their reverence, speaking in whispers, as one did in sacred places.

Following the trail farther, they came upon an ancient fir with the circumference of a small room. Paul stood agape. Amy walked into a fold in its trunk where the tree completely enveloped her. There she rested her cheek on its bark and draped her arms around it. Breathing in deeply, she softened and she listened—not so much with her ears as with her heart, listened for any advice such a living thing might offer about surviving so long, about enduring storms, about losing parts of itself but continuing to grow in other ways, about the divinity of symbiotic relationships. She wasn't sure whether the feeling that washed over her then came from the tree or whether it was inside of her all along or whether the feeling was the very voice of God, a voice she was finally able to hear in this green, living cathedral. If she were to put words to it, they would be that it's all okay—life is okay and death is okay and all the adaptations we make to survive everything in between is okay. And that no matter what, we would always be okay. If she were to give it a name, it would simply be peace. She felt it all the way down to the very marrow of her bones, all the way down to the deepest part of her soul, and it was such a blessed relief.

Opening her eyes, she looked around, then turned and walked deeper into the tree where the center had died and rotted, leaving a large den. Intrigued, Paul slipped in behind her, looked around, and said, "This place really *is* magic."

Amy sat down cross-legged and then Paul did. "This place is better than church."

"Now I understand why you had to go be with the big trees."

She curled up and lay down on her side, her head on his leg. "When I grow up, I want to be a bear."

Paul laughed and stroked her hair for a few peaceful moments.

After a while, she sat back up. He stood and helped her to her feet. Hand in hand, they left the tree and walked on down the path together, one foot in front of the other, taking the next step and the one after that, so much adventure and joy still ahead of them.

ACKNOWLEDGMENTS

Thank you to my agents, Meg and Christina, and to everyone at St. Martin's Press, for taking all the pressure off of me and giving me time—time to heal my body, time to heal my mind, time to find my will and desire to write again. Thank you to my editor, Eileen Rothschild, for not only her patience as this novel morphed several times over the years but the level of insight and understanding she brought to this final version. Deep respect, Eileen.

Thank you to Kari Morrison, my old high school friend, and her dad, Jack, for telling me stories about their summers in Mt. Rainier and Yosemite National Parks. Jack, not only did you give me great book material but you lifted me up out of the darkness on one of my lowest days. Thank you for transporting me to magical places with your stories.

Thank you to Rhonda Noah for information about the Oklahoma City bombing, OSU, and all things Oklahoma.

I read archived articles in the *Oklahoma City Herald* to learn about the Oklahoma City bombing and the effects of this trauma to the first responders. Thank you to the journalists who did such difficult and important work.

Thank you to Mark Stevenson, Joe Fountain, Vince Sianati,

Ramiro Espinoza, and Ross Green for answering my questions about experiences in the military and police and about trauma too.

Thank you to Ben Whitting and Kevin Walton for giving me information about remodeling houses.

And thank you to everyone who touched my heart so deeply with their love and compassion in all forms and expressions—practical help, practical gifts, donated sick leave, accommodation at work, quiet companionship on walks, gentle encouragement, soulful listening, and respectful honoring of my boundaries as I walked through a really tough time in my life. Extra thanks to Connie Celuska for playing her harp for me in the hospital when I came out of surgery because that was truly and deeply beautiful. And thank you to all my friends who survived breast cancer before me who informed me, encouraged me, and inspired me, but especially Patsy Everson, Annie Gerber, Patti Callahan Henry, and my cousin Angela McLaren. And again, thank you to my health team at Confluence in Wenatchee and to my loving parents for saving my life and being my heroes.